WILD CARD

MAGGIE RAWDON

Copyright © 2023 by Maggie Rawdon

Editing by Kat Wyeth – Editor (Kat's Literary Services)

Proofreading by Vanessa Esquibel - Proofreader (Kat's Literary Services)

Photographer: Michelle Lancaster - www.michellelancaster.com

All rights reserved.

No part of this book may be reproduced in any form or by any electronic or mechanical means, including information storage and retrieval systems, without written permission from the author, except for the use of brief quotations in a book review.

This is a work of fiction. Any names, characters, places or events are purely a work of imagination. Any resemblance to actual people, living or dead, actual events, or places is purely coincidental.

ONE

Scarlett

"DO YOU THINK IT'S OKAY?" I turn around for Harper one more time in the short black dress I'd pulled from the back of my closet. "I brought a second dress with me, just in case. Something more conservative. I was just thinking, it's my birthday, so maybe something sexier you know?"

"Um, you look hot as hell. And exactly, yes. It's your birthday, and Carter will die when he sees you in this."

I haven't been on a date in a while, too long really. With the museum losing its funding, moving all the collections into storage, and trying to find a temporary job while they prep the new building it's moving into, I haven't had a single second to think about anything that isn't work. So tonight I'm forgetting about all of it and putting myself first for once. And maybe, just maybe, this is the first night of something new.

Carter's a former coworker, and we've been meeting to catch up and talk about how he can help with the nonprofit

Harper's running with our friend Joss. But all the late nights chatting shop have led to drinks and other conversations. Including him confessing how he always had a crush on me when we worked together but didn't want to make it awkward.

Cue Harper who is now happily dating Alexander "Xander XXL" Xavier, the defensive end for the Seattle Phantom, and wants to get everyone else coupled up just like her. Her matchmaking plot between Carter and me started the second she saw us flirting and culminated in her suggesting that we double date for my birthday. Only now I'm nervous as hell, but also strangely hopeful. As I turn one more time in the mirror, I feel the little whisper of butterflies in my stomach at the idea that I might actually have found a guy I like for once—one who has a ton in common with me, understands what I'm going through at work, and loves all the same nerdy things I do.

Butterflies that are absolutely crushed to dust when we get to the restaurant, and I walk down to the bar to grab a cocktail before dinner to calm my nerves. I run into Carter on the way and stop dead in my tracks. He has another woman with him, and her fingers are laced with his as she trails behind him.

"Scarlett." He gives me a warm smile. "I didn't know you'd be here. I guess it makes sense if it's Harper's birthday."

"Oh um, yes," I mumble, and I can feel my cheeks heating. I don't want to correct him but the fact that he didn't even realize it was my birthday we were going out for makes me want to die a little.

"This is Chloe, my girlfriend. Chloe, this is Scarlett, we used to work together at the museum. She and Harper have been working on some fundraising and I've been trying to see how the CRM firm can get involved."

"So nice to meet you." Chloe smiles brightly at me and shakes my hand.

"You too. They're waiting to be seated. I'll be right there in a minute." I fake a smile in return and then start to walk away.

"All right." Carter nods and the two of them take off toward the table, while I continue my way to the bathroom.

Forget wanting to die a little. I want to die full stop. Launch myself into a black hole of nothingness to never return or have to think about this again. But I think my only mildly sane option might be escaping out a back entrance and claiming sudden illness.

Except I hate to do that to Harper when she worked so hard to get these reservations for me. It's a fancy new place with a waitlist that I'm fairly certain she had to namedrop to get to the top of. But we could eat here another day when things calmed down, and the four of them could have a lovely non-birthday dinner together. I just have to text her. I rustle through my purse trying to find which pocket I stuffed my phone in.

I could still have my own party tonight. Not completely waste the fact that it is my birthday. I could grab fast food on the way home and have a pity party for one. Crying into my milkshake about what an idiot I am for misreading the signals and watch a romcom that gives me false hope that the great guy I've always wanted is still out there somewhere. Sounds like a perfectly themed spinster thirtieth birthday party.

> So Carter brought his girlfriend. I'm mortified, and I'm leaving just as soon as I pull it together. Just tell them I didn't feel well.

HARPER

WHAT?!

Just wait!

I'm coming to you

A MOMENT later Harper comes hurrying down the stairs into the bar area, looking like she might rip someone to shreds. Namely Carter.

"What the hell is going on? Who brings a date to a date?" She looks at me.

"Apparently, this guy. He brings his girlfriend." The tears threaten to come but I manage to hold the dam back. Barely. "I'm so embarrassed. I must have misread everything."

"Oh, Scarlett! Don't cry. I'm sorry. I don't think you misread anything. He was flirting with you—heavily. I have no idea what happened. We're going to think of something. It's not going to ruin the night. We're still gonna celebrate your birthday. We'll just have to figure out how to get rid of them."

"I don't want to be the fifth wheel to your double date or the third wheel to your date with Xander. I'd rather be alone then sit through that. No offense. I love you guys and I'm so happy for you, but I have enough existential crises on my hands at the moment."

She sighs, staring down at the floor and shaking her head.

"I was clear it was a double date."

"Well, he thought it was a double date with you and Xander. He also thinks it's *your* birthday."

"My birthday? What the fuck? He wasn't listening at all then."

"Apparently not."

"The way he just fanboyed over Xander, I think that might have been all he heard."

"The dangers of a bestie with a pro-football player boyfriend." I manage a small laugh even though my throat is scratchy from holding back tears. "I'm just gonna go home. We can do a raincheck. You guys have fun though. Okay?"

"No. No way. I have your cake for later at my place, and then we have reservations in the VIP section at that club we talked about. You can't go home. I don't want to spend the night with Carter and his girlfriend."

"Harper. I love you, but I can eat the cake tomorrow. I can't do it tonight. Always being the sad spinster one now with you all coupled up is rough enough without having to do it on my birthday. Like there's a neon sign on my back."

"I understand. I just wish there was another way. Stupid fanboys not listening... Oh shit! I have an idea. Hold on."

I frown at her. "What?"

She starts texting fast and furious and smirking at her phone. I hear the little dings in response to several of her messages and my frown deepens.

"What are you doing? Who are you talking to?"

"A solution to the problem. Xander's just making sure they can put us at a bigger table."

"What solution? Please don't invite more people to witness my humiliation. I just want to sneak out of here quietly, unnoticed." My stomach knots as I think about Carter figuring out that I thought he was going to be my date and how awkward that would be.

Her phone dings again and she grins. "Problem solved."

"What do you mean, problem solved?" I can't think of a single fathomable way this problem could be solved without me just leaving.

"Tobias is coming. He's going to be your date for the night. Fanboy can eat his heart out."

I love Harper. I really do. But right now? I want to murder her.

TWO

Tobias

I'M in the middle of getting ready to go out for the night with a brunette I met at a party a couple of weeks ago. She'd been eager to give me her number and even more eager when I finally texted to see if she wanted to grab drinks somewhere.

She's currently texting to hint at how hungry she is and how something in her stomach might be a good idea before drinks. While I have no doubt she's right, I also know this is just her attempt to angle her way into a longer evening. Something I have zero interest in. I thought I'd made it pretty clear in my original offer. If drinks aren't enough for her, I'm out. I don't have the energy for more.

There's really only one thing we have in common, and I don't want to waste my time pretending there might be more. Our having dinner would just be one long slog of me pretending to give a fuck about anything she's saying, and her pretending she knows enough about football to care about what I do for a living.

I'm in the middle of typing out my drinks-only offer again when a text pops up from Xander, my best friend and teammate.

> **XANDER:**
> What are you doing right now?
>
> Trying to keep drinks just drinks instead of dinner with the hot one from Adam's party a couple of weeks ago. Why?
>
> No dinner plans then?
>
> You inviting me on a date?
>
> Yeah. An accidental triple one. Want to come rescue Scarlett on her birthday?
>
> Obviously. Give me the address and time.
>
> Time is now, and I'll send you the address. For all intents and purposes - you're dating her and you just happen to be running late.
>
> Got it. I'm already downtown at the condo. Be there in a couple.

I SEND off a quick text to the brunette to tell her something's just come up. Canceling will save me trying to remember her name and explaining my way out of dinner. Although it will mean the loss of what I'm pretty sure would have been a hot one-night stand considering I rain-checked the offer to blow me in the bathroom the night I met her.

But my friends come first, and Xander doesn't ask for favors often. More importantly, Scarlett is my favorite off-limits torment and any chance I get to return the irritation is one I'll take. So if she needs rescuing on her birthday, I'm there.

WHEN I GET to the restaurant the host takes me to the table. I greet Xander who introduces me to an awkward couple who seem a little too dazzled by our job titles for my liking. I flash smiles and make small talk for a moment to try and play the nice guy, but then I ask for Scarlett. Fictionally speaking, I'm her boyfriend and she'd be my first concern.

Xander tells me they went down to the bar for a quick minute. I excuse myself and walk down the stairs, spotting the two of them at the bar and pausing to watch her from across the room for a moment before I approach, and our sparring session starts.

Scarlett's long legs are on full display in the dress she's wearing, one that makes her look like a fucking smoke show. She looks like a modern-day Rita Hayworth during her redhead era and apparently, I have a weakness for it. That and the Mary Jane heels she has on with the thigh highs that have the seam up the back giving her that vintage edge that she always manages to pull off so well. The one that always has me dying to find out what kind of dress-up she likes to play behind closed doors. If I could ever get her to play with me, which would probably be the longest shot of my career. So absurdly unlikely it's not worth talking about.

We have more in common than she thinks we do, but I also know she's a good girl who's a lot like Harper. She wants things I can't ever give her and that means that I have to keep my distance. Remind myself why I can't ever have more than our banter whenever Xander and Harper force the two of us back into a room together—like tonight.

THREE

Scarlett

"OKAY. Okay. I'm sorry. Listen. Let's go to the bar, do a couple of shots really quick, and go back to the table. You can ride the rest of dinner out tipsy, and then we'll ditch everyone else and have cake at my place. After that, the night's up to you. But there is insanely delicious food on the menu, and I've been dying to come here with you. Plus, you're here and you're gorgeous, so... let's make the best of it?" Harper argues her cause.

"I will get you back for this. If he's an ass or makes this worse, I'm still leaving out a back door."

"I owe you. Big. Huge. Probably be repaying this debt for centuries. But I promise we're going to salvage the evening somehow. Okay?"

I take a deep breath. Salvaging the evening is the last thing I want to do. But I also don't want to be a giant crybaby who runs home, even if it is my first instinct. I can do this. Couple of shots. Delicious food. I could ignore the man I now hate, and the one I've hated for some time and still have a semi-decent night. I can do it if I just believe in it.

I nod, and Harper hugs me.

"I love you, and I'm so sorry I made such a mess. Let's get you some shots."

We sidle up to the bar, and Harper waves down one of the bartenders. It's dark and cozy in here, black and gold Art Deco motifs decorate the bar and seating. It feels like the kind of place you order delicate handcrafted cocktails—not shots. But I'll take any alcohol I can quickly down. At this point, I'm not picky.

I'm busy staring out into the abyss of the dark room, contemplating how my life got to this point on my thirtieth birthday when the bartender reappears with a small tray from the other side of the bar.

"Shots!" Harper slides the drinks to me across the granite, two green and two golden.

"What's this?" I hold the oversized shot up.

"Four Horsemen and a Scooby Snack to wash it down for old time's sake." Harper grins at me.

"You asked the bartender here for Scooby Snacks?" I laugh.

"I told them you were having an awful birthday. They were happy to help."

"You realize we're not young enough for this anymore, right? This is gonna hurt in the morning and some of us still have to go to work?"

"We'll get you hydrated and patched up before the night's over, but we have to properly welcome you into your thirties."

"I think the horsemen are gonna properly welcome me to hell." I hold the glass up and the light from behind the bar prisms through it.

"You got this. To another fantastic decade!" She holds up

her shot and we clink glasses and toss them back.

I press my eyes tight as the whiskey burns its way down my throat, blindly reaching for the sweet shot to chase it. The sugary liquid coats the harsh burn, but the taste is still unforgiving on my tongue. I frown and Harper hands me a lime to bite into.

"It's not tequila, Harp." I grimace.

"Yes, but you know it's my go-to. Works like a charm. Just suck on it for a minute, and the fruit will neutralize it." She pops one in her mouth.

"Fine. I'll suck on it." I roll my eyes because I'm not a believer, but I do it anyway because I love my bestie. She always has some trick up her sleeve for almost any situation. One of the many things I love about her.

"Well fuck. Sounds like I got here just in time." An amused chuckle interrupts my thoughts.

Speaking of the four horsemen and her tricks.

His voice makes my eyes open and every part of my body snap to attention. I'm seeing far more of him lately than I ever expected to in my life, especially outside of the confines of the screen in a sports bar. But Tobias Westfield is now not only the star wide receiver for the Seattle Phantom but my best friend's boyfriend's best friend. Which means we're together a lot lately, especially since Xander and Harper are in that honeymoon phase where they can't stand to be apart for more than a few minutes.

When I look at him his eyes are fixed on me and a smirk tugs at one side of his mouth. My cheeks heat in response, and I can tell the moment he sees it because his smirk only gets stronger in the wake of it. I *hate* the way I react to him. Mostly because I would give anything on this planet not to find him attractive. Seeing less of him would certainly help.

"Don't you have better places to be?" I look back down at

my nearly empty shot glass and drink the final drop just to have something to focus on that's not him.

"And miss your birthday? No way, Spitfire."

I should be excited. Fangirling my brains out because I'm a huge Seattle Phantom fan. Have been since I was a little kid thanks to my dad, and these guys are two of my favorite players.

Except you know that saying? Don't meet your idols. Yeah. *That*.

Xander might have actually improved now that I know him personally. Everything he's done for Harper—the way he looks at her, and how kind he's been to literally everyone in her orbit except her ex who deserved everything he got and then some—has made him seem like some sort of fairytale prince come to life. Or at least one that says fuck a lot and has neck tattoos, but hey... I like that kind for Harper.

Westfield on the other hand is... well. He's even hotter in person, but more infuriating in almost every other way. We argue about every little thing and can't seem to find anything in common. It makes these friendly little get-togethers an adventure—one where my attraction competes with my better sense.

The way he's dressed tonight, all in black with his sleeves rolled up showing his tattoos, two-day-old shadow on his jaw, and a smirk that makes his blue eyes practically glimmer with mischief—well, the wrong side of me is winning. But just give the man a minute. He can ruin anything by opening his mouth.

"What's in your glass tonight, Spitfire?"

Like when he calls me *Spitfire*. As if I'm some little girl on the softball team he coaches on weekends.

"Horsemen." I cough a bit when I try to talk, my throat still burning.

"Oh yeah? Going hard then?" He signals one of the bartenders who happily comes running when she sees who's summoning her.

"Something like that."

"Can we get some waters? A round of horsemen shots and then can we get a bottle of Dom up to the table, or do I need to wait and order that there?"

"If you let me know the table, I can send one up."

Tobias looks to Harper. She explains the location of the table before the bartender nods and hurries off to get started on the shots. When Harper returns her attention to us, Tobias smiles at her.

"So what's the situation?"

"Xander's up keeping them busy. When we get back to the table, I'll explain that I pulled her aside to do a quick birthday shot and then you finally showed up, late but apologetic."

Tobias nods his assent to the plan.

"Then you just pretend to be her date for the night."

"Or I could just go home like I wanted to in the first place. And you all can hang out together." I make one final protest. I know Harper won't budge, but I can't help one last attempt to squirm out of this uncomfortable situation.

A moment later, Tobias's hand is on my lower back, his thumb brushing back and forth while I freeze. His eyes search my face before he smiles.

"We got this. Now do we want to actually make him jealous or are we just toying with him?"

"We're doing nothing with him. We're pretending he doesn't exist. This is humiliating enough. I don't need any Westfield antics, okay?" I give him a pointed look.

"He doesn't exist. Got it."

"We just need to get through dinner and get rid of them. We can go to my place, get cake, and then go to the club. Then we can find some nice gentleman for you to take home." Harper raises her brows and grins.

"Or we just get cake and then go to bed. I'm in my thirties now, that's a thing, right?"

"Thirty, is it?" Tobias looks at me amused.

"Yes. I'm old." I flick a look back at him. Probably too old for him to be pretending to date.

"Nah. Thirty is when things get good, Spitfire."

"And please do not call me that ridiculous nickname at the table."

"Don't call you Spitfire. Got it." His amusement grows every time he talks and it's making me nervous.

"There was literally no one else you could think to call?" I look at Harper desperately.

"It'll be fine. He'll be too dazzled by two Seattle Phantom players to even notice anything else. Just enjoy dinner and then I promise we'll make the rest of the night better."

"Yes, don't worry Spit—Scarlett. We'll find you a nice gentleman." He grins, and I could punch him. I honestly could. The man inspires violence in my pacifist heart without fail.

"No thank you." I offer a false smile and he returns it like we're locked in some sort of standoff. One that's only broken when the bartender returns with the water and shots that Tobias ordered. Tobias raises his shot glass and the rest of us join in.

"To Spitfire—for turning dirty thirty! Here's to another decade of good luck." He glances at me and there's almost a sweetness in the way he looks at me. *Almost.*

I throw back another round of the horsemen but this time it's not the burn of the whiskey that makes me choke. It's the second half of the toast he whispers low enough that only I can hear.

"And to you getting railed tonight by a guy who's not a gentleman."

FOUR

Tobias

AS WE WALK UP the stairs, Scarlett and Harper lead the way. I can tell it's already under her skin that I'm even here. Because Scarlett hates the fact that she's attracted to me. It's written on her face every time she thinks I'm not looking. Right up until she remembers it's me and the flicker of disdain flashes in her eyes. But tonight, I get to pretend to be hers for a little while, and I can't say I hate it.

"Spitfire?" I call after her, taking the steps faster to catch up.

She halts and turns back to look at me while Harper continues to the table. Her eyes run over me, studying my face for a moment like she's trying to puzzle me out.

"Change your mind? Perfect. Goodnight."

"No." I frown at her and hold out my hand. She stares at it for a moment before she realizes what I want. There's a subtle shake of her head and she turns, but I catch her. My fingers sliding over her palm and then lacing with hers.

"We don't need to play it up like this." There's irritation in her voice, but I know it's because her feelings have been run through the grinder already tonight. For once it's not aimed at me, and I have the chance to help.

"Who's playing anything up? I just want people to know you're here with me," I whisper as we approach the table. She flashes a look in my direction but doesn't say anything else. I tighten my grip, and she returns the gentle squeeze as we approach the table.

Harper is in the midst of telling a story and the rest of the table is listening intently. Scarlett pauses suddenly and leans into me, bringing her lips close to my ear.

"They think it's her birthday instead of mine. So just play along. I don't want to embarrass him."

I frown in response, but she gives me a pointed look before tugging me along to the table again. I pull her chair out when we reach the table, and for her part, she gives me an adoring smile as she sits down.

We're not half bad at this routine, probably because in recent history we've watched Xander and Harper replay it like a broken record. They're sickeningly in love and we're just two sad single souls who look morose in comparison. But at least we can mimic the appearance of it.

"Thank you," she says softly, and I grin knowing it's probably killing her a little to say it.

"Of course, gorgeous." I lean over and kiss her cheek before I look up at the rest of the table and conversation resumes as I sit down.

A few minutes later the rosé champagne and glasses arrive, while Carter's girlfriend lets out a little squeal. The server works to fill everyone's glass as she makes her way around the table. Once she's finished, I raise my glass.

"To my birthday girl, who's so incredibly patient when I'm late and looks absolutely fucking stunning this evening."

I nod to Scarlett and smile because there's no way I'm letting this guy ride after he embarrassed her. Xander coughs, and I hear Carter's girlfriend whisper something to him before they take their drinks.

Scarlett stares at me for a long moment after the toast when everyone else is already taking their celebratory sip. Like she can't decide whether she hates or loves me for doing it. The fact that I called her mine makes her lashes flutter and confusion spread. Seconds feel like minutes until the moment snaps, and she downs her drink quickly. I raise a brow at her but reach for the bottle and refill her glass and get another surreptitious assessment from her before her attentions return to the chatter at the table.

Scarlett's cheeks are pink, and she laughs more easily when dinner arrives. I assume between the shots and the champagne, she's feeling better about the whole evening and less offended by my presence.

By the time we head to Xander and Harper's place for cake, she's almost in a good mood. Harper and her head for the kitchen to prep the cake and chat about the night's debacle while Xander and I head out to his terrace for fresh air and whiskey, which we'll both taste more than drink because we're in season and that means almost everything fun is off limits.

"Fuck me, that was brutal." Xander groans when we get outside.

"That guy was annoying as fuck. Clearly just there to impress his girl with us at the table. And he was supposed to be Scarlett's date?"

"I don't fucking know. They've been working with him on

fundraising stuff. Harper really had high hopes for them I guess, so she's pissed off on Scarlett's behalf."

"Scarlett can do better than that fucking loser anyway."

"Oh yeah?" He leans back on the railing. "Like who? You?"

I shake my head and take a sip from my glass, stealing time because my gut reaction to his question is complicated. I'm pretty sure I'm the worst and best she could do at the same time. It just depends on the context.

"If we're talking one night, I'd be perfect for her." I recover.

Xander's brow furrows, and he glances out over the skyline before he looks back at me.

"I'm not going to tell you what to do but remember that Harper and I are a permanent thing and that's her best friend. Be really fucking sure that however that night ends, you can still stand to see each other regularly in the future, yeah?"

"Yeah, happy for you and all but that permanency is ruining things for me a little tonight. Because that dress she has on... Fuck. I don't know if I can stay away."

"She's pretty good at resisting you, so I wouldn't worry too much." He laughs.

"Let's hope that holds. Cause if that icy wall ever melts, I'm in fucking trouble."

"That bad, huh?"

"One night would cure it. I've just got it built up in my head at this point. Listening to her tell me she hates me while we fuck." I grunt and raise my brow before I down more of the whiskey than I should.

The sliding glass door opens, and she appears in it, lit from behind like a fucking angel. Her eyes sweep over me, and she frowns.

"Harper has the cake ready if you want some."

"Be right in, thanks." Xander nods to her, and she closes it again. His neck craning to me. "I don't know if you can come out of that with all of *you* intact, so just be careful she doesn't take a part that's vital to playing football."

"Got it."

AN HOUR later we're in the VIP section of a club Harper has insisted on taking Scarlett to, even though I'm not sure she's really feeling it. It seems more like she just wants to keep Harper happy since she's planned this night for her. I watch her as she stands with Harper, overlooking the crowd below and chatting about their drinks. She laughs at something Harper says and leans back, crossing her legs at her ankles, and once again my eyes are drawn to them. Thinking about what they'd feel like wrapped around me, draped over my shoulders, and kneeling on my bed.

I should stay away from her. I know I should. She's a good girl which means even if I could convince the prickly historian to spend a night with me, the chances that it ends in disaster are high. And if it does, I won't escape it. Not when Harper and Xander are on a runaway train to the white picket fence, and she's involved with the nonprofit that Harper and Joss have spun up together.

But I also need her out of my head. Something to stomp out my curiosity for good, which means I'm tempted enough to press my luck tonight. Maybe the prospect of going home alone on her birthday will finally be enough to sway her my way.

When Harper and Xander disappear for a few minutes, I slink over to the spot next to her. She's sitting with one leg up and crossed on the couch as she peers down at the crowd, nodding along to the music. She doesn't notice me until I'm already next to her, and I tease my finger along the strap of her heel before I sit down.

Her eyes snap to mine and rake over me. She likes what she sees, even though she doesn't want to. I'm fairly certain she thinks I'm a dumb jock with shit for brains and the fact that she still imagines riding me probably gives her existential rage. The kind that could be channeled into the kind of hate fucking I'd die for.

"Decided which one you're taking home?" Her eyes flick to the women who had been leaning over the wall of their VIP section to talk to me. "Oh. Or is it a both situation?"

"It's a neither situation."

"Oh. Well, that's disappointing. I was rooting for the blonde."

"Why?"

"She seems like she genuinely likes you. The other one just seems like she'd brag to her friends about fucking you." She's been downing water with her cocktail for the last half hour, but her tongue is still loose from the shots earlier.

I glance back at the women and one of them catches my gaze and gives me a coy smile, but I feel none of the usual excitement. Too distracted by Scarlett to give a fuck about anyone else.

"Maybe. What about you? Pick someone out for your birthday?" I nod toward the crowd below us.

She laughs at the idea. "Yeah. The bartender down there. Gonna see if he'll rail me when he gets off his shift. He doesn't look like a gentleman, right?"

The guy looks like an absolute self-absorbed dick who probably fucks a different girl he takes home from the bar every night. One who definitely doesn't deserve to touch Scarlett. And while I'm all too aware of that irony, I can't help but want to stop to it.

"He looks like tomorrow morning's regret."

She looks back at me and raises an eyebrow, her eyes

flashing to the women I was talking to and then back to me without saying a word.

"They'd probably regret me too, I know."

Her lips quirk with amusement but she still stays silent. I slide my palm over her thigh, risking dismemberment.

"But you wouldn't, right?" I smirk when I raise my eyes to look at her, and her brow goes sky-high in response.

"Regret fucking you? Probably not. It's the murder and the twenty-five years that'll be a real source of remorse for me."

"Would make you pretty unpopular."

"I think my popularity's already waning." Her eyes float to the women across the way who aren't amused that I'm touching her. "So you'd better go back to your fan club."

She stands then and leans over to grab her purse. I feel a little swell of panic that she's headed off to flirt with the bartender. If he has any brains at all, he'll definitely sign up to be hers for the night. I hate the thought of the two of them fucking. Of anyone touching her but me tonight.

"Leaving?" I slide my fingers up the back of her knee as I look up at her.

"Need the powder room. I'll be back." She looks down at where my fingers brush over her soft skin.

"Good. I'll drive you home when you're ready." I lean back, looking up at her to make sure she knows I'm not joking. Her mouth moves like she's about to say something, but she closes it again and heads off to the bathrooms instead.

FIVE

Scarlett

I PRACTICALLY RUN to the bathroom to put some distance between Tobias and me. He's taking the gentleman thing a little too far this evening, being ridiculously attentive and borderline charming. I know he can't possibly be implying what I think he is, but if he was any other guy on Earth, I'd assume he is.

I need a break, fresh air, and probably a whole lot more ice water than I've had so far. But if he did want a one-night stand... would that be so bad? I might hate him, but he is incredibly fucking nice to look at and rumored to be pretty good in bed. I could do worse for my birthday, and he'd probably treat me better than some random bartender given that he's guaranteed to have to see me again in the future. I think I might not completely hate the idea, but I'm definitely not going to embarrass myself for the millionth time tonight by saying something first and being wrong. Since apparently, when it comes to signals, I'm clueless.

By the time I get back to the VIP section we've been in, I have my answer. I feel stupid for even thinking of leaving with him. The blonde from before is curled up next to him drinking champagne and running her hand up his forearm while she listens to whatever he's saying. Across from them Harper and Xander have returned ahead of me and are so focused on making out that they don't even realize I'm standing here. I've come full circle this evening, back to being the fifth wheel. Which is my sign to go home, get in my pajamas, and sleep this embarrassing day off.

I hustle my way back out and down the stairs before I'm spotted, pausing on the landing to get a ride before I make my way through the crowd. I don't want to tell Harper I'm leaving because she'll insist on taking me home and the last thing I want is to be around any more adoring couples this evening.

So when the car arrives and I climb in, I send off a quick text to her to tell her I'm on my way home and that I love her and appreciated the amazing birthday she gave me. Then I collapse in the back seat, staring out the window for the long ride back to the suburbs while the rain starts to come down hard.

IF I'M HONEST, I hadn't been dreading turning thirty the same way some people do. I'd been looking forward to it. My twenties had been a long marathon through school and crappy relationships that didn't work out in the end, and I'm ready for a blank slate. A whole new decade to see what comes next.

I did not, however, anticipate starting that decade and ending this night in the cold pouring rain sitting in the back seat of my driver's broken-down car on the side of the road while he trudges down it to get a tire because he refuses to get a tow.

I tap my nails on my phone for several minutes, wondering what the hell I should do. If I'm safe here and who I could tell just in case. Not many people I know are likely to be up at this hour, and I don't want to wake someone up just to worry them. Which means there's really only one person to call. So I text Harper about my dilemma. A moment later the phone rings.

"Are you telling me you're sitting in a stranger's broken-down car in the middle of the night alone?"

"Something like that..."

"Scarlett. No way. Especially not when you've been drinking. Something could happen to you! Why didn't you walk with the driver? Or better yet just tell me you needed a ride!"

"Because being trapped out in the cold rain with him if things got weird seemed worse than being alone in the warm dry car." I realize now that my plan sounds a bit nuts.

"No. We're coming to get you."

"No. Harper! You don't need to drive all the way out here. You're in the city and you're within walking distance from home. Don't be silly. You've done enough rescuing for one night. I'll just call a car or something. I just wanted someone to know where I am in case."

"No, no more strangers. Just send me a pin and we'll be right there."

"Harper—"

"Don't argue with me. I'm serious."

"Fine."

"Love you and be careful!"

"Love you. And thank you."

. . .

BRIGHT LIGHTS BEAM through the back window less than half an hour later. I lean forward to try to get a peek at it. Whatever it is, it's fancy as fuck which makes me think it's Xander and Harper, and not a serial killer. But then you never know. Honestly, at this point, I think I might be ready to take my chances. The door opens and a tall figure steps out just as I start to open the door and get out, the rain battering my face as I do it.

But when I look closer, the figure is definitely not Xander, and there's no Harper on the passenger side. I reach back for the door handle, but it's locked behind me. Fucking automatic locks, or maybe I hit it on accident. Whatever the case, panic is welling in my chest. The figure comes closer, and I hold out my hand to stop them.

"Stay away! Just stay there. I don't need help. I have a friend coming any minute."

The man answers but it's unintelligible because of the rain, and I take two steps backward, bumping into the car mirror in a way I know is going to leave a bruise on my shoulder blade tomorrow. If I make it until then.

"Stay away!" I scream, but they keep coming.

So I do the only thing I know how. I run through the wet grass on the side of the road screaming for help.

I don't make it far. My foot catches on a rock and I stumble, tripping forward and desperately trying to regain my balance. Apparently, thirty is as far as I'm going to make it, and I'm going out like this—murdered face down in a muddy ditch on the side of the road. I start to scream one last time, just as arms wrap around my waist and pull me back up. A hand slams over my mouth half a second later.

"Jesus fucking Christ, Scarlett. I know you're fucking drunk but calm the fuck down!" If the booming voice doesn't let me know who it is, the scent of his cologne is a dead giveaway.

I turn around, ripping out of his grip, and shove him back with my hands.

"What the fuck, Tobias? Why didn't you say it was you?"

"I said it was me, twice!"

"Too quietly! I couldn't hear you over the rain! I thought you were a murderer. You were supposed to be Xander and Harper. Where are they?"

"I told them I'd come to get you so they didn't have to go out."

"Jesus. She and I are going to have a fucking talk. Like I need you rescuing me twice today."

"That's fucking funny. That didn't sound like a thank you."

I glare at him, and he just silently raises his eyebrow in return.

"We just gonna stand out here in the rain then because you're too stubborn to say thank you?"

"I am not too stubborn, and I always say thank you."

"And yet..."

"You make it very fucking hard."

"Likewise, Spitfire."

"Stop fucking calling me that!"

"You done throwing a tantrum or you want us to get completely soaked out here?"

"I'm not leaving with you. I'll call another car. I should have done that in the first place."

"You're going to call another car and wait out here in the dark and pouring rain for it?"

"Yes. So go home or off with your little blonde, okay?"

Then he does the last thing I'm expecting—he laughs, full and loud and wild. Two seconds before he grabs me and throws me over his shoulder.

"What the fuck are you doing?"

"Taking you home."

"You are not. Put me the fuck down!"

"Nah. We're done doing things your way now."

"If you don't fucking put me down, I'll..." I trail off. I have no idea what I'll do. Before I can think of a plausible threat, we're already at his car, and he's opening the door and pulling me down off his shoulder.

"You'll what?" He pins me against the car.

"I hate you."

"I know. Now get in the car."

"No."

His teeth grit and turn into a saccharine smile.

"Scarlett, you get in the car, and you put your seatbelt on, or I will grab the bands I have in my gym bag, tackle you in the mud when you try to run again, and hog-tie you before I throw you back there. Your choice."

"You're insane." I glare at him, but the glimmer reflecting off the headlights in his eyes tells me I'm right. "You'd do it," I mumble, realizing I'm going to lose this fight whether I like it or not.

"I would, and I would enjoy every single moment of it. So what's it going to be?"

I plop down, the splash of water against his expensive leather seats audible and flip my wet hair over my shoulder. There's a bitter grin on his face before he shuts the door and rounds the car to get into the driver's seat.

"Should you even be driving?"

"I barely had anything, and it was all at the beginning of the night. I'm fine."

"You can just take me to the gas station up here, and I can call a car."

"Give me your address so I can put in the GPS."

I let out a sigh, cold and muted, but then I give him the address. Resigned to the fact that any other plan than him taking me home at this point would probably be a battle I don't have the energy for and a way for him to embarrass me more than I already am.

The ride home feels longer than it is, more sobering than it should be. Because the warmth of the car and the light hum of the engine are just enough to calm my anxiety and make me realize how ridiculous I've been tonight. How much I've acted unhinged when I could have just thanked him and let him help me. I just hate the way he gets under my skin.

When we pull into the parking lot the guilt is hitting hard. So hard I feel like I don't want to wait for another time to do this. So I go for it. Ripping off the Band-Aid. Still shivering as I manage to say what needs to be said.

"I'm sorry," I blurt out. "I'll pay for the seats to be cleaned or fixed or whatever."

"It's fine," he answers, and I can't bear to look at him. "You should get upstairs and get warm."

"It's not fine. Just... do you want to come up? I can get you some towels for you and the car. Make some tea, something."

"Scarlett—" He sounds pained. I should probably just let the man go home, but I don't want the night to end on this awkward note.

"Please, can we just call a truce? Let me do something. You did a lot tonight, and I want to make up for it. We're going to have to keep being around each other because of Harper and Xander, and I just don't want to have to wake up to being the complete bitch in all of this."

"Okay..." he says softly after a moment and turns the ignition off.

He's so reluctant, I almost tell him to forget it. Feeling like

I'm asking him for another thing that's too much. But he gets out of the car, and we both make our way through the rain up to my apartment.

SIX

Tobias

THE LAST THING I should be doing right now is following her into her apartment. I should be leaving her alone. Shouldn't have even intervened with Harper and Xander in picking her up. A thing that Harper might have been enthusiastic about, but I could tell by the look on his face Xander wasn't excited by it. Because he knows what I know. I can only take so much around Scarlett before I crack and give into temptation where she's concerned.

She's shivering next to me, and I just want to get her inside right now. Her hands are shaking as she tries to put the key in the lock of her apartment door. I gently take them from her, sliding the key in, and turning it for her.

"Thanks. Sorry. Just so freaking cold still."

We enter the apartment, and she flicks on the light, revealing a place that's small but cozy. It can't be more than one bedroom. A small hallway that looks to open up to two or three doors, a living room that's about the size of the mudroom in my house, and a galley kitchen with a small island that juts out. The cabinets are dated, and the apartment looks older, but it's comfortable and warm. She's put effort into decorating the place. A combination of things that look new and vintage, probably thrifted or hand-me-downs if I had to guess. But it looks and feels like her. Like she's put her magic touch on everything and somehow made all the ordinary bits seem like they add up to something more. The same way she does with everything she wears.

"I'll turn the heat up a bit and put a kettle on. Feel free to sit at the dining table. The chairs are from college anyway. Won't hurt to get a little water on them." She offers a small smile as she heads into the kitchen, filling up the kettle with water before she puts it on the stove.

I watch her more closely than I should. Because the dress she has on is absolutely plastered to every curve of her body and her wet hair curls at the ends where it's trying to dry. Her makeup is smudged but still looks gorgeous and that's all before we get to the thigh highs that are still accentuating every long line of her legs.

"God, it almost feels worse in here. Colder. Are you okay? I can get some towels. Just give me a minute." She doesn't wait for an answer before she disappears.

When she returns, she's got one dabbing at her hair and holds another out for me. I use it to get the worst of the water from my hair and down my neck. She watches me for a moment and her eyes drift down my body. I'm in a similar state to her, my clothes still soaking wet and glued to my body.

"You should take those off." She nods to my clothes, and I go still. Trying to figure out if she's saying what I think she is. "I can put them in the dryer really quick. So you don't have to drive home like that. Between that and the tea, it'll warm you up."

So no. Not what I thought she was saying.

"Oh, I'm fine."

She steps forward and presses her palm to my forearm. "You're freezing. You're not fine. Just let me have the clothes. I can see if I have a robe or oversized shirt or something if you're feeling modest. It's not like I haven't seen you mostly naked though."

I frown for a moment, trying to recall when that was and then it hits me. The photoshoot I did for Joss to help Scarlett with some museum thing she was doing. It's followed by memories of the way she looked at me. Subtle appreciation she tried to hide. One that I can only imagine will be worse now that she's had a bit to drink and trying her hardest to be nice to me. But I feel ridiculous refusing, so I just deflect.

"You should get out of yours first. Make sure you get warmed up and put something dry on." I nod toward her.

"Fine. I'm going to go change in my room. In the meantime take those off. There's a blanket on the couch if you want to cover up."

"All right."

She disappears then, satisfied with my answer, and I start undoing my belt and pulling my wallet out onto the table. Setting it next to my phone which is already out and safe from the water. I manage to get my shirt off and am in the process of stepping out of my pants when she returns. She glances at me and then away like she's trying to be respectful.

"So, slight problem. The dress is wet and so is the zipper, so I'm having trouble getting it off. Can you try?" She turns her back to me and slides her hair over the front of her shoulder, exposing the long line of her neck and spine.

I finish taking my pants off and set my clothes on the chair before I move to take off her dress. My fingers feel icy cold and less than dexterous with the strain of it, but I make an effort. At first, it doesn't budge for me either, but then I finally feel it start to give way. I tug gently, pulling it all the way down her back. It gapes at the sides, revealing the dimples at the base of her spine and the lacy edge of her panties just beneath it. And fuck me, do I want to rip them all off and run my tongue over her.

"Got it," I whisper instead.

She turns her head, looking over her shoulder back at me, hesitating before she moves. I run my fingers over the base of her neck and across her shoulder, pushing the strap to the side as I watch it reveal more of her skin. She lets me, her eyes glued to the spot where I'm touching her before her lashes flutter suddenly, and she turns her head away again.

"Thanks." She pulls forward.

Then, like she's trying to prove a point that she's unbothered by all of this, she steps out of the dress and piles it on top of my clothes, taking them off the chair.

"I'll just put these in the dryer."

She turns back to offer me a half smile and my eyes fall to her bra. A sight that nearly takes me out cold. Because her bra is see-through lace. Both of her pale peach nipples are hard little beads that are pressing against the fabric and her lacy underwear is leaving almost nothing to the imagination.

"Fuck," I mutter and avert my eyes to the ceiling.

"What?"

"Your bra or lack thereof." I shake my head, closing my eyes.

"Oh. I forgot it was this one," she mumbles.

"So yeah, Carter's a fucking idiot for missing out on that."

She lets out a small, amused laugh. "I didn't wear it for him."

"Who did you wear it for then?"

I know it can't be me. She didn't even know she'd see me tonight, but fuck I wish it was.

"Me. I wanted to feel nice. I didn't expect anyone else to see. Sorry."

"Do not fucking apologize for that. You look fucking gorgeous. Cold, but gorgeous." I grin and open my eyes when she stays quiet. She's still standing there, holding our clothes, and looking at me.

I take a step forward, closing the short distance between us, and run my hand up the side of her arm. I lean forward because I'm close, so close to giving in to temptation and kissing my way down her throat and over the curve of her breast. Peeling back the edge of the bra, so I can take one of her nipples in my mouth and warm her up.

"You're so cold," she whispers, her lashes lowering as her eyes run over my body.

I slide my hand under her chin, tilting it up and staring down at her plush pink lips that part just the slightest bit under my watch.

"We're working on fixing that, right?"

Her lashes flutter because she knows what I'm asking.

"Right," she says softly.

I lean in to kiss her neck, my lips achingly close when the kettle whistles, and she jolts back. She blinks like she's come out of a daze.

"*Right.* I'm going to put these in the dryer." She presses the wet clothes closer to her body and takes a step back. "Could you take the kettle off the heat?"

SEVEN

Scarlett

I HURRY off to put our clothes in the dryer and put distance between Tobias and me. I have no idea what the hell is happening tonight. My brain is struggling to keep up, and it's still muddled from the cold. I can't tell if he actually wants me or if this is some sort of pity thing on his part because of the multiple times he's had to come to my rescue in one day. Maybe he thinks he needs to save me from my dry spell too.

I put the clothes in the dryer and turn it on to a low cycle, leaning my head against the door of the stacked machine for a moment before I turn back toward the kitchen. I pause for a second, briefly considering putting clothes on, but then I don't want to seem like a coward. Plus he's seen me half naked already, so in for a penny and all that.

When I get back to the kitchen he's opening the cabinets looking for mugs, and I smile at him in his underwear rooting through the cupboards. Watching his tight ass flex in his boxer briefs. Ones that are plastered against his skin thanks to the rain, giving me a view that I'm going to mentally catalog for later.

"It's the one on the far right."

He looks back and grins at me before he moves to it and pulls out two mugs. He holds them in his hands for a minute, reading them, and then cracks up.

I'm thankful for my punny taste in mugs for once because it breaks the tension between us and relaxes the knot that's been building in my neck since our clothes came off. I grab the tea bags and place one in each.

"You want to make a tea bagging joke too?"

"Maybe. You into that sort of thing?"

"Mmm, no. Not my kink of choice." I smirk as I pour the water into the mugs.

"Don't talk about kinks, Spitfire. And while we're on the subject, you should really put some clothes on. Walking around here looking like that. It can't be warm."

"Just trying to keep it fair since you can't change. You sure you don't want me to see if the robe would fit you?"

"I'm good. I prefer cold dignity to warm humiliation."

"Fair…" I grin and dip the tea bag in and out of the water. "We could get under the covers in the bed. That would at least help. See if there's something we can watch on TV while we wait for your clothes to dry."

His eyebrow creeps up as he looks at me, glancing down at his mug and then at me.

"You're suggesting we both crawl half naked into your bed?"

"No. I'm suggesting two cold people get under a blanket and watch some TV so they don't freeze to death while they wait on the dryer."

"Right." He stares down at his mug.

"Can't handle it?" I taunt him, not even trying to hide the little smirk that comes to my face.

"How about you change out of the lingerie into something warmer, and I'll get under the blankets while you stay on top of them?"

A laugh tumbles out before I can stop it, and I bite my lower lip. A grouchy look crosses his face, and he frowns at me.

"This amuse you, Spitfire?"

"That Tobias Westfield is worried about being under a blanket with me? Yeah. I'm amused." I take a sip of my tea. "I think you can handle it. Let's go." I nod toward my room, but he doesn't follow.

"Scarlett... I'm doing my fucking level best here thinking the unsexiest thoughts I can imagine, keeping my eyes down, and trying my fucking hardest not to cross any lines with you while you stand around in see-through lingerie and talk about your 'kinks of choice'. A lesser man would have caved by now and put you on your fucking back in the bed." His eyes lift from his mug and under his thick lashes, his blues are smoldering with the threat.

I'm pretty sure I don't get a second chance like this, and I'm thirty now, so fuck it.

"I think I'd rather have the lesser man tonight."

Apparently, I've given him the permission he was looking for, or the bait, because a second later he slides his mug on the counter, grabs mine out of my hand and deposits it on the table, hauling me up into his arms. He crosses the apartment and pushes the door to my room open, depositing me on the bed a second later, pinning me to the mattress.

He opens his mouth to speak when something catches his eye, and he turns his head. He stares at the desk in the corner of my room. It's set up to film my History Harlot videos, with two cameras, a large monitor, and a big comfy chair. His eyes narrow and he blinks, and then he looks back at me.

"Are you—I'm asking this without malice or judgment to be clear—but are you a fucking cam girl, Spitfire?"

I burst out into laughter, and his frown deepens.

"No. I wish."

His eyes widen, and he blinks.

"I film history content. Educational content. I have a video channel that people subscribe to, so kind of a cam girl. Doesn't pay nearly as well. I've thought about trying it, but I chicken out every time."

"What do you mean you chicken out?"

I feel the heat of his gaze, and I swallow against my dry throat. "Um... I've tried filming a few times. But deleted them."

"Holy fuck." He groans closing his eyes.

"What?"

"Sometimes I think you're cosmic punishment. Sent to torture me for all the wrong shit I've done over the years. Too many fucking coincidences for it otherwise." He takes a breath and blows it out slowly like he's trying to regain his composure.

"Lucky me."

"I need you to tell me this is a bad idea. Remind me this is gonna make things worse between us in the long run."

"Or maybe we just fuck it out and can finally stop driving each other insane?"

He looks down at me, his eyes dark with lust, and his jaw tightens.

"Now you are baiting me." He grabs my hand and hauls me up to my feet again. I look at him quizzically. "Go take a shower."

"What?"

"Like a cold shower? Ice cold. Go take one. Think this

through. You still feel that way when you get back, then fine. But I'm calling a timeout after everything tonight."

"Are you serious right now? You want me to take a cold shower when we're trying to warm up?"

"Then take a warm shower, or a hot one—even better. Get your body temperature up and make sure your head is clear. Okay?"

"Tobias."

"Go." He gives me a look followed by a playful smack on my ass and I, for my part, listen to him.

EIGHT

Tobias

"TOBIAS?" I hear her call from the bathroom after the water shuts off.

"Yeah?"

"Could you um... in the hurry to get in here, I forgot a towel. There's some in my closet in the bedroom. A little hanger cubby that has them in there. Would you mind?"

"No problem." I hop up and head to her closet, opening the door to the small walk-in.

I turn the light on and look for the cubby she's talking about. I spot them and grab one, but out of the corner of my eye, I see a flash of Phantom colors. Which makes me curious. I know she's a fan of the team. That she comes to games. I'd heard her and Harper talk enough to not be surprised they're in here, but when I look closer, I realize one of the three shirts is a jersey. So I do the thing I shouldn't and push them back to get a better look.

The T-shirts are from our division win and the conference championship a few years ago. The jersey is older too. A style we retired a while back. I slide the hanger back so I can see the name. Assuming it'll be St. George or Lawton. It would fit with her temperament to love one of them, and it would've been Colt's first year with the team when he was putting up insane rookie numbers. So my heart slams against my chest when I see WESTFIELD in big letters and my number on the back.

"Did you find it?" she calls out.

"Yep!" I practically croak the word, hurriedly pushing the jersey back into place.

I shut the door and then hurry down the hall, rapping my knuckles against the frame.

"I'm looking away," I say preemptively as I hold the towel out and turn my head in the opposite direction.

She reaches for it and I feel her fingers brush over mine as she takes the towel, a waft of her shampoo and body wash enveloping me along with the steam from the shower.

"Thank you," she whispers, and even looking away, I can feel her eyes on me.

I nod and then hurry back to the bedroom where I stand in the middle of it, running a hand over my face. I'm so utterly fucking confused right now. I've flirted with her endlessly since I met her and nothing. She's never once acted like she was dazzled by being around me or even tried to pursue me. If it wasn't for her occasional clandestine eye fucking, I wouldn't even know she found me attractive at all. Yet she's got my jersey in her closet, one she's had for *years*. This woman is going to be the death of me.

I edge the closet open again, the jersey taunting me, and I pull on it, flipping it over to the back again to look at it. Confirm one more time that I hadn't just seen what I wanted to see there. That it isn't all just a complete figment of my imagination.

Which is when I see it. Scrawled over the number on the back of the jersey.

My signature. My handwriting.

I rip it off the hanger and throw it on the bed. Because now I'm gonna need an explanation.

NINE

Scarlett

WHEN I COME BACK into the room wrapped in a towel, I grin at him sitting on the edge of the bed watching me. Meanwhile, I'm taking in all the skin and tattoos on display. But when my eyes meet his, there's something stormy there. The little bloom of anticipation in my chest fades.

"What?"

"Forgot clothes too?"

"Yeah. You kind of rushed me out of here."

"Good. Put it on." He nods to the spot next to him on the bed.

Which is when I spot the jersey—his jersey. The one that hangs in the back of my closet. The one he never would have seen if I hadn't asked him to go looking for a towel. *Fuck.*

"Tobias..."

"You hate me and yet you have an old jersey of mine."

"Having your jersey is a crime now?" I ask defensively.

I'm honestly a little shocked. I thought this would have bolstered his ego, not made him grumpy as fuck.

"It's signed. *I* signed it. When the fuck did that happen?"

"Shortly after I bought it—years ago. When I went to an open training camp day."

"I don't remember it."

I laugh at the idea that he would, and he frowns.

"Why would you? You've probably signed thousands of them over the years."

"I feel like I'd remember you." There's a defensive edge to his voice.

"You barely even looked at me. You were too busy flirting with my friend and asking for her number so she could meet you at a club that night."

A panicked look flashes across his face. "I didn't—" He stops as abruptly as he started.

"Fuck her? No. She had a boyfriend and wasn't interested. She told you that before trying to get me to give you my number. Which you responded to with... 'Nah. I'm good, sweetheart' before you waved us off."

His eyes soften, and his jaw flexes.

"I think I'm beginning to understand why you don't like me."

"It was a million years ago."

"So nothing to do with why you've seemingly hated me since the first day we met?"

"I mean, I didn't forget that it happened. But the animosity since is mostly to do with the fact that you seem to get off on irritating me. I have no idea what I did to deserve that."

"You're fucking hot when you're pissed. I honestly can't help myself sometimes. It's like an addiction."

I laugh at the honesty, and he smiles at me for a moment

before a devious smirk spreads in its wake. He pulls the jersey off the bed, turning it over to look at his name again.

"So does this mean you've had an unrequited thing for me all these years? Just pining away for me?"

I raise a brow at him.

"It means I liked watching you play."

"Past tense?"

"No. I still like watching you play. I just also fantasize about strangling you to death sometimes while I do it."

"Yeah? I think about wrapping my hands around your throat too, Spitfire, but the ending's a little different in my mind." He reaches out and runs his fingers up the inside of my knee, and I freeze. I don't even try to stop him.

"No murder?"

"No... but you still get all your frustrations out on me in my version."

"Oh yeah?" His fingers climb higher up the inside of my thigh, and he presses gently to pull me closer to him.

"Yeah. You ride them out until you come hard." He looks up at me and smirks, and then his eyes drift over to my camera. "And then we watch the replay until it makes you so wet you beg me for more."

"That sounds ambitious." I have whiplash from how fast this side of him appeared.

"You've watched me play. You know I'm an overachiever when it's something I'm serious about." He grabs my wrist and turns me before he pulls me down in his lap, my back to his chest and my legs barely touching the floor between his. My towel is still hanging on me by a thread.

"And you're serious about this? What happened to me taking a shower to cool off and think about things?"

"Then I found this." He tosses the jersey in my lap. "And

now I know you've been thinking about fucking me a lot longer than tonight."

I let out a stuttered laugh. "You think so, huh?"

His hand wraps around the damp ends of my hair until he has a fistful, and he pulls back on it, exposing my neck.

"Lie and tell me when we fight you don't think about fucking me, Spitfire," he whispers against my throat before his mouth follows, kissing a slow trail up the side.

"Sometimes I think about hurting you."

"Good."

"You're due some for being such a dick all the time." I press on because the tension is so thick, I feel like I have to talk to make sure it's real.

"That's probably true. You want to make me hurt, sweetheart? I'll let you. As long as at the end you let me watch while you ride me, I don't care." He grabs the edge of the towel and presses a kiss under my earlobe. "Let me see you."

I nod, and he doesn't hesitate to rip it off. It drops to my waist, pooling around the tops of my thighs on top of the jersey. The cool air assaults my skin and whatever warmth I'd managed to get back is quickly dissipating, right along with any resistance I have to the idea of having him inside me tonight.

"Fuck me. You're even more gorgeous than I imagined you would be. This body, Scarlett. Fuck... I don't know how I ever saw anyone but you." His fingers trace a line down the center of my body as I lean back against his chest. His palm splays over my abdomen, and I follow its descent with my eyes until he stops just past my belly button. "Tell me I get a fucking taste of you tonight after all the torment."

I don't answer. I can't because words just won't come for me right now. So instead I spread my thighs and put my palm over the back of his hand, pushing it down until I hear him curse against my skin. He parts me and the pad of his middle finger grazes over my clit. I'm wet and on edge from listening to him talk. So much so that I'm sensitive enough that it nearly hurts, and I gasp at the contact.

"Oh, you've been waiting for me. Fuck. Scarlett... You should have told me. I could've taken care of you earlier. You just have to ask," he mutters against my skin as he adds his index finger, giving me the extra friction that I need as I roll my hips up to meet him.

"Fuck. I'm going to come already..." I whisper, half-embarrassed at how little of his touch it takes to bring me close so quickly. If he didn't think I was obsessed with him after the jersey, he will now.

"That's okay. This is just the first one. You let me; I'll make you come so many times tonight you won't even remember this one."

It's a lie. Because I'm definitely going to remember the first time I let him touch me. How gentle he's being, how sweet his words are, and how good he is with his hands.

"You've been wound tight all fucking night. Let me take the edge off." The pads of his fingers circle my clit faster, and I bury my face against his neck, the stubble on his jaw rough against my cheek as I moan against his skin.

"That's right. Come for me. So fucking sweet and wet for me. Like a fucking dream."

A dream because I've definitely never come this fast before in real life. My whole body shivers under his touch and the hot flush warms me again. Something I'm trying to process as I start to come down from the orgasm, and he slows his rhythm, sliding his fingers back up my body and smirking at the trace of wetness that trails behind. I don't know if he's this good or if my body is just this needy at this point, strung out from stress and a lack of sex.

I don't have much time to dwell on it though because he's

hard beneath me, and after everything he's done for me tonight, the least I want to do is make him come. I also don't mind scratching that off the bucket list. An item that's near the top of it even if I'd never, ever, tell him that.

I stand and turn, slipping down to my knees between his legs and reaching for the elastic of his boxer briefs before his hands catch my wrists.

"Nah, birthday girl. You don't get on your knees tonight. Birthday rules. I only come if it's in the process of getting you off."

"That sounds made up."

"It is. Literally just now. But I like it, so we're sticking to it."

"What if I want to?"

"It'll have to wait for another time then."

"Fine. Then I want you inside me now."

"Fuck, you're bossy." He grins.

"So are you."

"Fair enough. I'll have to run out to get my bag. I don't have a condom on me."

"There's some in the drawer." I nod to my nightstand, and he raises a brow.

TEN

Tobias

"HOLY FUCK, Spitfire. You have an arsenal in here." I stare down at the open drawer that has at least three kinds of vibrators, and one I've never seen before.

"Have to keep it interesting."

I glance back at her before I pull a condom out of the box and there's a small unreadable something in her eyes that has me wishing I could read minds. I had no idea there was this side to her. One so sweet that she's willing to get on her knees for me.

She crawls up the bed and leans her head against the palm of her hand as she watches me, a devious little smile on her lips. I'm imagining her sprawled out on the bed as she is now with her toys, filming herself like she's making spicy audition tapes to be a cam girl. I almost want to ask her to do it for me. Let me watch her while she films herself. My cock gets harder at the thought of it, but I need to stay focused on the task at hand—her.

If anyone had told me this morning that I was going to be having sex with Scarlett tonight, I'd have thought they were fucking insane. That there was no possible path from where we were to where we're about to be. But I'm here, somehow, and wondering if I've fucking lost my mind. A concussion taking me out the same way it's taken Colt, and I just don't realize it. All of this is a dream while I'm passed out on the field.

"Find one you like?" she asks when I'm taking a little too long.

"Perfect," I answer as I peel the boxer briefs I have on off and open the condom wrapper.

Her eyes fall to my cock, and I can feel them on me while I roll it on, tracing my movements and watching everything I do. Her tongue darts out over her lower lip, and I almost regret not letting her suck me dry. I want it, so fucking badly. But I also want tonight to be about her, and only her.

"You were different tonight," she says suddenly as her eyes trace their way back up my body.

"Different?"

"Rolling out all the good manners. With the chair and the drinks. Playing the gentleman. What was that?"

"Me trying to make sure you had a good time for your birthday. Why?"

"It was nice, but now I want the opposite of whatever that was." Her lashes lift, and her eyes meet mine. "More of the guy who grabbed me and threatened to tie me up in his backseat." She grins.

I raise my brow at her. Fuck, she's good at these games. Surprising me left and right. I half expected her to say she was tired after she came. Tell me my clothes were dry, and I could go now. Instead, she's stretched out on the bed baiting me.

"You want it rough, Spitfire?"

"You did promise to put your hands around my throat."

I reach out and grab her by the back of the neck. Dragging her up off her side and toward me. I hold her eyes as I climb onto the bed. Her gaze travels up my arm, tracing the tattoos, and her teeth dig into her lower lip as her eyes light with excitement.

"That make you wet already?"

She nods.

"Fuck. I always hoped you'd be this way. Have this dirty side to you. I love it." Her lashes flutter with the statement and her eyes meet mine, an intensity in them that matches my own. My heart skips. Just for half a second. So quick I could have almost missed it, but just enough I know it's there. Even if I want to ignore it.

So I try. I sit back on the bed, leaning against the pillows and headboard and pull her toward me. She straddles me, her sweet little cunt so close to my cock I can feel the warmth of her.

"I want to watch you take my cock, sweetheart. Every fucking inch of me."

I slide my hands down the sides of her body. It's a balancing act now, giving her what she wants while still making sure she's the one really in control. I'll give her the illusion that I'm in charge. Tell her what to do, make her come more times than she can count. But for my sanity, I need her to be the one who decides here.

"Ride me. *Now.*"

She rolls her lower lip between her teeth, her eyes going to my cock before she lines herself up. Teasing the tip before she slides down on me. Her cunt, so fucking tight, I curse when she's fully seated, blinking when I open my eyes to take in the feel of her and her perfect fucking body. She looks like a goddess right now with her thighs spread, taking me deep, head back as I pull her hair. I want the full image. Fuck, I need it.

"Move, sweetheart."

She rises up and down once, her eyes closing. Licking her lips and then a soft moan escapes from them. A small gasp follows on her next try and then she finally starts to take me in a steady rhythm. Her breasts sway with the movement, and I release my grip on her hair to watch it fall down over her shoulders.

"You feel so fucking good," she whispers. "I needed this."

It's probably the best thing I've heard someone say to me in years.

"Yeah, you've needed me for a long time, Spitfire. I know. You're a good girl, and you deserve it."

She moves in perfect rhythm as if she was made for my cock. Made for me. Taking all of me so well each time her gorgeous thighs meet mine. The sound of our fucking's so loud and the smell of her fills the room, all the while she gets wetter and wetter as she rides me.

She's so fucking sexy; I can barely focus. She has a body full of perfect curves, full hips, a rounded belly, and breasts that have me dying to fucking have her on camera. Some way to revisit this image again and again when I need it the most.

I run my hands under her breasts, supporting the weight of them, and then brushing my thumbs over her nipples. They bead up under my touch, and I lean forward to take one in my mouth, circling my tongue around the tip. One of her hands goes to the back of my neck, running up my spine and into my hair. The scrape of my teeth elicits another moan as she writhes up and down. I turn my attention to the other one, nipping at the underside of her breast and then licking my way up over the tip of her nipple before I suck it into my mouth and roll my tongue over it.

"Fuck me harder, Spitfire. Take me deep like the dirty fucking girl we know you are now. Riding my cock like this. So we both remember how much you've been craving having me inside you." I grab her ass and squeeze, urging her on as she does what I ask of her.

"Just like that. The way you take me, the way your perfect little cunt feels... Fuck, Scarlett. You're gorgeous. I can't take my eyes off of you."

Her eyes flutter open, meeting mine for a moment before they drift down over my chest. She puts her hands on my shoulders, bracing herself as she starts to move faster and takes me deeper. She's so tight and wet that I don't know how much longer I can last.

I slide my hand down over her stomach and the soft curve of her abdomen, resting my thumb over her swollen clit, countering the rhythm of her body with each stroke.

"Oh fuck. Yes. Like that," she mutters, her eyes closing as she concentrates on chasing her own pleasure. She looks wild, a few pieces of her damp red hair stuck to the side of her face before I reach out to sweep it back behind her ear with my free hand. She turns her head then, kissing my palm, and I slide the backs of my fingers down the side of her jaw.

She lifts her chin, letting my hand slide to her throat and her eyes flicker open again, the same intensity in them as before, and I realize what she wants. I wrap my hand around her neck, stroking her throat, and feel her swallow against my palm. I squeeze and pull her forward.

"That what you need, dirty girl? My hand wrapped around your throat while you take my cock?"

"Yes. Please, Tobias." The plea goes straight from her lips to my cock, and I can feel myself getting close.

I squeeze her neck tighter and quicken the pace of my

thumb over her clit. The sounds she makes in response are fucking taking me to the very edge.

"Come for me, Scarlett. I wanna feel how hard you come on my cock."

She gasps a few times and then she starts to moan—a mess of curses and begging that ends in my name on her lips as she collapses forward. I kiss my way down her chest and over her shoulder again as she rides out the last of her release. Then I turn us, putting her on her back but never fully pulling out of her.

I lean over and stretch to reach into her nightstand, grabbing one of her vibrators. Her eyes go wide, and she looks up at me. I smirk at her, flicking it on and then pressing it against her clit while I start to fuck her again.

"Oh fuck..." she mutters, closing her eyes and wrapping her legs around me. "Oh god. Tobias. Please it's so much."

"You can come again for me. I know you can. This greedy little cunt needs it, and so do I."

She whimpers, throwing her head back against the pillow, and I start to fuck her harder, never letting the vibrator slip away.

"Tobias, please. Oh fuck..." The curse rips from her lips, and she slams her palm back against the headboard as she rolls her hips forward to take me deeper, and I watch her ride another orgasm out. She clenches down on my cock this time, and it takes me over the edge. Her sweet little cunt holding me tight as I come hard inside her.

She bats the vibrator away with a murmured curse, and it falls to the comforter beside us, but I want one last orgasm out of her before we finish. Especially if this is the last one I get. So I pull out of her and move down the bed, quickly taking care of the condom before I slide between her thighs again.

Her eyes are still closed, head back on the pillow, and hand across her forehead as her breathing starts to shallow out again. Just as I slide my tongue over her in one long slow drag. She gasps immediately, legs drawing up before I catch them and pin them down. I tease her again with my tongue and she cries out.

"Tobias. What are you doing? Fuck. There is no way I can again."

"Just one more. Last one. I promise."

"Tobias..."

"Please. For your birthday. For me." I smirk up at her, and she takes a deep breath but relents, her thighs falling open for me. I pull her down then, burying my face against her and taking time with her clit. Slow long drags while I try to bring her back to me. She fists the comforter at first, but then slowly after a few seconds, she starts to rock forward the slightest bit. Her hips seeking my warmth, and I work her clit in my mouth, kneading it with my tongue and then sucking hard.

She gasps again but her fingers thread through my hair, pulling me closer and I feel the swell of satisfaction when she speaks again.

"Fuck. I'm close. Somehow. Oh my fucking god. You're good at this. A little more."

I do as she asks, sucking a little harder and sliding two fingers inside her, bending them as I stroke her from the inside, and it doesn't take long before she's writhing against my face and crying out for me. Repeating my name over and over like it's a prayer, and I'm her god.

When she's finally spent, I release my grip on her, standing slowly and finding the trash for the condom and the wrapper. I open her closet and grab a washcloth from the same cubby where the towels are, taking a quick trip to the bathroom to wet it down with cool water before I return to her.

She's sitting up when I get back, looking dazed and vulnerable. I hold up the washcloth before I slide it between her thighs and she takes it from me, a small smile on her face in return. I sit next to her on the bed, brushing her wild hair back over her shoulder.

"You are gorgeous. So fucking perfect, Scarlett," I say softly, running my fingers up her thigh.

A little sound of amusement before she closes her eyes and rests her head against my shoulder.

"That was not what I expected." She breaks the silence after a moment.

Honestly, me fucking either. She's breaking me tonight in so many ways, and she doesn't even fucking know it.

ELEVEN

Scarlett

I'M STILL a little lost for words and shell-shocked from the sex we just had. I gladly signed up for this because I expected him to be rough and selfish. To take me like I was a doll, come inside me, and then tell me he had to leave. Which honestly, I would have been up for. A new mood for my thirties. What I definitely did not expect is this version of Tobias or any of the sides I've seen of him tonight.

"Didn't think I could make you come? Ouch. No faith in me, huh, Spitfire? I see how it is." He grins at me, and it melts a little more of my resistance, making me nervous. I shift against the pillows.

"Just not that many times. I never have, like that..." I trail off because now I feel awkward talking about fucking other people with him still naked in my bed.

"Yeah well, I could give you a lot of things you've never had. Just have to let me."

Another thing my stupid heart kicks up in response to. This is just post-sex haze clouding his judgment and his words. But it makes me smile that he's still so sweet and playful. Because I had fully expected him to bolt after he came too, and not be nearly this thoughtful. It's having a dizzying effect on my post-sex recovery. I need a minute and some distance to recover my wits.

"I'm gonna get cleaned up and check on the laundry really quick."

"Sounds good. Okay if I grab some water from the kitchen?"

"Of course. Go ahead."

We go our separate ways then, and I definitely did not have watching Tobias Westfield's gorgeous naked ass walk across my living room on my bingo card tonight. But I don't mind it. A slight improvement on the boxer briefs that looked like they were painted on. I bite the inside of my cheek and hurry off to the bathroom, glancing at the time on the dryer on the way. It's almost done, which means our time is almost up too. I can mentally process all of this once he's done and gone. A thought I reassure myself with while I clean up and get ready for bed.

WHEN I EMERGE, I grab his stuff out of the dryer and double-check to be sure it's really dry before I head back into the bedroom. He's sprawled out on the bed flipping through channel options on the television, looking every bit as sexy as when I left. He grins when he sees me naked and hurrying into the closet as I drop his clothes on the bed.

"You could just stay naked, you know. I wouldn't complain."

"The neighbors might if there's a fire alarm in the night," I counter as I pull on a set of pajama shorts and a tank. I don't bother with the bra. Considering the man's been inside me tonight, there's really no reason for false modesty. When I reappear in the room, he hasn't moved to put on his clothes or leave which is curious.

"You mind if I take a quick shower?"

Ah. That makes sense. I smile at him, taking in one last look before I lose this for good.

"No. Go ahead."

"Thanks, Spitfire." He brushes a kiss on my temple as he passes by me.

Once he disappears into the bathroom, I climb into bed, realizing how exhausted I am from the day when I hit the pillows. I'll just close my eyes for a few and be up again when he leaves to lock the door behind him.

THE NEXT MORNING when I wake up it takes me a minute to remember the previous night's events. I blink awake, realizing I never said goodbye to him and checking to make sure the bed is empty next to me. His clothes are gone, and the other side of the bed is cold, so I'm guessing he left after he took his shower last night and didn't want to wake me up. I'd been counting on him slinking out in the middle of the night, so I'm not surprised or distressed to find myself alone.

Which is why I nearly jump at the sound of his voice.

"You're up." He leans against the door frame in a way that is entirely too sexy for this early in the morning. "I got donuts and coffee. I didn't know if you had a potential hangover routine, so I went for something tried and true."

"I'm not hungover," I announce as I practically jump out of bed, and immediately realize from the throbbing sensation in my temples that I am in fact a little bit hungover.

"Right. I also got something with electrolytes in it, just in case. You know. For your *not* hangover." He grins.

"Okay. Um. Thank you. I'll just get dressed and be out in a minute."

He nods and heads back to the living room while I dodge into my closet. My mind is spinning with the *slight* hangover and the fact that Tobias is still here and being all cheery and thoughtful. Very much not the fuck-and-run I expected.

Once I change and run a brush through my hair, throwing it up off my shoulders, I head out to face whatever fate is awaiting me in the dining room. When I walk out, he looks up from his phone, his eyes dropping over my outfit and then back up to my face.

"Not always vintage. I wondered." The smile I get this morning is the same charming one from last night, and I can't help but return it.

"Not always. No."

"I realized when I got there, I didn't know how you take your coffee. So I got ice, creamer, milk, sugar, and a couple of shots of vanilla on the side. Hopefully one of them works?" His brows knit together, and I nod.

"Yeah, that'll work. Thank you, so much. You really didn't have to do that. I figured you would have left last night."

"Nah. Can't get rid of me that easy, Spitfire."

"Don't you have practice?"

"Yeah. I have to go in a few minutes, but I just wanted to be sure I got you something. Between the horsemen and the pink champagne and all."

"Yeah. I think I'll have to try to pick one vice at a time in the future."

"Only turn thirty once."

"True. The champagne was amazing by the way, and I'm sure it was expensive. So again, thank you."

"Worth it to see you relax a little at dinner."

"And after, apparently." I feel weird that we're dancing around the subject of last night. His face flickers with an emotion I can't read at the mention of it.

"We're good though?"

"Yeah. Like you said, I only turn thirty once. Throw in the cold rain with the champagne and apparently it makes for an interesting night."

"It was definitely that." His eyes drift over me again.

"I don't think we should tell Xander and Harper that you came back here."

"No?"

"No. Harper is in matchmaker mode for me, and I worry she'll read into this and think it's an opportunity. She's so happy with him and now she wants everyone around her to be as happy as she is, you know?"

"Right." He doesn't argue but something about the set of his jaw as he says it makes me think he doesn't like it.

"Is that a problem for you? I mean I'm not embarrassed or trying to keep it a secret necessarily. I just think she'll make it awkward for us anytime we're around each other again or try to set us up and... Yeah..." I shrug. Not knowing what else to say.

He looks down at his coffee cup, frowning for a moment before he looks up at me again and his expression clears.

"Nah, Spitfire. It's smart. Can't disagree with you there." Another flash of the genuine smile has me smiling again and turning my attention to the coffee before I start looking like a crushing teenage girl.

"You saved the day though. Seriously, I owe you. For the double rescue." I pour the coffee over the ice and add some of the milk and vanilla, putting the lid on and shaking it a bit before I pop the straw in to take a sip.

"You don't owe me. Minus having to chase you down the

side of the road and tackle you, it was a really fucking good night."

"Oh god. Yeah. Let's never talk about that part again." I cringe. I'd blocked that part out temporarily.

"I don't know. I didn't hate it. Ending was pretty good." He grins and then takes a sip of his coffee.

"Well, again. Thank you."

"All right." He stands. "I'm getting out of here before you thank me again. But make sure you eat some donuts and drink some water, yeah?"

"Will do. Have fun at practice." I walk him toward the door and lean against it as he walks out. He looks back at me one last time and then disappears down the stairs.

Maybe my thirties were going to be better after all. A little bad luck followed by a lot of good luck. It could happen.

TWELVE

Scarlett

I'M OVERSEEING the last of the boxes being moved onto trucks and heading off to go to storage, thanks to dozens of volunteers. Because it's been a massive undertaking that we've had to move up as the museum can no longer continue to pay the bills. The final exhibit we'd planned to put on has been moved online, and now I'm trying to figure out where I'm going to go in the meantime while I wait for the new museum to open.

It'll be months before the new building, that Harper and Joss's nonprofit has helped fund, is completely remodeled which means all of our staff are busy looking for temporary work. Most of the senior staff have found positions at other museums or universities nearby, but I've been struggling.

I'm starting to think I might need to return to waiting tables or working in retail in order to make sure I can continue paying my rent. The only upside is that I might actually make a little more money every month doing that than what I'm currently being paid by the museum. Silver linings, I guess.

I sigh when I get back to my office, seriously looking forward to the drinks I'm having with the girls tonight. I hang my coat up and make my way down the hall when Allison, our registrar, stops me in the hall.

"Hey. A messenger was just here a bit ago and had a package for you. I put it on your desk because I didn't know where to find you."

"Thanks. I was out with the trucks. Back and forth. Did you text?"

"Yeah. But I know it's hard to hear over all the noise and stuff. Anyway, just wanted to tell you, so you don't miss it before you leave for the day."

"Thanks."

I head back to my office wondering what would be so important it needed to be sent by messenger. I can't think of anything, but it's possible there was some paperwork or something that needed to be signed off on in a hurry. I feel like that's all I do most days right now—either for my own job applications or on behalf of collections.

So I'm puzzled when instead of a manila envelope, there's a small box sitting in the middle of my desk. I grab the letter opener to break the seal on the tape and pull out the small card that's sitting on top. There's a handwritten note scrawled on it, and I have to look at it for a moment before I can read the writing.

Thoughts on another truce? Text me.

A number's scrawled underneath the note, and I raise a brow. I can only think of one person who it could be from, and I feel the little wingbeats of excitement in my chest. Ones that are entirely involuntary because I'm levelheaded. Sensible. I don't fall for this kind of charm.

Except when I pull the box up and unwrap it, it's a box of candy—rosé gummy bears. Him being his charming self and taking me by surprise again that he went to the trouble. I stare at the number.

I could text him. It wouldn't harm anything just to text him and thank him, right? That doesn't mean anything other than I'm being polite. I could do that much.

> Rosé gummy bears? Thank you.

TOBIAS:
Didn't think your work would appreciate sending alcohol in the middle of the day.

Or that you'd want the attention. You know... in case Harper shows up.

> Good plan.

Is it?
The truce I mean.

I stare at the message. My head is telling me no. But every single other bit of me is telling me to do it. To say yes. For a million reasons, some of them being as vain as the fact that Westfield wants a repeat, and others being more grounded. The worst part is, I think I like him. When he's like this, at least. Sweet, thoughtful, with a sense of humor about the things that shouldn't make sense. Like the two of us somehow having the best sex of my life.

> Will there be actual rosé if another truce is called?

TOBIAS:

You can write your requirements into the negotiations for the cessation of hostilities.

> That's a lot of big words. Where'd you learn those?

Getting my degree, Spitfire. You'd be shocked by how many words I know. Some I already know you're going to like.

> I'd consider a truce if I get to find out what they are.

Tonight?

> Can't. Have a thing.

After?

> No car and ride costs are eating me alive while I wait for my car to get out of the shop. Plus I'm less excited to use them when they break down in the middle of the night.

Well, can't argue with you there. I could pick you up, but why don't you have a rental?

> Rentals are more expensive than rides.

I'll loan you a car.

> You're funny.

I have five. I can spare one. I'm going out of town to play anyway. You can give it back when you get yours out of the shop.

> Are you bribing me into a truce?

This is separate from that, but if it helps my truce chances I won't complain.

> Are you sure?

Yeah. I can have my assistant drop it off at the museum in a bit.

> I don't know how to handle all this villain being the hero stuff.

I can help you think of ways to say thank you since you've decided you like those words now.

> And there he is.
>
> Also... thank you. A lot. It should be ready on Monday, so I can have the keys back to you Sunday night or Monday depending on when you get back and want them.

Penciling in a Sunday night truce, Spitfire. Don't let me down.

> As long as there's rosé.

Done.

And just like that, I've signed myself up for a second one-night stand with Westfield.

THIRTEEN

Scarlett

SUNDAY NIGHT I'm at Harper's. Joss and Violet have come over and we're having a girls' night after having watched the afternoon Phantom game and ordered a bunch of takeout for dinner. Now we're deep into the wine and talking about guys, museums, Joss's boudoir photography business, and what it's like to have to sleep in airports.

I drove over in Tobias's car so that I could return it to him since he lives in the same building and the shop was able to get the part and get the car patched up. The only trouble is, I now owe my credit card company a small fortune for it, but that's a problem for another day. Joss is pouring the two of us another glass of wine when the door pops open and Xander, Tobias, and a gorgeous brunette walk in.

"Hey! That was fast." Harper smiles and kisses Xander who picks her up with one arm and gives her the kind of kiss that has the rest of us looking at the ceiling and the floor.

"Traffic was light," he grunts when he's done, tossing his bag on the floor. "Hello, ladies." He nods at the rest of us. "I just gotta get Tobias a charger. His phone's dying."

"You don't have one upstairs at your place?" Harper raises a brow.

"No, my spare one was in my car and I... put it in the shop." His eyes drift to me.

"Ah. You going to introduce me?" Harper's eyes fall on the tiny brunette who shifts on her heels. I feel like I'm staring at his latest hookup, and I'm surprised by how nauseous I feel.

"Sarah this is Harper. Harper this is Sarah. She's just coming up to help me with the outfit for tomorrow's media thing."

I feel my stomach untwist the slightest bit.

"Oh yes. For the record setting thing. We saw tonight, it was amazing. And nice to meet you, Sarah."

"Nice to meet you too. Xander's talked a lot about you. Tobs and I have just been missing each other all week and now we're down to the wire. Plus he promised me he's got some new wine I have to try."

"He always has something good." Harper studies the woman and smiles as she talks.

I can tell just from the subtle look on Harper's face she doesn't like her, which makes two of us, and I have so many questions already. Ones I can't ask without sounding like I have an out-of-pocket crush on Tobias. One I most definitely do not have. Because I can have one-night stands. I don't have to be *that* girl. The one who always chases something more. The new thirties thing can work. I can watch my one-night stand go and hookup with his new one-night stand, if that's what she is, and feel okay with it.

One hundred percent okay.

Either way, he's forgotten our penciled-in meeting or it got bumped when she decided she needed his time. So I feel silly for staying here so late when I'm not waiting for the guys to come home. I down the glass Joss filled and push it toward her for another. She's remarkably quiet, and I watch her silently studying Harper and me but not saying a word about anything.

AFTER THEY LEAVE, I walk out onto the terrace with what's left of my wine. I need a breath of cold air and a moment to get my shit straight. I was going to have to pull it together and hang out with the girls for a while before I ran the keys up and got a car home. I didn't want to interrupt them at an awkward time, but it would also be weird for me to run up there after him now.

This is why I don't do things like this. Get involved with men like Tobias. Let them in. It's too much for my heart to take. The sex is hot as fuck. The best I've ever had in my life by a wide margin, but I'm not sure it's worth my sanity and my dignity when I fall apart because I can't keep my stupid head from thinking about more.

"So... how long have you been fucking Tobias?" Joss walks up silently behind me before she speaks, and I nearly jump when she does.

"What?" I try to act stupid, but she smiles in a way that lets me know I've been caught.

She grins, sipping her wine and waiting me out.

"Just once. Last week. It was stupid. Harper doesn't know, and I don't want her to yet. She'll... want to help, and I don't want help."

"Help with what exactly?"

"Playing matchmaker, and Tobias is not the one for that sort of thing, you know?"

"Oh, I know. He and I..." She points toward the general direction he might be in. "We're the same."

"Oh. Oh... Did you guys? Shit. That's awkward."

"Oh no. No fucking way. If Colton is anywhere near, I can't even look at another man. It's the reason I have to stay on another continent most of the time."

"Colton and you?"

"Officially, yes. Still working on spreading the news. Happy to be your confidant, but I've definitely fallen victim to a matchmaking bestie. Maybe we can decipher the things I did wrong and help you in the process."

I grin. "Sounds like a plan."

"So..." She bumps her hip into mine. "You did the one-night thing and now what? You want more, and he said no?"

"No. I went in with my head completely clear. It was just a little... birthday experiment. Push my comfort zone. Try new things, you know? But now we have to be around each other, and I have to see the next hookup." I gesture back toward the apartment and frown. "And it's a bit awkward."

"Ah. I can relate on the being around each other bit. Again, with Colt being around so much... was hard not to want to dive into bad habits."

"Right, and we see where that got you." I grin and she laughs. "Plus I need to return his keys, and I brought them tonight, but now I have to go up there with them and... Ugh. Awkward. You know?"

"Want me to do it for you?"

"No. I appreciate it. But I think I have to be a big girl. I'll definitely look jealous and crazy if I send up a substitute."

"Well, that's true. But I would still do it for you." She smiles at me. "I think I like it by the way. You and Tobias. Makes sense in a weird way. Especially with your hobbies."

"What do you mean?"

"Oh, you don't know yet? You'll see."

I want to ask her what she means, but instead, she changes

the subject, and we spend the next hour chatting about her former life in the Alps and all the mountains she hiked during her summers there.

EVENTUALLY, I work up the courage to go upstairs. So I say goodnight to everyone and grab my coat, jumping on the elevator pretending like I'm heading to get in my car and instead going up to see Tobias. I rap lightly on the door, and I take a step back when it opens and it's her again, smiling at me from the doorframe. She has a glass of rosé in her hand and looks like she belongs here. My stomach quivers a little bit, threatening to relaunch fresh nausea on me, but I hold tight.

"Is Tobias around?"

"He's in the other room getting dressed."

"Oh. Okay. Could you give him these? He'll know what they're for. Thanks!" I hand her the keys, and she looks at them perplexed for a moment, but she nods.

"Okay, sure. You sure you don't want to wait?"

"No. I've got a ride to catch but thank you!" I grin brightly and then I hurry down the hall, slamming the down button and being incredibly grateful when the elevator comes almost immediately. I tuck inside it and press the close button. Watching as the doors shut and finally letting myself breathe.

This is fine. It's good really. I've ripped the Band-Aid off. I fucked him. Then we called it good and did the friend thing. Now I've had a polite conversation with the latest girl. I'm adulting the fuck out of this whole situation. I should be proud of myself.

Except, I can't help the tiny bloom of want I can still feel. I hadn't believed we were actually just one and done, even though I should have known. It tracked with the Tobias I've known all along. The one who could flirt with anyone including my friends and who rarely took anything seriously. I was stupid for thinking it could be anything else but just him being friendly and trying to keep things normal between us. I just can't help the little crushing feeling it has on my spirit.

The elevator dings, and I step out into the dark hall. This building is gorgeous, dark blue carpeting spills out in front of me, and I start walking toward the lobby area where a low-hanging chandelier illuminates a leather couch. I lied about the car, so I was going to be waiting for a few minutes before it got here. But just as I start to clear the threshold, I hear footsteps echo in the hallway and the crash bar to the stairs clicks, so I turn around.

It's Tobias looking winded and pissed off.

"You" is all he manages to get out.

"Me?"

"Don't play stupid. I'm not doing this chasing thing, Scarlett. It's not who I am." He gives me a once over, disappointment in me etched in his features.

"What the fuck are you talking about?" Now I'm pissed.

"You couldn't wait two seconds for me to come get the keys and you fucking press the close button instead of waiting for me when I yell for you? Not very mature."

The last bit stings hard.

"Um... I was just dropping off the keys. I didn't know I needed to wait. She said you were getting dressed, so I assumed I was interrupting. And I did not hear you call when I shut the elevator. I was just trying to get out of there."

"Interrupting what?"

"Don't play stupid, Tobias. You were obviously fucking her. And the rosé? Jesus. Do you at least change up your bit or did you have a gummy telegram set up for her too?"

His tongue wets his lower lip, and he runs his teeth over it in the wake, his lips pulling up in a smug little grin.

"Jealous much?"

This fucking prick. I can't believe I fucked him. Or that I thought he was different. That I'd misread him.

"Over you?" I force a laugh. "Get a grip."

His arm darts out faster than I realize it's happening, and he pulls me with him, smashing into the crash bar again and pulling me into the dark stairwell. His fingers tighten around my pulse point, and he backs me up against the cinderblock wall. His hand encircles my throat and his thumb brushes gently under my chin.

"Enough for you, or you want it tighter?"

"Tobias—" His thumb shifts up and presses hard against my lips.

"Nah, Spitfire. I just ran down sixteen fucking flights of stairs on a travel game day to catch you before you walked out. The least you can do is admit you were fucking jealous."

I dart my tongue out and lick the pad of his thumb, his brow raises with the action, and he swipes the dampness over my lower lip. I use the opportunity to bite down hard on the tip of his thumb. Because fuck this man and his ego.

But he just grins and watches me, leaning in when he whispers.

"That's not gonna have the effect you want, sweetheart. We haven't gotten that far yet, but I like that kind of play. Biting me? Makes me hard as fuck watching your teeth sink in like that. Draw blood, and we'll stain those pretty fucking lips with it before you wrap them around my cock."

"I hate you. This was a *giant* fucking mistake. I think we just need to go back to how things were before where we tell each other to fuck off and keep our distance."

"We could do that." He tilts his head to the side. "Or you could admit you're jealous. Then I can explain how I was getting dressed because she's my stylist and helping me pick out something for a media event tomorrow. And she's drinking champagne because her husband moonlights as a sommelier and we like to compare collections. She didn't know I was saving it for you and apologized before she left." His brows raise, and he stares at me pointedly.

I close my eyes, feeling my stomach churn with embarrassment.

"I don't bring women back to that condo, Spitfire. It's just my place near the stadium. Business only."

It's my turn to give him a pointed look.

"Admit to the jealousy."

"It wasn't jealousy. It was just... soon. And new. And you let me borrow your car. I don't know what we're doing."

He takes a deep breath and raises his brow impossibly higher.

"Fine. I was a tiny bit jealous."

FOURTEEN

Tobias

"GOOD. Because I can't get you out of my fucking head either."

"So what now?" Her gray eyes turn on me.

"I don't know. You don't do one-night stands. I don't do relationships. We're a bit fucked, honestly."

"I think you were probably just supposed to go home after you dropped me off the other night, and this was just supposed to be a weird friendly-banter-tension thing between us. It was working pretty well. Now we've fucked it up."

"Yeah, but then you wear those fuck-me thigh highs with the seam up the back and the little vintage style dresses that make me want to hear you beg for me. You have this mouth on you, so fucking smart and such a good girl. And fuck... I'm just a fucking mortal, Scarlett."

"Yeah well... the sex was really good. Not that your ego

needs to hear that. I thought you probably just did the bare minimum. But you actually live up to the hype."

"I think that might be the nicest thing you've ever said to me."

"Don't start." She gives me a warning look, and I grin. "It's just... the sex the other day and talking to the girls about their sex lives. I realize I've been missing out, you know? And I just thought... the way you were talking that maybe we might at least... I don't know. We could try some things while we fuck this out or whatever we're doing."

"We could maybe do that." I can't help the smile, but it doesn't do me any favors.

"Don't be smug. It's ruining the gentleman thing you've had going for you," she teases.

"Isn't that the reason you like fucking me so much?"

"Maybe." Her eyes lift to mine, and I catch the hint of a smile.

"In that case, I think we need to head upstairs, to try a few things." I lean over and drop a kiss just beneath her earlobe, running my hand up her side, and she melts into the touch.

"Agreed," she whispers, her hands traveling up my chest.

"Anything special in mind?"

"Could start here. Somewhere we could get caught." Her voice is soft when she suggests it, and it stirs something in me that I can bring this out in her. That she's like this for me.

I slip my hand under her shirt, running my palm over her bare skin and up under her bra while I kiss my way down her neck. She arches into my touch, little sounds of appreciation as she lets me have what I want.

"Yeah, we can do that. Give you a taste of it before I take you upstairs and fuck the jealousy out of you."

She runs her fingers over my lats. "That sounds like a plan."

"Good. Then take the panties off for me."

She uses me to balance as she slides them off past her heels and then playfully tucks them into my pocket. She looks up at me expectantly after, and I pin her against the wall, kissing her throat and sliding my hand up the inside of her thighs until I hear her breathing go heavy with anticipation. I love the sound of her like this, knowing how much she wants me, that I'm the only one she's thinking about in this moment.

I test her gently with my fingertips and listen to her breath catch in her throat before I push two fingers inside her and she relaxes into me, letting me take her where I want. Her breathing picks up as I massage her clit with my thumb. She leans her head back against the cinderblocks just as a door opens higher in the building.

Her eyes flicker open, and she looks to me, a hint of anxiety behind them.

"You're good. Focus on how you feel."

Her lashes lift, and she looks up the stairwell as we hear footsteps descending on them. Her brow furrows as she tries to concentrate, nearly closing her eyes again. But the footsteps keep coming, hitting landing after landing and her eyes return to mine. Something like panic in them. I pick up my pace, sliding in and out of her faster and circling her clit, forcing her attention back to where I have control over her body. She whimpers and then slaps a hand over her mouth. Her eyes going to the steps.

"Focus, Scarlett," I remind her.

"I can't. They're coming," she whispers.

"You're coming first if you focus." I raise my brow at her and half a smile flickers over her face.

But she's still distracted as the sound of the steps comes closer. They're only a few levels above us now, and her lashes flutter back and forth between the door and the stairs. She panics then, pushing me back and taking a step away as they get too close for her comfort.

I choke back my own groan of disappointment at losing her when I was so close to having her come for me. Reminding myself that she's new at this and we have to take our time. I don't want to ruin her eagerness this early in the game.

She moves toward the door just as a door latch opens two floors above and our potential intruder exits through it. It slams shut behind them, echoing down the staircase to where we stand. I look at her amused as her expression morphs from panic to disappointment.

"Sorry," she whispers.

"You're good. Let's go upstairs." I nod to the door behind her, wanting to take the elevator because climbing all those flights after running down them is the least appealing idea I can think of. Especially if I'm going to save my energy to fuck her.

"But... what about?"

"Upstairs. Or on the elevator."

Her brightness returns, and she leads the way out the door, hurrying toward the elevator and pressing the button. It comes quickly, and I punch in the number for my floor as we wait for the doors to close. I lean back against the railing at the back of the elevator and a sly smile crosses her face as she comes up to me. Her fingers wrap around the edge of my T-shirt, and she raises onto her toes to kiss the side of my neck. I dig my hand into the soft curve of her ass to pull her closer and her warm lips trace their way over my throat and the curve of my shoulder.

"I want you so much," she confesses as the doors start to close, and just those words and her mouth have me hard as fuck.

I slip my fingers back between her thighs, and she pulls

closer to me searching for the friction she lost earlier. A soft moan escapes her when I slide inside her again.

"Spread for me." I barely say the words before the doors pop open abruptly and a man gets on. I feel her whole body go tight with tension, and I turn us so that my body shields her, but I don't let her go this time.

FIFTEEN

Scarlett

I'VE GOTTEN MY WISH. This experiment has gone from almost caught on the steps to caught immediately on the elevator. The good-looking guy who gets on is dressed like he's headed out for a date and the flowers he's carrying up with him pretty much guarantee it. His eyes flick over Tobias and me as he gets on the elevator, a knowing smirk forming before he turns his back to us and presses a floor just a couple below the one that's already lit up for us.

The smell of his cologne rivals Tobias's, and I struggle to keep my focus on his fingers and his attention. Wound too tight by the fact that this man is standing a few feet away and is pretending like he doesn't know what's happening behind him. Tobias continues to taunt me with his touch. He teases my clit with the perfect amount of pressure and an involuntary gasp comes out before I can stop it.

The stranger looks back over his shoulder, his eyes drifting up my legs to where Tobias's hand disappears under my skirt. His smirk widens and then his eyes flick up to meet mine, a knowing look of amusement in them. I can't stop myself from staring back, returning his smile, and we're caught like that for full seconds before I feel Tobias's hand at my throat and his lips at my ear.

"Eyes on me." The words are so rough they're practically a growl, and my eyes snap back to his. The blue there deep and stormy as fuck as he glances up over his shoulder and then back to me. I keep my eyes on him as he picks up his speed to an almost punishing pace, and I rock my hips forward to counter him.

Another moan comes, and I crush my teeth into my lower lip to try to stop it. Closing my eyes when the stranger clears his throat in response. I try not to whimper when Tobias takes the pressure of his thumb away again, opening my eyes to try to make sense of it. His eyes search my face, and he looks even more pissed off than before as the elevator comes to a stop and the doors open.

"Have a good night!" The stranger calls behind him as he exits, and Tobias and I stand there staring at each other, his fingers slipping in and out of me, torturing me with the faintest pressure imaginable as the doors close again.

"What's wrong?" I ask, frowning at him but his expression doesn't change and there's no answer. The elevator climbs a few more floors and his fingers slip out of me as he searches for his keys. He's quiet while we exit it and he unlocks the door for us. He tosses them on a bench before he grabs me and pins me up against the wall in the entryway. Kicking the door shut with his foot.

"First rule if we play these games Scarlett... If I'm touching you, your eyes are on me. I get your full attention."

The words make my heart flutter, and I feel a flush on my

cheeks, half from the embarrassment and half from how badly I need to come after two back-to-back almost orgasms.

"I'm sorry. You have it now," I apologize because I want him back.

"I want it always." He grabs my chin and his eyes drift over my face. "At least when we're doing this. I fucking mean it, Scarlett." Something in his eyes looks lost despite the firmness of his tone, and I circle my arms around his neck.

"Eyes on you, promise." My fingertips slide over his traps as I try to reassure him.

His gaze drops to my lips, and I run my tongue over the lower one. The tension is palpable, and I feel like even breathing too much could spin this whole thing out of control. So I hold it as I wait for him.

"I hate kissing," he mumbles, like he's trying to remind himself and explain to me at the same time. "Especially when I fuck. Ruins the mood."

I puzzle at the statement, realizing that despite everything else we've done, we have not in fact kissed. I hadn't missed it, which says something because I do like kissing. Being kissed. Especially if he's good at it, and I imagine Tobias would be, or would have been if he was more practiced at it. But I can live without it. He more than makes up for it in other ways.

"Okay. I don't mind."

"But I want to know what you taste like. If your mouth is as sweet as the rest of you."

My stomach twists, and I don't have a chance to respond before his lips are on mine. He takes my mouth the same way he takes every part of me, without hesitation or apology. Like I already belong to him. His kiss is exploratory at first like he's just tasting me to see if he likes it, and then firmer, and more insistent like he needs everything I can give him.

He grabs me and hauls me up against the wall and I wrap

my legs around him. He grinds himself against my core, teasing pressure that makes me writhe against him for more as I feel him going harder. He pulls me down a few moments later and carries me out of the room while I kiss my way over his throat, one hand gripping his neck and the other traveling down his back.

"I need you inside me."

"I know you do."

He sets me down on my feet in a bedroom, one that I assume is his and we both start stripping out of our clothes. He grabs his phone out of his pocket and sets it on the nightstand and my eyes go to it as I toss my bra and shirt on the chair next to it. I imagine him filming me, rewatching it after I'm gone and the thought of it lights everything inside me on fire. Suddenly a thing I thought I might want is a need.

I pick it up and hand it to a naked Tobias, pushing him back into the chair as I slide to my knees.

"Scarlett?" He nearly chokes on my name.

"I want you to film me while I get you off."

"But—" He frowns, starting to protest.

"It's not my birthday, so no excuses. Unless you don't want it now?"

He curses under his breath, but the way his eyes light I can tell he likes the idea. "I want it, but I just want you to be sure. Extra fucking sure if I'm recording it."

"I'm extra sure," I reassure him.

"Anytime you want it to stop, you say so. You want to delete it, we delete it. Okay?"

"Okay," I agree as I wrap my hand around him, slowly stroking down.

His cock is unbelievably perfect, just thick and long enough without being too much and curved up just that little bit where he hits every spot. Attached to this man, with the tattoos and the body, that makes me want to die a little every time I get to see it, makes it feel like the universe was a little too unfair when it made him.

I can't imagine many men compare when you've had Tobias first. Maybe some of the models he dates go on to get other athletes or actors who can compete with the memory, but I will certainly be returning to average Joes after this and will be summoning this memory to get me through the inevitable future crappy one-night stands and ill-advised dates.

So I'm going to make the most of it while I can. Including recording a few moments when he's into it.

"You're sure?" he asks again, his brows knitting together with concern, and I smile at his need for reassurance.

"I'm positive," I answer as I slide my tongue down the length of him, and his eyes shutter on a curse.

"Fuck, Scarlett... I don't deserve this."

SIXTEEN

Tobias

I HIT the record button on my phone just as she takes me in her mouth, and it's too much at once. The sight of her through the screen, the feel of her mouth, and the fact that she's encouraging me to take the video in the first place. I can barely hold it still, and I have to close my eyes for a second when she takes me deeper, concentrating hard on not just fucking coming right this second all over the back of her throat.

"Fuck... Fucking fuck. Slower, Spitfire. Your mouth is too fucking good." I groan as she slides further back on my cock dangerously close to the base, taking me deeper than I expected her to.

I might be an ass for thinking it, but I didn't expect her to be very good at this. In my head, she's the good girl in a cardigan, making notes at her desk and taking crumpets and tea at night. Too good to know how to hit her knees and take cock down her throat. So having her kneeling before me and taking me down like she manages men like me on a normal night is a surprise.

Her hand wraps around the base of my cock as she devours me again, and she slides it in rhythm with her mouth. I move the screen out of my way, so I can watch her for real. Seeing her concentrating hard, wanting nothing but to get me off is a memory I want as much as a recording. There's only one thing missing, and it's a thing I hope will slow her down enough that we can make this last.

"Touch yourself."

Her eyes lift to mine as her tongue works over the tip of my cock, and I have to close my eyes for a moment to regain my composure.

"Please? For me." I brush the hair out of her face and cradle her jaw in my hand. A soft blush on her cheeks forms as she slides the hand that's not wrapped around me between her legs.

"Rub your clit for me. I want to feel you moaning on my cock while you do it. Think about how it's going to be my mouth there later."

Her eyes shutter as her fingers circle, and I reposition the camera and lean back just to listen to the sound of her. Her mouth on my cock and her fingers sliding through her wetness while she hums her approval. It's fucking perfect.

Something I put out into the universe must have been phenomenally, cosmically, profoundly fucking good. Because this right here with Scarlett so soft and eager, so willing to do things we both love. It feels like a massive fucking reward. The kind that comes so rarely I'm half enjoying it and half worrying about how soon it's going to be over. So thank fuck for recording this for posterity. I just pray she doesn't want me to delete it because this is going to be the star of every fucking self-session I have for years to come.

But right now I can't take much more.

"Fuck I'm close, sweetheart. I need you on the bed. I want to feel you come with me."

After another few moments of her torturing me before she pulls away, teasing the underside of my cock before she releases me, she lets go. She looks up at me with her swollen pink lips wet and her cheeks flushed from the exertion of sucking me off. She runs her hands down her thighs as she stands, a playful grin on her face.

She walks to the bed and bends over it, spreading her legs, and then glances back over her shoulder at me. She waits patiently while I grab a condom and watch her.

"This how you want it?" I run my hand over her ass when I get back to her.

"Yes."

I rub the side of her left hip and push on the back of her thigh.

"This leg up on the bed. You want it deep; I'll give it to you." I motion to it, and she follows my direction. "Good... just like that."

I run the backs of my fingers down her spine before I grab her soft round hip with one hand and guide my cock inside her with the other. She moans when I start to move, and my eyes are fixed on the spot where I slide inside her. She's so wet and perfectly tight, desperate for my cock with the way she pushes back against me.

"Fuck. You're so good," she murmurs into the comforter as she buries her face in it.

"Yeah? Better than that fucker in the elevator would have been." A flash of her eyes wide and her mouth parted, looking at him while I touched her comes to mind, and I hate it. Which is entirely new for me and a little bit frightening.

"Yes. Better than any—" She moans before she can finish the last of her words, but I know what she means.

The admission goes straight to my cock and my ego, and I start to take her harder and faster. Wanting to make her fall apart and give her everything she gives me. It feels like more than just the sum of its parts with her—that she's willing to be vulnerable for me. Willing to try new things. So trusting that she'll let me film her on her knees.

"So close..." Another soft plea from her that makes me want to give her anything she wants.

"Come all over my cock dirty girl. I want to feel how much you love it."

She comes hard a moment later, begging me to go harder on her, and the sound of her moaning and whimpering makes it so I can't hold back any longer either. I grab her hair and pull her up, biting down on the side of her neck right where it meets her shoulder as I come. She gasps at the sensation before she begs for it on the other side. I give her what she wants while I massage her clit, taking her to the edge again now that we know she can—*for me*.

"Tobias... oh my god. Please." She whimpers and I drag one last wave out of her before we both collapse.

"Scarlett, fuck sweetheart... You wear me out." I run my fingers over her stomach and she offers up a small satisfied smile in return.

"You sound surprised." She raises a brow.

"A little. You always seemed so quiet before. When you weren't ripping my head off anyway." I grin at her.

"You bring out the worst in me I guess."

"Yeah well, I think I like your worst." I kiss her.

She laughs and kisses me back. "Okay. Shower and then sleep?"

"Sounds like a plan."

My heart is still pounding in my chest when I watch her get up. Half because she is a fucking workout and half because she makes me feel things I'm not sure I can even put a name to yet.

SEVENTEEN

Scarlett

I WAKE up in the middle of the night and sit up, the moon coming in through the window, and looking outside I see other high rises glowing with the reflection of the moon. It takes me a second to remember where I am and remind myself this isn't a dream. I've just managed to fall asleep in Westfield's bed instead of leaving like I should have.

I glance over to see his side of the bed empty and cold. I wonder if he already left. I glance at the time, pulling my phone over to get a closer look at it. It's 3:30 a.m. and I groan inwardly. I should have left after the sex. Now I'll have to creep out in the middle of the night or lay here for another hour or two until it's acceptably "morning" and get a car home.

But first I need a bathroom. I look up and see the door's ajar and dark, further evidence he's probably gone. I still hurry in and close it behind me, quickly using it to freshen up—

splashing water on my face and finger-combing my hair. I look exactly like I feel. Well-fucked but not completely well-rested.

I need to resume my job search later in the morning, but I can at least sleep in for a while once I get home. This late-night hookup thing with Westfield can't last for a number of reasons, but one of them is the fact that thirty is also apparently the age when not getting enough rest is going to catch up with me. I freshen up and try to pull myself together before I hit the light and start to tiptoe back to the bedroom to gather my clothes.

When I get out though, Westfield's sitting on the bed staring at me. He's pulled a pair of sweats on, but he's still shirtless, and every inch of his gorgeous, tattooed skin is on display. He's lit beautifully by the moonlight coming in, and he looks more like something out of a dream than an actual mortal who lives on the same plane as I do.

"Hey, Spitfire."

"Hey. I thought maybe you were gone. I was just gonna get dressed and get a ride home."

He frowns and looks at the clock by the bed.

"It's the middle of the night. You think I'd just abandon you here in the middle of the night?"

"I don't know. If you had practice or something in the morning."

"Not this fucking early."

"I mean I know but... never mind. I don't know. But I'll be out of your hair so you can get some sleep."

"Insomnia. Can't sleep. Didn't want to keep you up, so I was in the living room watching some TV."

"I'm sorry you can't sleep."

"Actually, that's a lie. Not the fact that I can't sleep. But the TV bit. I've been rewatching the video we made."

"Oh." I bite my lip because, in the heat of the moment, I

felt brave as fuck. But now in the cold light of not quite morning, I feel like maybe that I pushed things too far.

He picks up on the discomfort immediately.

"I'll delete it if you want. If you regret it, no problem. I just... I'm gonna be honest, Scarlett. It's the hottest thing I've seen in my life. I think I might already have an addiction to it. I'm not into most porn but watching that... Fuck..."

"I thought... Or I guess I heard that exhibitionism was a thing for you."

"It is."

"You haven't made a video before?"

"Oh. No, I have... but not like that. I usually delete them, honestly." He frowns. "Fuck that sounds like I've made dozens. I haven't. But occasionally it's kind of a rush to have the camera on, you know? Course you know since you've made some solo films." He grins at me. "But watching it back isn't really my thing. Cringe-worthy most of the time. But fuck, Spitfire, you could definitely be a cam girl. I'd give you whatever you were charging."

"Uh... thanks, I think? I'll keep that in mind in case this job hunt doesn't work out."

"Fuck. That sounded bad. I didn't mean it like that." He runs his hand over the back of his neck nervously, a slightly awkward Tobias is hot as fuck.

"Okay."

"I'm asking if I can keep it."

"Sure, I guess. As long as you're not showing anyone else."

"No. Fuck no."

"Okay, then no, I guess, I don't mind. Not entirely fair if you have one, and I don't though."

"That brings me to the second part. If you're up for it."

"What's that?"

"You take one of me."

"Oh. That's okay. I'm just teasing you. We don't have to do that. It's fine."

"No, I don't think you understand. I want it. Again, assuming you're up for it? You'd just have to lay back and film it. I'll make it easy for you."

I blink. I might need to pinch myself. Because I'm standing in his expensive fucking condo in the middle of the night naked while he begs me to let him go down on me while I record it. This is not my life.

"I can make it worth it. We can film a few different takes. Try a few positions to see what you like best."

"Do I get to keep a copy?"

"As long as you promise when you're using your arsenal and watching it, that you're thinking of me. Sure." Another playful grin, and I'm going weak.

There's a long pause, and I sit on the bed next to him while I try to process. His hand runs up my thigh.

"That a yes?"

"Yes." I agree, not entirely sure I'm ready for it even if I want it. I don't know if my heart can take this Tobias. His eyes light with my agreement though, and he hands me his phone.

"Get comfortable. However you want."

I scoot back on the bed reclining against the plush stack of pillows, nervously watching as he makes his way up the bed. I press the phone to my lips, shielding part of my face as he kisses his way up my legs. This isn't the first time, but I still feel shy at the idea of recording him doing it. I tap the phone against my lower lip and take in a shaky breath when he takes me in his mouth, and his warm tongue drifts over me.

I'm already wet from the anticipation—just thinking about this man doing this to me does things for me, watching him is another story entirely. The way his hands grip my thighs, the way his brow furrows as he concentrates, and the deft way his tongue slides over my clit in a perfect, subtle arch that wakes all my nerve endings is so good, I'm finding my braver side again.

I swipe to the video button on the phone, bringing it up from the main screen and hitting record a second later. The frame shakes a little along with my hands, and my hips raise at the next stroke of his tongue, the anticipation building with each round.

He pauses, his gaze shifting up when he notices I have the camera on, and he grins.

"Spread for me. I want my tongue on every inch of you."

I let my legs fall wider for him, and he grabs my hips, pulling me closer to him before he starts another round of assault on my senses, his lips closing around my clit to suck me. I cry out and thread my fingers in his hair, pulling gently when it's more than I can take. He relents, but only enough to make the torture that much sweeter.

I nearly lose my grip on the phone, shifting and holding it tighter. I glance at the video again instead of him, and I'm distracted by how sexy he looks. How unreal it feels to watch the man I've secretly lusted after in our friend group be prone on the bed, arms wrapped around my thighs while he uses his perfect tongue on me.

"Oh fuck," I curse, gripping his hair tighter than I should have. "Sorry. I just. Sorry," I mumble, trying to scoot back on the bed to escape him.

He kisses me and takes a breath, his hands and mouth massaging my skin with featherlight kisses and touches that have me writhing underneath him.

"Don't apologize. I love it when you lose control like that. I want you to use me however you need. Grab my hair. Fuck my tongue. I just want to taste you and feel you come for me, Scarlett." He glances up at me, lashes low and blue eyes rich with the knowledge that he has me however he wants me.

"Okay," I whisper, gasping when his lips graze my clit again. I take his direction, raising my hips and grabbing his hair, moaning as I help get him to every spot I need him. He slides two fingers inside me, pumping them in and out in rhythm with his mouth, and it doesn't take much after that. The crest of my orgasm hits me like a massive crashing wave, so good I feel like I might actually melt.

"Oh my god. Tobias... please... please," I'm begging when he continues to hold me close, his tongue massaging the last few sensations out of me until I collapse a sated and exhausted mess underneath him.

I close my eyes for a minute before I remember the phone is still going and look over to see it recording the blackness of the sheets, taking a breath as I hit the stop button. He kisses his way over my abdomen and chest, grabbing his phone as he settles in next to me.

He hits play a moment later, turning up the volume and the sounds of us echoing in the room are painfully hot. I'm moaning so much louder than I thought I was, and I go to pull a pillow over my face. He grabs it, yanking it back.

"This is... wow," Tobias mumbles, his eyes fixed on the video.

"Like yourself that much?" I tease him about his vanity, but he shakes his head.

"Like watching us this much. I'm up for as many takes as you want of this."

It's a dangerous proposition, because as much as I like watching us—I think I might like the man even more. Especially when he looks at me like I'm one of his favorite things.

EIGHTEEN

Scarlett

I'M in a good mood despite the fact I'm cleaning out my office on the last day in this building and currently have no job prospects to speak of. I'll have some unemployment pay and savings to let me squeak by for a few weeks, but then things are going to get dire if I can't find work. I've applied for dozens of jobs already but so far they don't want to train someone who will just go back to an old job when it comes around again. I can't really blame them, but it's making it hard to find anything.

But despite all of that, I've had a good week thanks to the last man on earth I expected. Now I'm just trapped somewhere between hate and hope. So when I see a text from him, I feel the tension of those two emotions rising in my chest.

TOBIAS:
Can I stop by your place after practice tonight?

> Sure. I can make dinner and you bring the rosé?

I grin at my phone. I know I shouldn't let myself get carried away. This has to end eventually, and it needs to happen in a way we can both still be friends. Which will be difficult if I let any kind of feelings be involved. So it has to be just sex. Us both needing a release and weirdly being a good match for each other in that particular space.

TOBIAS:
> Okay. See you in a couple hours.

WHEN HE GETS to my place that night, he's not all smiles and charm like he usually is. He looks tired—exhausted really—like he's been run ragged.

"Rough practice?"

"Rough day."

"Well, I've made dinner. I wasn't sure what you'd want or what you eat after practice but—"

"That's sweet of you. It looks amazing. But... We should talk first."

The tone of his voice makes a pit form in my stomach, and I set things back down on the counter to look at him.

"Okay," I say softly, studying his face and realizing it's more than just tiredness there. I feel like the conversation I've been dreading is here. I'd been prepared for it, reminding myself over and over that this is how it ends. Although it's weird that he'd agreed to dinner when he knew it was coming.

"You should sit down. I have to tell you something, and I don't know how." He nods to the dining chair, but I refuse it.

"I'm good." I shake my head. "And you can just say it." I urge him on.

I'm not going to fall apart just because he's not interested in me anymore. A bit ridiculous that his ego is so big he thinks I would.

"Okay. Your choice." It's a gruff dismissal, but he scrubs a hand over his face like he's trying to recenter himself. "I got a call from my publicist today, and then my agent. Word is out that a tabloid has a video of me and a woman."

"Okay." I frown, trying to make sense of this and why he's telling me.

He looks up at my face and he must see the confusion. "A sex tape. They have a sex tape of me."

"Oh fuck." I gasp. "That's awful. I'm sorry."

I'm trying to wrap my head around this discussion when I'd been expecting another one entirely. Now I can understand why the anxiety had been rolling off him ever since he came through the door.

"The implication being that it was a video pulled or hacked off a cloud. You and I used the record feature a few times, remember?"

It suddenly comes back to me. Because in all my confusion I'd forgotten that we'd used his phone to record us. I see flashbacks of the other night. The things we'd done. The things we'd said. I imagine all of that going viral on the internet. Click after click. View after view, and I feel like I'm going to be sick.

"Fuck. Sit down. I knew this wasn't going to go well, but I couldn't just not tell you. I couldn't put it off anymore either because they're going to release it any day now. I don't know when, but that's not how I wanted you to find out."

"Are you sure it's real? That it's us?" I start bargaining with the possibility of this kind of fate, hoping that there's some way out of it. By the look on his face, I'm not the only one.

"I hope they're lying. Bluffing because they want a comment or to trick me into a bigger story, but I don't know. It really sounds like they have it. It's the only thing that was on my phone recently."

I sink into the chair. The room feels like it's spinning. I imagine everyone I know seeing that video. Harper. Xander. My family. People I work with.

Oh my god.

I'll lose my job. Lose everything. I'm having enough trouble trying to find work. If there's a sex tape like that out there? I'll never get another job working at a museum again. They'll be too afraid I'll tarnish their reputation.

I probably won't be able to get a job anywhere. At least not anywhere that sex isn't part of the brand. They might want me at a sex shop. Or as a cam girl... I might not have a choice about being shy anymore. Tobias kneels down in front of me and runs his hand over my knee in a reassuring gesture.

"I have everyone working on it. PR, agent, lawyers. They're doing everything they can to validate whether it's real or not and shut it down if it is. Okay? I just wanted you to hear it from me first."

"Okay." I nod because I don't have other words. What else can I ask him to do about it? He's been hacked. It wasn't like he leaked the video or had control over it. I doubt he wants this out any more than I do.

"If it gets out, we'll figure something out, Scarlett. Don't worry too much, okay?"

"Kind of hard not to worry. It'll mean my whole career is over."

I take a deep breath. Doing my best not to panic or cry. It's not like it'll change anything. My fate's in the hands of his lawyers apparently.

"I'll do everything I can. I'm really sorry. You don't deserve any of this, and I fucking hope they can take care of it in time."

"Well, I guess that's what we get for thinking we could get out of this without consequences, right?" I force a small laugh and try to crack a smile.

He looks at me doubtfully, half a smile fading as quickly as it appears. He starts to say something, but I can't take any more of this awkward "are we about to be porn stars" conversation.

"Dinner's going to get cold." I stand abruptly, and he follows. "If you want to stay. Or maybe you have somewhere to be. I guess I misread the situation. Do you want a to-go box?"

So much for not being awkward. I'm hoping he leaves because I'm internally freaking out and I don't want to melt down in front of him.

"Um. Sure if you don't want to..."

"I don't have much of an appetite anymore. But I don't want it to go to waste. Just give me a sec, and I'll get a bag for you." I start putting a few portions in plastic tubs before he even has a moment to respond, quickly sliding them in a reusable grocery bag I've stuffed under the sink and handing it to him.

He stares at it and then at the door before he looks up at me. He looks as untethered as I feel right now, but I don't know how to fix it for either of us.

"I'll keep you posted on anything I know."

"Okay. Thank you." I open the door, and he walks out. A part of me wondering if it's for good.

I can't imagine his publicist will want us around each other stirring up speculation and gossip. It's going to make it hard for me to even see Harper if this goes down like this given how often Tobias is part of the Harper and Xander package deal. We'll have to timeshare our own best friends. This is why this was all a massive mistake in the first place. Why I should have never invited him up.

Once he's gone, I let out the sob that I've been holding back, and release the tears. I'm already in danger of not having a job. All the financial cuts that had to be made meant that most of the positions were reduced already and they're trying to decide who's going to replace Harper. Which means my position is likely to go in favor of that one, but no way am I getting promoted to head curator if there's a sex tape of me floating around. One that'll be in the tabloids because I decided to fuck a guy who can't stay out of the limelight.

I had a few thousand subscribers on my video channel, which is also likely going to turn into a cesspool of trolls once they put two and two together and realize I'm the woman getting fucked by Tobias Westfield on camera. This is *my* cosmic punishment apparently for trying to act like I'm not the quiet good girl. Trying on this other version with someone whose celebrity could destroy me.

Pretending like I can live the kind of life the rest of my friends do when I have none of the same advantages. No NFL contract, no wealthy boyfriend with a host of lawyers, not the kind of job that can withstand this sort of scandal or maybe be improved by it. Because I have no doubt if Joss and Colt suddenly had a sex tape, or Harper and Xander, that it would only make them more loved because of it. The public would probably rally around in their defense. But Tobias and some no-name acquaintance of his? I'm going to take the brunt of that humiliation, but he probably won't escape it either.

I knew things had been going too well. That something bad was due any day. And now it's here, or almost here. The worst torture of all is I just have to sit around waiting for it.

NINETEEN

Tobias

THAT AFTERNOON after the end of an early practice I'm at the house getting stuff together for my costume. Ben and Violet, my fellow wide receiver on the Seattle Phantom team and his wife, are hosting an engagement party for Colt and Joss, my quarterback and his fiancée. It's Halloween themed because of Joss's obsession with the holiday, and we're all required to dress up.

I'm pulling things out of the closet and grabbing some of the bits my assistant brought over for me that I'd asked him to find when my phone dings with a text message. It's my publicist and my heart sinks when I see there's a link attached. One that goes to a tabloid website.

I drop down on my bed and click it. There's a blurred-out photo over the play button and an NSFW warning, but enough of my tattoos are on display that everyone will know it's me the second they see it. My gut churns when I hit play, but I need to see it for myself.

It only takes half a second for me to realize it's both better and worse than I'd imagined. Because while I watch the view count multiply at an astronomical rate and it's most definitely my bare ass on display, it's not Scarlett on the couch with me in the video. It's another woman I'd met at a party. She'd been sweet and we'd been mutuals before she'd asked me over one night. I can't even remember her name, and I have to scroll down for the reminder. Grunting when I see the name Alexis and her screen name underlined in the article, some of it coming back to me.

She'd asked to take a few shots while we were fucking. Said she wanted them for personal use later, and I'd been stupid enough to agree. I'd filmed them on my phone, but I'd sent one to her. This one. So now I don't even know which one of us was hacked.

I fire off that information to my publicist and lawyers before I open the video back up and finish watching it. I'm an exhibitionist to my core. I love fucking, and I'm not remotely ashamed of it. But I only enjoy it when everyone involved is consenting to watch and being watched. And having this video shipped out to hundreds of thousands of thirsty assholes who just want to tear the two of us apart and try to shame us? Not something I signed up for.

I glance at the comments for two seconds before they make me nauseous, and I close them out. I toss the phone across the bed, and lay back against it, staring at the ceiling.

It won't take long before all the vitriol starts to roll in. Before I start to hear from my father about how I've disgraced the Westfield name. About how many times he's told me to get my act together. How he didn't put me through expensive schools with top football programs and all the best training camps with all the best connections to watch me fuck up left and right. To make the Westfield name a laughingstock.

And like I'm a fucking psychic my phone lights up with the call, and I answer it.

"Why the fuck am I looking at your bare fucking ass above the fucking fold on a tabloid website?"

"Because someone hacked the video."

"Why is there a video? Is this a girlfriend or just some random woman you picked up for the night?"

"She's not a girlfriend."

"Fan-fucking-tastic. So who knows what she'll say to the media. If she'll fucking blame you for it. I hope you have your people on this."

"I have them on it."

"This is going to wreck your mother's nerves. Jesus Christ. You know what that does to her. She doesn't fucking need it, Tobias." He pauses for effect and as he intends, the guilt of making my mother miserable rolls over me. A fresh new horror in all of this. "And now Easton and I are going to have to answer these questions from the media. Talk about your bare ass instead of talking about my guys and how well they're playing. I'm gonna be fielding questions about you fucking some random girl because you're too fucking stupid to think about consequences."

I feel my chest collapsing in on itself as it all hits me. He's not wrong. I hadn't even thought that far. Too worried about Scarlett, the woman in the video, and me to think about how this would radiate out from us.

"Is there a point to this call?" I'm used to grey rocking this man, but sometimes, like right now when the wounds are fresh, I can hardly stand all the fucking salt he pours in them.

"This is your last fucking shot, Tobias. I swear to all that's fucking holy, I didn't spend my life's work on this family, on you boys getting your shit together just to watch you squander it. You're too old for this shit. Too fucking smart for it too, frankly. I expected Easton would turn out like this, and yet somehow, he manages to be the least problematic of the fucking three of you."

"What does my last shot entail exactly? Gonna make me change my name?" I summon up the courage to taunt the man.

"I'm not gonna do shit, but the league will. You're old. You're getting slower every fucking season. I can see it on the tapes. You've got a few years left at best and no fucking ring to show for it. You'll be lucky if they don't replace you with someone they draft next year. You have all these off-field scandals and when the Phantom offloads you, no one else will want you either. You'll be relegated to some fucking foreign team or an indoor league at best. A few used car lots might have you throw a sport coat on and smile along to their fucking jingle. That how you wanna go out?" He pummels me with all my worst fears. The ones he knows will set me back in line. Make me think twice about speaking in the future.

"Thanks for the pep talk, Dad."

"Don't fucking Dad me. Get your act together. Put a cease and desist out, and I highly recommend you track this woman down and kiss her ass. Give her a car, a house, a fucking ring if she wants it, and worry about a divorce later. But make sure she doesn't trash you in the tabloids just to save herself."

"Fuck up my whole life because someone stole something private of mine. Got it, *Dad*. Will get right on it." I'm too angry to care about pissing him off more right now.

"You have the fucking privilege of having the name you do. The chances you do. Sometimes that means you gotta deal with the consequences of that privilege, *Son*. Do what you gotta do to fix it."

I don't answer. I just stay silent because I have no answer to his demands. There's no point in arguing.

"Call me tomorrow when you've got a fucking plan, but if you go under, you're on your own. I'm not trying to save you again. Not going to watch the rest of the family suffer because you can't stop being a fucking train wreck."

"Thanks for the consolation, Dad. Appreciate you. Have a good fucking night."

I hang up the phone. It usually sends him into a full-on rage, but tonight I don't care. He can rage at me and everyone else all he wants.

My phone dings again and I look down at it when I see SPITFIRE as the name that pops up. I open the message, hoping she's seen that it's not her and at least one of us can be relieved by it all.

> SPITFIRE:
> Saw the video pop up. I'm so sorry.
>
> Have your people figured out where the leak is from and how many of these there are?

I hit the call button, too tired to try and type this conversation out with her. Too emotionally broken to try to come up with all the perfect words and hoping that hearing her voice will at least be a little bit of a balm to how fucking rough this all feels.

"Hello?" she answers.

"Hi. Just thought I'd make this conversation easier. They don't know where the leak is from. They're looking into it. She had a copy of that video too, so I'm going to talk to her and see if she thinks the leak could have been on her end."

"Got it."

"Dodged the bullet for now though."

"Yeah."

"Everything okay?"

"Yep. Just probably should go, so I can get ready, and you can talk to anyone you need to. You still going to the party?"

"Yeah, I'll be there, Spitfire." My heart warms that she's still asking, wanting to see me.

"Okay. Well, I just... I'll probably keep my distance. I don't want anyone asking questions or wondering. You know?"

"Right. Of course..." I answer, swallowing past the lump in my throat.

"Okay. Well, I'm sorry... that all this is happening to you. I'm sure it's not easy even when you're as confident and untouchable as you are. Sucks that anyone would do this to you and invade your privacy like this. Fuck that tabloid for wanting to profit off of it too." There's a sympathetic tone to her voice that nearly breaks me.

I clear my throat, trying not to choke on my next words.

"Thank you."

"Of course. If there's anything I can do, let me know, okay?"

"Definitely. See you later."

"See you later."

The call ends, and I toss the phone across the bed. I want to crawl out of my skin right now knowing this is just the beginning of days of endless exchanges around this subject with people. Of my dad's ranting and my agent and publicist trying to help me slog my way through the mire of trash this is going to pile on top of me and my career.

I just want to fucking get away from it all. Hop on a plane like my sister does and take off for a new location. Somewhere I could start over again. Not be a fucking Westfield. Not have a sex tape. Not have the reputation that comes with everything I've done for the last decade plus.

Before I know what I'm doing, I head for the garage, grabbing my keys off the wall for my bike. I rarely take it out anymore. I'm not supposed to do it during the season, and it's frowned upon even in the offseason. But today I don't give a fuck. I just want the open road. Wind in my fucking ears so loud I can't hear any of my own thoughts.

I pull out, down the hill, and off my property, the tire sliding a little when I take a turn a little too close on the semi-slick roads that are still drying out from earlier rain. When I get to the main road, I gun the engine. Whipping out around an SUV in front of me, so I can have an open road to ride like I want.

I feel the stress starting to melt away, my guts untwisting from the mess and my head clearing from the fog already.

This is nothing that can't be fixed. It's going to be miserable for a while, but then I'll get past it. Move on and start fresh. My dad overreacts to every minor issue, and that's all this is going to be. Minor in the grand scheme of things.

I can still talk to Scarlett. Explain that all of this is fucked up, but that the woman in the video is from a long time ago. That it doesn't have to change anything between us or what we're doing. Fuck... Not only is she the only one on my phone, I can't even picture anyone but her when I close my eyes lately.

I convince myself it's all going to work out. It has to. I just need to go back, get ready for the party and I can talk to her. Explain everything and we can move on from this. Be with the rest of my friends who will understand and support me through all this bullshit.

I start to slow down to turn around just before a car pulls out from a stop sign without looking both ways. There's no way I can hit the brakes fast enough. Not with how slick the roads are and the way the bike keeps its momentum.

Laying the bike down is my only shot, so I take the risk—immediately regretting the fact I skipped putting on any of my usual gear when I ride. I lay it down and let go, praying I get enough distance before the car that I don't end up splattered by one or the other.

The bike skates over the slick pavement, skipping and then tumbling before it slams into the car. I'm not far behind it and I'm wondering whether I'll have to worry about this whole video problem at all.

It's the last thing I think before things go black.

TWENTY

Scarlett

I'M at Colt and Joss's engagement party despite the fact it's the last place I want to be. I'd rather be home with a pint of ice cream stressing over the fact that I might still have a sex tape released and that things are going to be well and truly over with Tobias now. There's no way I can keep up the illusion in my head that we're in some special secret bubble. That I'm special to him, and he might actually change for me.

Not when I'd seen cold hard evidence to the contrary and watched it one too many times in an attempt to compare the way he treated her to the way he treated me. It was wrong, but I also couldn't help my curiosity. My overanalyzing brain wanted to know if I'd read too much into every interaction we'd ever had.

But when I'm surrounded by friends and celebrating Joss & Colt who are some of the best people I know, I forget all the potential problems. For a while, I even forget that Tobias is supposed to be here tonight. Until the time gets later, and he still hasn't shown. Fashionably late is his thing, but this is way beyond that. Food, cake, even presents have been finished off at this point, and he's not here. I'm starting to wonder if he stayed at home to eat his own pint of ice cream and avoid the crowd. Maybe he doesn't feel like discussing his sex tape with everyone—I know if I'd been the woman in it, I definitely wouldn't be here.

I'm not the only one wondering about him though because a few minutes later Colt asks if anyone has seen him. Joss and Xander discuss he's missing and it's obvious they haven't seen the tape.

"You guys haven't seen the news?" I ask, dreading the idea of having to tell them but also feeling like it'd be weird if they found out I knew and didn't say anything.

"What news?" Harper looks up at me suspiciously.

"Uh... If you don't know, I don't think I want to be the one to say," I respond nervously when I confirm my suspicions. Now I have to explain how I know, and they don't. Shit. "I just accidentally found out when I was scrolling earlier because it's trending now." That's close enough to the truth. I could have found out that way.

"What's trending?" Joss's eyes snap to me. "I've been too busy helping Violet prep."

"Same," Harper answers.

Everyone in the room turns to stare at me, and I feel the heat crawling up my neck. I keep reminding myself that I'm not the one in the video. This video at least. But it still feels awkward as hell to be the one to tell them.

"Uh... here. I'll forward it to you, Harper." I look at my best friend as I reach for my phone.

Harper's suspicious look grows, but she doesn't say anything, pulling her phone out of her purse instead. I send the message, hearing it ding on her phone and bracing for her reaction. She opens and her eyes go wide. She gasps as she turns to Xander.

"Oh. Oh fuck. Um, Alex. Here, you can... yeah, you can look at this." She throws the phone to him, panicking no doubt at the site of staring at his best friend's ass on full display in the video.

"What is it?" He looks between the two of us confused before he looks at the phone. "Oh..." Sudden realization laces through his tone. "Yeah. Fuck..." He takes a deep breath and shakes his head.

"Is someone going to fill us in?" Joss looks to me and then to Harper, her brows climbing.

Xander turns the phone so she can see, no doubt reading the clickbait headline and glimpsing the above-the-fold still shot from the video.

Colt's face goes stark white before he yells.

"God fucking damn it! I've told him so many times."

The conversation descends into a discussion of what it will mean for Tobias's career and whether he took the video, or the woman did. Joss is particularly defensive of him, glancing up at me.

"It doesn't even look like he necessarily knew this was being taken," Joss comments as she looks closer at it, and Colt teases her about her intense interest in his friend's sex tape.

"I'm just saying. Talk to him first before you assume he did it." Joss looks at me pointedly when she hands the phone back to Harper.

Everyone agrees to quit discussing it until Tobias is here to explain himself and goes off to their various Halloween-themed activities around the party. Half of them bobbing for apples and the others playing some board game where one of them pretends to be a ghost helping them to solve a crime. I follow with my drink and watch amused at everything that's going on, but I can't bring myself to participate.

Still too shellshocked by the sex tape and concerned that Tobias not being here says a lot more than anyone else thinks it does. I wonder briefly if he's with his agent and publicist right now, and if they'll ask him to do something similar to what Xander and Harper did. He might have to date her, or at least fake it.

Whatever they decide, it's going to be his new priority and any fun we might have been having before is probably over. I knew this would be short-lived, but I hadn't truly accepted how soon that end was coming. Now I'm going to have to figure out how to keep attending get-togethers like this with our friends, seeing him with other women—for real —and not acting like I'm still hoping for one more one-night stand.

THE PARTY IS WINDING DOWN, and I start thinking about heading home when Xander bursts into the room looking distraught and overwhelmed. My heart bottoms out when I see him. Somehow, I just know. Between him not being here, the gut feeling I have, and the panic on Xander's face. I know something happened to Tobias.

He confirms my fears a moment later, announcing Tobias has been in a motorcycle accident. My heart shatters in my chest, tears threatening, and I can't even move for several seconds.

I have instant regret that I didn't go to see him. Insist we come to this party together or even offer to skip it and eat that stupid pint of ice cream together. Do something—anything—to let him know he had someone here for him.

But I have to figure out how to look calm. As far as they know, he's just an acquaintance to me and the whole room is spinning with movement.

Everyone grabs their stuff and practically runs to their cars, piling into as few as possible while Ben furiously dials Tobias's brother, Easton, and a friend of Ben's from college. I get into the car with Harper and Violet. Staring ahead into the void because I don't know how to keep my emotions concealed. I feel like crying. I'm heartbroken for him and so scared for what lies ahead at the hospital.

THE WAITING room closest to where they have Tobias looks like a combination between a crisis management center and the Seattle Phantom locker room. I have no idea why I'm still here because there are at least a dozen friends and family members standing around, and it's well after midnight at this point. I'm sure everyone else is starting to wonder why I'm here too. But I can't bring myself to leave, even if it seems like I don't belong here.

Tobias is ultimately nothing more to me than a one-night stand and a possible costar in a sex tape that thankfully turned out not to be ours. If it wasn't for the fact that we share so many friends, I wouldn't be allowed in here at all—probably be banned from coming anywhere near him. But as it stands, I can stay close, and selfishly I want to.

So now I'm just curled up in the corner, listening to the chaos around me as everyone tries to decide their plans for the evening. Who needs to go home and shower, who hasn't eaten, where his brother and his brother's wife who came straight from the airport after a short flight up from California are going to stay for the night. How and if they'll get back in time for the Monday night game he's supposed to be playing in California.

I haven't officially met him yet, but anyone could spot Tobias's brother, Easton, from a mile away if you'd ever seen him. It helps that I watch a lot of football and knew the Westfield brothers and their father from all the Sundays of my past. But it'd be hard not recognize them as brothers anyway.

A nurse walks in then, reminding all of us that it's past visiting hours and there's nothing we can do from the waiting room.

"But one of us can stay with him, right?" his brother's wife asks.

"Yes. He's in the private wing so up to two of you can stay in the room as long as you're signed in and on the approved list. But that's it. The rest of you really should go home. Get sleep. Come back during visiting hours. He's stable now. He just needs rest."

"The guys really need to get home and get sleep. They've got a game in less than twenty-four hours." Easton looks to his wife.

"Yes, but you have one in a little more than that. We need to at least find a place to stay. Get a room."

"I'd offer to let you stay with us," Ben offers. "And it's open if you want, but we're not very close to the hospital."

"Tobias has a place close by, doesn't he?" Easton looks to Xander.

"Yeah. Same building as us. But I don't have the key right now, and not sure where he has it. You can stay with us though. I have a guest room."

"Are you sure?"

"Yes. Absolutely." Harper nods.

"All right. We won't be there much. Just to get settled and changed. Maybe get food before we come back."

"So who's staying?" Waylon asks. "I'd do it, but I've got to get back. And Mac has the kids."

I realize looking at the room that everyone either needs to get back because they're playing tomorrow, or they had more than their fair share to drink tonight because they weren't playing tomorrow and were enjoying the alcoholic offerings at the engagement party.

"I'll stay," I say it before I know what I'm doing. Harper turns abruptly to look at me.

"Are you sure?"

"I mean, at least until his family can get food and get settled. I can stay until you all come back. Sit with him for a few hours," I offer, suddenly feeling very awkward when everyone looks at me. To all of them, I'm a virtual stranger to Tobias. Someone he only knows in passing because of Harper and Xander. We're more acquaintances than friends really in their eyes.

"That could work." Xander shrugs as he looks around.

"He'll probably be sleeping the whole time. But are you sure you don't mind?" Easton's wife asks me.

"I'm sure. I don't mind. He knows me well enough, and if you give me your number, I can text or call if something comes up. And I can text Xander and Harper too," I answer softly, trying to respect the fact that it's so late and lots of patients are probably trying to sleep. Not expecting a celebrity patient to have a small entourage in the waiting room for him.

"Thank you, so much. I'm sorry I didn't get your name?" Easton reaches out a hand.

I stand and take it. "Scarlett. Nice to meet you, minus the circumstances."

"I'm Easton's wife, Wren." She holds out her hand.

We exchange quiet smiles and then numbers before everyone scurries off to make things right in the rest of the world and then come back to the hospital to be with Tobias.

WHEN THEY SHOW me to his room the lights are already dim and he's asleep, the monitors blink and hum in the dull light, and I glance at the nurse.

"He's out. Probably for the night. Trauma has taken a lot out of him, and we've given him meds so he can be comfortable and get some rest. If he wakes up and needs anything, just page us, okay?"

I nod. Setting my purse and coat down on one chair, I sit in the other. He doesn't look anything like the man I'd just seen a couple of days before. He's covered in hospital blankets and bandages, propped up with pillows. What little I can see of his face is swollen, and I don't dare approach the bed to get a closer look. My stomach churns with anxiety, hoping he doesn't wake up and wonder what I'm doing here.

I have no idea how he'll react. If he'll be happy I'm someone he knows, or if he'll think I'm a psycho for sitting by his bedside imagining I'm some doting girlfriend.

Despite all the amazing sex and the surprising kindness he's shown through all of it, we've never talked about feelings. Never thought about whether or not it'd be appropriate for me to visit or sit with him in a situation like this. So I just pray he stays asleep through the night, or at least until his brother can get back here and sit with him.

It's a relief to see him for myself. See the monitors and know his heart's beating. Seeing his chest rise and fall with regular breaths. Because for the interminably long ride over here, I wondered briefly if he'd be dead or on so many machines, he might wish he was. A few tears of relief form in my eyes, dropping down my cheeks before I can wipe them away.

I'm glad that our friends are close enough and trust me enough to sit with him because some part of my stupid heart, the part that won't be convinced that he will never belong to me, belongs to him. So being able to sit here and be with him during the darkest moments of his life is all I want right now.

TWENTY-ONE

Tobias

When I wake up my whole body aches, every inch of my bones throb, and my muscles feel like they might just tear off my limbs. The skin down the whole right side of my body feels like it's on fire, and somehow, I think even my hair hurts. I blink and try to open my eyes.

The light that pours in is glaringly bright, and I have to close them again immediately, wincing at the fact that my eyeballs hurt now too. I have no idea what the hell I did for my body to hurt this badly. Even the most brutal games where I've been tackled hard or hit blindside haven't left me this bruised in the morning. I try to remember how the hell I got here, and the first step to that is going to be getting out of this bed.

I groan as I try to sit up, joints cracking and muscles stretching in ways that make it hurt even more than it did before.

"Fucking hell..." I mutter.

"Fuck. Tobias... Be careful." I hear my brother, Easton's

voice and that makes my eyes snap open again despite the pain.

"Tobias. Bro... listen to me. Go easy."

"East?" I blink, trying to adjust to the lights. Just talking is a struggle as my whole mouth feels like cotton. "What are you doing here?"

If East's here something has to be wrong because we both play in the league, and he has no business being in Seattle. It means he's missing practice with his team and that shit will get you on the wrong side of your coaches fast.

"You're in the hospital, bro. Just be careful, okay? You got hurt pretty bad."

"Do you need anything?" It's his wife, Wren's voice, and I crane my neck to look at her which is a mistake. I lay back again resting on the pillow, trying to confirm what they've told me.

Sure enough, the walls are that horrific shade of cream, beeping machines are keeping an irritating rhythm around me, and I'm buried under scratchy sheets that are paper thin. I go to ask what the hell happened that I ended up here, but my mouth is so dry the words don't want to come.

"Water?" I manage to rasp.

"Here you go," Wren answers, handing me a bottle with a straw in it.

I take a sip but it's lukewarm. It takes the edge off the worst of the desert-dry feeling, but I frown. "Ice?"

"I'm sure I can find some. Let me see if I can find a nurse or a tech. I'll be back." Wren shoots me a sympathetic look before she hurries out the door.

I take another sip of the water because some is better than none and look at my brother. He's standing at the side of my bed, arms crossed and looking more like our father than I've ever seen him look in the current moment. Can't imagine that's a good sign.

"How you feeling?" Easton's concern turns into a full-on

frown as he assesses me. So I'm going to guess I look about as good as I feel.

"Like fucking shit," I grunt, trying to sit up.

"Easy. *Easy*. What are you trying to do?" He jolts forward, hands out like he's gonna try to make this easier. Which is pretty much impossible. I flick him a look, and he just raises a brow in defiance.

"Sit up more," I grumble.

"There's a button for that." East presses something at my side and the bed starts to move slowly, a small metallic sound accompanies it. He hands me the remote then and takes a step back.

"Thanks."

"You remember what happened?" he asks after he studies me for another moment.

I stare blankly at the sheets bunched at my waist. Trying to think back to the last thing I did. But my head is killing me almost as much as everything else. I go to reach up to run my hand through my hair and my fingertips meet with rough cotton bandages. I look to East for answers, and his brow furrows. He glances at them and then down at the floor like it hurts him to see me like this.

"They've got your head wrapped. You were in a motorcycle accident. Thrown into a car on impact."

My heart drops to my gut and my first thought is to make sure I can still wiggle all my fingers and toes. I hadn't thought to check or pay attention to make sure all those things still worked, too focused on my need for water and all the pain. I breathe a sigh of relief at their movement before I think of what most people look like when they've been hit by a car. The injuries. Ones that might prevent you from doing your job, especially when your job is to run down a field lightning fast and snatch a ball out of the air while guys try to pound you into the turf.

"How bad?" I look for his reaction, half-afraid he'll lie to me. I might if the situation was reversed. Looking him in the eye and telling him his season was over would be a nightmare. Worse if it was his career.

"Well... it's not good but it's a miracle it's not worse. You've got some really fucking terrible road rash, but you at least had a leather jacket on. You've got a badly bruised jaw and some orbital bone trauma. They reset your shoulder, and you have a hairline fracture in your hip. You didn't need surgery, thankfully. They've got lots of instructions for you though. If you want to get out of here and back on your feet, I suggest you listen to them."

The knowledge burns through my gut like fire. Because it means I won't be playing this weekend, or any other weekend for several weeks at least. Maybe not the season. It means sidelines and rehab. A miserable stretch of shit I don't want. Tears start to well in my eyes, and East walks up and puts his hand on my arm.

"A few months out is better than dead, brother. So just keep it in perspective." Now he fucking sounds like our father. The famous Westfield serenity even in times of stress —at least publicly speaking. But I feel anything but calm right now. The way my life is headed, I'm not sure if it's better.

"Ice!" Wren returns and holds it up in a pink cup she procured from the nurses' station. She pours half the ice into the cup that's sitting on my table and turns the straw toward me like I'm a child.

"Thanks." I stare at it for a minute because I've forgotten why I even wanted it in the first place. Why it matters in the face of everything else.

"You told him?" Wren looks into my eyes, the pity there obvious.

I take another sip and the cool water coats my tongue and throat, bringing a little relief to the least of my problems.

"Just the basics of the accident."

"Is there more?" I frown.

Easton scrubs a hand over his face before he speaks again. "You know about the tape?"

My gut manages to drop lower. It's practically in hell at this point, dragging the rest of me with it. I'd managed to forget the sex tape that'd been leaked in the midst of all of this pain. That's been one blessing of hurting this badly, I guess.

"Yeah..." I admit.

"Well... That's why I'm here instead of Mom. Dad was gonna come but when it was serious and not critical, I told him I'd come. With coaching and everything... You know. Mom wanted to be here, but I figured with everything it'd be more than you want."

"Right. Thanks." The last thing I need is my mother here lecturing me about a sex tape and motorcycles. Telling me I need to finally grow up and settle down.

"I'll have to fly back tonight, but Wren can stay a few more days if you want. Waylon and Mac offered her a room at their place. Xander and his girlfriend have been in and out checking on you. They just went home for a bit to shower and get some sleep."

"I'll be fine. Don't change your plans for me. I know you've got practice and Wren's got the business to run." I shift in my bed, trying to find some comfort on the stiff mattress. East leans forward and helps me move some of the pillows again, and it takes a little of the pressure off my aching lower back.

"You need someone with you. Especially when they send you home. You don't want to be alone."

"I won't be alone. I've got friends to check in on me. An assistant. The ability to have food delivered. I'm good."

East gives me a skeptical look, and I know what he's thinking. It's not wrong either. I have a lot of friends who are more acquaintances than anything. Happy to come to a party or a game, and travel if I want some friends to head to the mountains or beach for a long weekend. But they aren't the kind of people you call when you need someone. Those people, the ones I can count on, all play on the same team as me—fellow Phantom football players—and while they would jump to help me, they're all mid-season and overwhelmed with practice and games.

"I really think—" Wren starts.

"I'm good. If it gets bad, I'll call Mom," I mutter. Moving my mouth too much hurts right now, I assume from the swelling in my jaw.

"If you're sure." Easton frowns again, marring his otherwise serene face. One that looks like mine and yet not quite the same. Less angry. Younger. A touch less rugged.

Another thought hits me. One that's stupidly vain. If I fucked up my face, my jaw... there's no fucking telling what I look like now. It's low on the list of reasons to be depressed at the moment. I shouldn't care at all, but half my sponsorships are based on my looks.

"Mirror?" I ask.

East frowns and shakes his head, so I look to Wren. Wren looks at him, a reluctant one that sends a whisper of anxiety through my nerves.

"Mirror," I repeat, and she reaches into her bag and hands me a small compact.

I open it up and bring the mirror up to my face with my left hand, the one that fucking hurts less. When I see myself, I feel like I might throw up. Everything looks bloody and swollen. My whole head is wrapped in bandages and huge parts of my right cheek and jaw are obscured by the gauze they've put there. The colorful green and purple stain of the bruise spreads beyond them and under my eye where I look like I've gone way too many rounds in the ring. I click the compact shut and hand it back to Wren.

"There's a lot of swelling and bruising right now. They said the bruising will likely get worse before it gets better. They've got ice packs for you to put on them in intervals. The nurse said she'll be back here in a few to explain things to you now that you're awake. They didn't think you'd need surgery, but they said you could decide once the swelling goes down if you want plastics to work on you." Wren expands on the explanation Easton had already given.

"Plastics. Jesus!" My stomach turns. "My porn star career is gonna be short-lived if I'm that fucked up."

Easton lets out a muted laugh. Wren just shakes hers at my dark humor.

"It might not be that bad. It just looks bad now. You have a lot of swelling from the trauma your face took when you hit the car, you know. Gotta give it a chance to recover," Wren says as she runs a hand over the back of mine. Trying to soothe me. "The important part is you're going to be okay. You scared us all, you know? You've got to be more careful."

I smile at Wren because my brother's wife is probably the only one I'm willing to take this lecture from right now. She's the kindhearted one in a family of assholes. Minus my sister, but she's crazy as fuck and would just show up, kick my ass, and give me shit. And I'm not ready for that kind of tough love yet either.

"I know," I agree. Because between the sex tape and the accident, I'm starting to question the immortality I'd always relied on getting me through.

TWENTY-TWO

Scarlett

"HEY, COME ON IN." Harper welcomes me into her and Xander's condo. She asked me over to talk and my stomach's been going rounds on the drive over worrying about what it is she wants to talk about. She takes my coat and then I follow her into the living room where Xander's already sitting, scrolling through his phone.

He looks up, giving me a smile and a chin tip when I sit down on the couch across from them, putting his phone away a moment later. Xander and Harper exchange glances.

"All right. You guys are making me nervous, like I'm about to get a lecture or something."

"No. Not at all. Nothing like that. It's just Xander's got a big ask for you and we're nervous about talking with you about it."

"Oh... Okay." Now the nerves are worse.

"Well, now you've terrified her."

"I mean... if you think the worst it might sound better in comparison," Harper jokes.

"Okay, let's just discuss what it is." I look back and forth between them.

Xander's expression clears and something more pensive replaces it.

"It's about Tobias. He's refusing to have any sort of nursing service or help come to his house. Easton had to go back, Wren needs to leave too, and his sister can't come out right now. She's got a commitment she can't break, and he doesn't want her to. But we all play, and the girls all have the nonprofit, and Violet has her business so... he's alone a lot. His assistant comes and goes but he has other work and can't be there all the time."

"That doesn't sound good given what I've heard of his recovery and mental state," I say softly, staring at the rug on the floor.

"It's not. He needs someone there right now, for the foreseeable future. Even if they're just in the house in case he falls or something. Help make sure he gets to PT sessions here soon. That kind of thing." Xander looks at Harper.

"And we thought we'd ask you," she takes over where he left off. "Xander would pay you of course, or Tobias might want to. We haven't said anything to him. We didn't want to have that fight until we knew if you'd be up for it. But it'll pay more than your salary at the museum, and it'd be temporary obviously. Just until he gets better." She looks at me thoughtfully.

"The money part makes me a little uncomfortable. To have you guys or him paying me. I mean, we don't always get along, but I do think of him as a friend, and I'd be happy to help."

Harper shakes her head. "You need the money; he needs the care. It makes sense. Don't think about it like that. Also... to be honest Scar, he's a nightmare right now. Trust me when I say you'll want the money to put up with him. He's miserable, and he's taking it out on everyone and everything around him. I wouldn't want someone there who wasn't getting paid."

"It still feels awkward."

"I get that, but you'd be doing us all a favor. Give Xander and the guys peace of mind. Be able to let his family know someone's there who cares," Harper adds.

"Also," Xander says, looking up at me. "Part of his excuses have to do with the fact he doesn't want someone there he can't trust. He's worried nurses or other staff are going to take pictures or talk to sports reporters about his condition. Or worse, another tabloid opportunity. And you're one of us, we all know you would never do something like that. He knows that. So I think he'd be more likely to agree to it."

I can understand his paranoia, honestly. With everything that's happened. The fact that we still don't know if our tape got leaked. I guess if it does and I'm working there, there's at least the chance to spin it positively in his favor.

"Right. Obviously, I would never do anything to disrupt his privacy. I just... I'm not his favorite person. Are you sure he's going to agree to this?" I frown.

"No," Xander answers immediately. "My guess is he won't. But I'm not going to give him a choice. I'm going to pay you and give you my key to his house. Tell him when you're going to be there, and he'll have to learn to live with it."

Harper makes a disapproving sound. "I don't think that's the way to sell it."

"He's stubborn as fuck right now, Saint. It's gonna be the only way. I just want her to know, so she goes in prepared." He looks from Harper to me. "I'll pay you extra, and if he's an asshole tell me. We'll get you hazard pay. Okay?"

"I'm not worried. I've dealt with plenty of jerks at work before. Harper can tell you that."

"Well, that's true. Fucking Paul." She rolls her eyes. "And Carter can be added to that list now."

We both laugh a little, but the thought of Carter reminds me of my birthday and then of Tobias. My heart twists and my gut turns a little at the thought of being with him again. I'm both anxious to see him again and nervous that he's going to reset to the cruelest version of himself. But I want to help if I can.

"As long as you're sure. It would be a relief to have some sort of work. I'd treat it like a job. I could cook and keep the place clean and stuff."

"He has a maid, and he orders in or his nutritionist has meals ready for him."

"Yeah, but it might help if he had some home-cooked food and things like that, you know?"

Xander and Harper exchange a look, and she smiles at me.

"Then you'll do it?"

"Yeah. I mean if he's okay with it. I understand if he's stubborn on the issue, but if he really doesn't want me there, I don't want to force the issue. He's had enough trauma." I try to keep it lighthearted.

"I'll talk with him and let you know." Xander nods.

"All right. If there's anything else I can do in the meantime, let me know."

Another nod and then Harper hops up.

"Okay. Now that that's out of the way... pizza?"

TWENTY-THREE

Tobias

"I DON'T NEED A FUCKING BABYSITTER." I bellow at Xander, annoyed he's acting like some sort of Trojan horse.

He came over under the pretense of us hanging out for a bit together, giving me some company, so I'm not staring at the same four walls. Now he's revisiting the idea of me having someone stay with me during the days to keep an eye on me. Which is the last thing I'm interested in.

"You do. You need help while you recover, and if you won't have a nurse stay here then you need to come up with a different plan. You know Easton and I can't be here. We would if we could. Harper and Wren can give you intermittent help but—"

"I don't need help."

"I'm not arguing with you on this. I'm telling you. You need someone to keep an eye on you, to be here when you're doing things like taking a shower, make sure you get your meals, take your meds. You need the help."

"And what are you proposing my backup plan is?" I glare at him because I can tell when Xander is angling for something.

"I'm not proposing it. I've already arranged it, and you're going to accept it whether you like it or not."

"I knew you'd done something already. What did you do?"

"Scarlett is—"

The mention of her name makes me feel sick. It's worse than I could have imagined.

"No. No fucking way!" I shake my head.

"Too late."

"I can't have her here. So whatever you did—undo it. Cancel it. Unfuck it." She is the absolute last person on earth I want to see me like this. That's all I need, her witnessing my every struggle, trying to help, and having those big sad gray eyes look at me with pity. No fucking way.

"She's out of work right now. She could use the income and you could use the help."

"*Not her.*"

"Why?"

I flash him a look. One that we only use when we don't want to talk details but need each other to understand. The man is like a brother to me, and I don't know why he won't just fucking listen.

"You fucked her." He scrubs a hand over his face, shaking his head and staring at the ground. "I told you—"

"Do you honestly think I need an 'I told you so' lecture right now?"

He folds his arms over his chest and stares at me.

"No. What I think you need is to accept the consequences of your fucking actions. I told you if that's how you chose to go that you'd still need to be able to live with being around her after. Remember when I didn't want to play fake relationship with Harper? When I said that was a terrible fucking idea?"

"This is not you and Harper. I was saving your ass from getting benched or worse."

"You fall when you're alone here, you don't have help when you need it—it could be worse for you too. Not just the season but your whole career."

"I don't need to hear that shit right now."

"But you do. That's half the problem. You're worried about the things that don't matter, and not worried enough about the ones that do. And to be fucking real with you friend, I don't think your mental health is in a place where you can spend weeks alone holed up in this place without spiraling out."

"Scarlett isn't going to help my fucking mental health. She hates me."

"She agreed to do it."

Fucking wonderful. Xander has already filled her in on what a fucking mess I'm in right now and her bleeding heart couldn't help but agree.

"Then the pity she feels must be fucking overwhelming."

"I don't really care what's motivating her. She's your option. You don't want strangers in your house right now? You want someone you can trust not to run to the sports gossip blogs and tell your secrets? She's the one you pick. She's a good girl, and she'll keep your fucking business secret. Fuck, the fact that you fucked her, and she hasn't said a word to Harper or anyone else. Just fucking endured whatever shitty treatment you gave her in silence and still shows up to the hospital and—"

"She was at the hospital?"

"Yes. She stayed with you that first night when the rest of us needed sleep and Easton needed to find a place to stay before he came back. You didn't know?"

"No."

The news takes my words away for a minute. I didn't think she'd been there at all. I hadn't seen her once during my entire stay even though she'd texted a couple of times to check on me. So it's a shock to find out she was there that first night when things were the worst.

"You were asleep when we left, and maybe East got there before you woke up." Xander shrugs.

"She can't possibly want to be here taking care of me."

"She didn't hesitate. She agreed even before I offered to pay her so she could stop looking for work while she helps out around here. She didn't want to take it either, said that she considers you a friend. And maybe it is pity motivating her. I don't fucking know, but frankly, you need pity or whatever she's fucking got for you right now. Maybe what you really need is a fucking wife—but in the absence of that, a scorned ex fuck-buddy who will agree to put up with your shit is better than nothing."

"A wife. Jesus. I knew you were gone on Harper but hearing you say anything about marriage..." I laugh but Xander doesn't look amused.

"I'm glad you think it's funny. But you know who will be there for me when I decide to go launching myself off a fucking motorcycle—or better fucking yet, who would talk me out of getting on the motorcycle in the first place?"

I grit my teeth and shake my head. I've already seen how marriages work out with my parents—with everyone miserable and pretending they aren't.

"You and Colt both want to join Ben, go for it. I'm not made for it."

"It's your life. If this is how you want to spend it, that's up to you. But I've listened to you when I really needed to. You need to listen to me now—our time fucking around and not dealing with the consequences at the end of the day is over.

Yeah? Cosmically, karmically, however you want to think about it. Time's up. You've got a fucking sex tape, a fucked hip, a whole lot of people pissed at you, and very few people available to be here for you when you need it. So make damn sure this is how you want to keep living. Because I fucking love you like a brother, and it killed me to pick up the phone the other night. I want better for you. You deserve better."

I feel something like tears clawing at my throat and I refuse, fucking absolutely refuse, to cry like a bitch in front of Xander or anyone else right now. So I just nod my head and look away.

"Scarlett will be here in the morning. I'm giving her my extra key until she can make a copy. Either talk nice to her or don't talk to her at all, but you need her, so don't fucking piss her off and make her quit. If she does, you'll have to get a proper nurse or aide to come and stay here until you're back on your feet."

"Fine," I grit out the word.

"Hate me now. But someday you'll realize it was the right move."

I could do both. Because as much as I hate the idea, the small flutter of excitement I feel in my chest at seeing her tomorrow is the closest I've come to hope since the accident.

TWENTY-FOUR

Scarlett

I TALK Harper into going with me to Tobias's house the first day I'm working there. It's a cold morning and we're both bundled up while she works on the security pad and lock. I've brought a box of donuts and some coffee as a morning peace offering. I'm hoping it'll ease the tension that I'm sure is going to fill the room.

She lets us in, and we shake off the cold and hang our coats up. I've seen his condo downtown, but I've never had a chance to be here—the site of his legendary parties. I could already tell from the outside it's massive, but inside just from where I'm standing it already looks labyrinth-like. I might have taken on more than I can handle, but then again, I doubt he's moving around much based on what I've heard.

"Here, we can set things on the dining room table, and I'll get some napkins and things out of the kitchen." Harper nods in what I assume is the direction of the dining room, and I follow.

A massive table sits in an enormous dining room with a fireplace, just off a huge chef's kitchen. His condo is a beautifully decorated bachelor pad, but this place looks like him. His personality is etched across every wall and on the furniture. I can tell that this is the place he likes to spend most of his time.

"I texted him when we got here, so he should be in. He's still on crutches though, so he's a little slow moving. Might be a minute," Harper says to me as she disappears into the kitchen.

I start to open the box of donuts and fold the lid back. Placing coffees at each person's spot. Between Harper and I, we managed to narrow down his coffee order, and I set the cups at the end of the table and pull out some of the extra creamers and sweeteners they put in the bag with the donut holes. Just as I put those out, I see movement out of the corner of my eye and look up to see Tobias on the threshold of the room.

I haven't seen him since that night in the hospital. We haven't texted other than a few get well wishes from me that went unanswered at the start. I haven't been invited to see him either, only getting updates through Harper and Joss. So I've just hoped for the best for him from afar.

The last time I saw him he'd been swollen, bruised, and battered, fast asleep on pain medication, and buried under a blanket at the hospital with bandages around his head. He looks better and worse now. Better in that much of the swelling has gone down and he's standing with the help of crutches. Worse in that the peaceful look of sleep has been replaced by a stormy look of malcontent. He frowns when he sees me and the donuts, moving slowly into the room until he grabs the chair at the head of the table.

"I got donuts and coffee." I try to keep a cheerful tone to my voice, but it sounds shaky.

He glances at them and then up at me.

"I can see that," he deadpans. None of his usual sarcastic banter or playfulness. The words bite even though nothing about them is particularly cruel.

He looks down at the coffee again and the side of his face catches the light. Instead of the bandages, there's a nasty scar, one that's very fresh and bright pink across the whole right side of his face. Surface level in some places and considerably deeper in others. My eyes drift down to his arm, remembering that he'd been bandaged there too, and I can see where fresh road rash is fading across his tattoos, leaving me to wonder how they'll survive the scarring.

"Make sure you get a nice good long look. Catalog it all, so we don't have to do this every day." The tone of his voice is dead weight, wrapping around me and throwing me into a dark pool of deep water. One where I'm floundering because I don't know what to say in response.

"I'm sorry. I just hadn't—It looks painful." I trip over my words, hurrying to try to cover up the offense I've committed.

"And hideous. I'm aware."

"Sorry, I didn't mean—"

"Morning!" Harper interrupts cheerfully, saving me in the process. "We got a couple of different coffees. We both had different guesses on what you drink."

"Morning. Thanks," he grumbles.

"We got donuts and donut holes too. I was going to show Scarlett around so you don't have to, and then I'll leave you guys to it."

"Fine." He takes the coffee I picked for him and puts a donut in his mouth before he moves to awkwardly leave the room on his crutches again.

"I could carry that for you," I offer, trying to be helpful.

He glares into the distance.

"See I told you you'd be useful," Harper chirps, and I know it's more for his benefit than mine. Her coded way of telling him to be nice.

He holds the coffee out and I take it from him, snagging the donut from his mouth before adding a couple of napkins to the mix.

"Lead the way," I say softly.

He doesn't say a word as we walk down the hall, but I'm thankful to get away from Harper for a minute. Before she leaves, I want to make sure that he really wants me here. That he's okay with this arrangement. Because the last thing I want is to be part of bullying him into this and have him hate me for it.

He turns down a hall and into a room which must be the master because it's huge. A small bar area to the right of the door and then two doors. One that leads to—from what I can tell—a massive bathroom and the other to a cavernous-looking closet. It tracks with his vanity that he'd have all this. He probably has a whole separate closet for his sneakers alone. But I smile a little at getting to see this part of him. His condo is for sure just a place for business because it has none of the personality of this place.

He sits down on the bed, another oversized piece of furniture with messy sheets that are wrinkled and look like they're in desperate need of a wash. A stack of containers is on the nightstand and a trash can in the corner is full. I'm starting to think he's not letting the maid in here.

"What are you gawking at?" He catches me staring, and I look up at him.

"The state of this place. Guessing you're not allowing the maid in here?"

"Fuck no. I don't need her snooping around or being in my business when I'm trying to recover."

"Okay well, I'm going to start on the sheets today. I'll have Harper show me where the laundry room is."

"The fuck you are."

"You going to do it then?"

He gives me a pointed look, turning his eyes to the crutches and back on me before he rests them against the headboard.

"Then I'm doing it. You can't live like this. It's not good for your mental health while you try to recover." I set the coffee and the donut on the nightstand.

"Jesus Christ. If you come in here and fucking start bitching me out like this, it's lasting a few hours max."

"You got a backup option? You want whatever random nurse they can find? Maybe she'll be a fangirl and talk your ear off all day about how amazing you are—or worse yet maybe it'll be a teammate of yours she can't shut up about. All day, every day you'll have to hear about Xander's arms or Colt's eyes—"

"Holy fuck, Scarlett. Enough," he interrupts me, and I give my best saccharine smile.

I look around the room and suddenly my concerns about bullying him evaporate. I get why Xander felt this was an emergency.

"Then don't argue with me. It's what I'm here to do. It's what Xander's paying me for."

"What I'm paying you for. I'm not fucking having you take his money to take care of me. Fucking ridiculous idea." He takes a bite of the donut.

"From what I've heard, you're the one who forced him to get creative about things."

His eyes snap up to mine.

"I'm fucking fine."

"It definitely looks like it." I circle my finger around the room and smile again.

"I don't want you here."

"I'm aware."

"So why are you?" His eyes narrow.

"Friends help their friends even when they think they don't need it, Tobias."

His eyes flick over me, assessing me, like he's not sure how he feels about the statement.

"Or you just needed the money," he says flatly.

"I did need to be gainfully employed to keep the roof over my head. And I can't be here and waiting tables at the same time. So yes."

His eyes narrow that I've flipped his nasty remark over on him.

"Just don't be fucking snooping around or getting too comfortable here. You're out as soon as I can move a little better. So keep those callback numbers close."

"I have no interest in snooping. You're the one with that particular habit." I raise a brow at him, and his eyes darken with the accusation.

"Yeah well. Don't worry. I don't have a secret shrine to you in my closet."

"Made sure to clean that up before I got here? That's good. It'd have been awkward if I had to see it." I grin at him and the irritation on his face grows. He takes another bite of his donut and grabs the coffee.

"Do you know what you want for lunch?"

"I don't give a fuck. My nutritionist has meals in the fridge and freezer."

"All right. I'll see what's in the fridge and pantry. Maybe I can cook something for dinner."

"I just said I have meals. You don't need to cook."

"I know." I shrug. "Am I allowed in the closet and bathroom to clean things up?"

"If you fucking must."

"All right. I'll leave you alone and have Harper show me where things are." I start to leave the room.

"Scarlett," he calls after me.

"Yeah?" I freeze, a tingle in my spine because I'm hoping he says anything that could possibly bury this tension.

He takes a breath and then there's a long pause.

"Nothing, just... don't fucking move stuff around too much."

"Of course." I walk out and close the door behind me, feeling like I've just signed up for the longest few weeks of my life.

TWENTY-FIVE

Tobias

"HEY," I answer when I see my brother's name light up my phone.

"How are you feeling?"

"Like fucking shit, and now Xander's got me a fucking babysitter."

"Did you need one?"

"I'll remember you asked that someday."

"I'm just saying... Xander's usually one to live and let live so if he intervened, I'm guessing there was a reason." Easton plays devil's advocate.

"I just don't want people around right now."

"I can see why he was worried then."

"I'm aware that I'm usually the one who has everyone around, but right now I just want to be alone. I don't need people gawking at me and watching me struggle every minute of every fucking day."

"I get that. I'd feel the same way, but you need someone there with you. This isn't the kind of thing you do alone."

"I was a fucking idiot for letting him convince me to have her do it. I should have just picked an aide service and had them come in. Risked the fucking bullshit that would come along with that."

"Who is her?"

"Scarlett. He said she was at the hospital. I never saw her, did you?"

"The redhead?"

"Yeah."

"She stayed with you the first night. Said she was happy to. Texted me and Wren updates about things until we could get back to the hospital. I assumed she was a friend of yours."

"Something like that."

Easton's laugh comes through the phone. "Did he assign your latest one-night stand gone wrong? Punishing you for your bad fucking behavior? Sounds like a thing Xander would do if he's tired of your shit. If that's what she is I don't think she's half bad. She seemed like she genuinely cared about you."

"She's his girlfriend's best friend. We fucked a couple of times. I thought... I don't know what I fucking thought. It was obviously before the sex tape and the accident."

"Yeah? Do you know what she thought?"

"No. If we're not fucking or fighting, she doesn't say much."

"But she's there for you now."

"Getting paid for it."

"Oh."

"I mean... not like that. She's in between jobs. She's a history curator and the museum she works for is temporarily closed. She needed work and Xander insists I need fucking help so..."

"So she's helping?" Easton's amused with himself.

"Not fucking like that. Jesus."

"If you say so."

"Trust me, when she saw my face and all the fucking road rash... Pretty sure that was the last thing on her mind."

"I got that scar from the knee surgery. Wren says it's sexy as fuck."

I roll my eyes, wishing I could smack my little brother upside the head.

"Wren would praise every fucking thing you do. And it's your fucking knee. Not your face."

"You look fine. Better than fine. Pretty sure when they do their yearly 'Westfield brother' coverage and run the fucking social media polls you'll still get voted prettiest. So don't fucking worry about it."

"Whatever," I grumble.

"You gonna tell her you've got feelings for her?"

"I don't have feelings for her." I frown at the phone. Most ridiculous shit I've heard.

"Which is why you've been talking about her for the last five minutes."

"She's in my house every day. What do you want me to talk about?"

"The party you're throwing when this is over, how your PT is going, whatever hot chick you met that you're fucking. How much we both can't stand the old man. The usual."

"My agent and publicist are on my ass about the party behavior after the sex tape. PT is painful. I can't fuck anyone right now until this hip is fucking healed up, and after the sex tape, I don't fucking trust anyone either. And the old man can't stop shitting bricks about all of it, so still can't stand him. Still have to answer the phone when he calls. Good enough report for you?"

"Making progress with PT though?"

"Slow. Too fucking slow for my liking. They won't let me push though. They keep telling me it could set me back. So it's slow and steady."

"You'll get through it. Probably come back better than ever."

"Stats for the season will still be trash and the bonus will be out of reach. And the team is fucking struggling without me there. We've probably lost too many games at this point to have a chance at the playoffs."

"Next year."

"Yeah. At some point, there isn't another year."

East sighs on the other end of the phone.

"Are you seeing someone?"

"I just said I can't."

"I mean for the depression."

"Fuck you."

"I'll take that as a no."

"Do you see someone for yours?"

"When I was in my head a couple of seasons ago about all the drops? Yeah. I did."

Well, fuck. The Westfield way had always been to pretend it wasn't fucking happening.

"Wren talked me into it. But I think it was worth it. I'd do it again if I thought it would help."

"And on that note, have a good night."

"Tobias..."

"What?"

"I want my fucking brother back. I know this shit is hard. I know you're miserable. I was all there to defend you the first couple weeks. Told everyone you needed time to wallow and sit with this. But now, fuck. I'm worried too. I don't want to tell you that. I don't want to make it worse, and I don't want you fucking pissed off at me. But listen to me and Xander, yeah?

We're not that much different, and you know we fucking have your back—always."

My chest tightens with the sincerity in his tone. East doesn't normally talk like this. We dance around things. Make jokes. I must be a fucking wreck if he's lecturing me.

"I hear you."

"Okay. That's all I'm asking."

"I should probably get going."

"Okay. Love you bro."

"Love you."

TWENTY-SIX

Scarlett

I'VE MANAGED to get all the food, his supplements, pills, and drinks on one tray, and I'm carefully balancing it all as I walk down the hallway trying not to spill anything. I did the waitress thing in college, but it's been a minute and the skills are rusty.

When I get to the door, I realize I have no way to knock or use the doorhandles, so instead I'm stuck using my hip to lean at just the right angle to pop it open as I back in. Thankfully it yields to me, and I still manage not to spill anything. I'm calling it a win considering these first few days have been a struggle.

"Knock, knock," I announce as I turn around and then almost drop the tray along with my jaw.

Because Tobias is definitely shirtless, with his pants pulled down and his hand wrapped around his cock watching what I assume is porn on his phone. I freeze but it's too late. He's heard me.

"Fuck!" he shouts, grabbing a blanket and throwing it over

his lap as his phone tumbles across the bed and onto the floor rolling and tumbling over the carpet until it lands near my feet. It disconnects from his earbuds and suddenly the sound of two people fucking is in stereo.

"Can't you fucking knock?" he shouts at me, and he starts to move across the bed to reach for the phone until he grabs his leg. "Fucking fuck!" He winces in pain.

"Don't. Don't move. I'll get it!" I quickly set the tray on the small counter near the door and grab the phone, just as I hear his voice come through the phone.

"I want to feel you moaning on my cock while you do it."

I blush bright red as I hit the pause button, too lost for words to say anything when I see the freeze frame shot of the two of us on the screen.

"Give it to me!" he growls from the bed, and I lean forward to hand it to him.

When I look up, I nearly make an audible gasp because Tobias fucking Westfield is blushing. And not like a little bit, but a full-face flush. I'm not sure whether it's the embarrassment or the activity, but I have to bite my lower lip hard not to smile.

"This fucking funny to you?" He stuffs the phone under the blanket and glares at me like he wishes I was dead.

"No," I whisper.

"Good because you should fucking knock."

"My hands were full with the tray, and I didn't expect you to be—" I stop abruptly because I don't want to embarrass him any further.

"Just leave the fucking food and get out! I knew it was a bad fucking idea to have you here. Shit like this is exactly why."

"Tobias, I'm sorry I didn't mean to." I do my best to look remorseful as I move the tray to the table beside his bed.

"Don't fucking look at me like that."

"Like what?"

"Like you are right fucking now. Jesus." He swallows hard, and I can see the flash of hurt and humiliation in his eyes, and my heart twists with it.

So I do a thing I shouldn't. I sit down on the bed next to him and slide my hand slowly over the blanket. But just as I wrap my fingers around the edge of the blanket to pull it back his hand darts out and wraps around my wrist.

"Scarlett, what the *fuck* are you doing?"

"Helping." It sounds stupid when I say it, but I don't know what else to say at the moment.

He closes his eyes and grits his teeth, his jaw ticking with the motion.

"I don't want your fucking pity handjob."

My eyes drift over his chest, over the tattoos that swirl across it and down his arm to where it meets his hand. The one that currently has mine in a vice grip. I hate that he's hurting. I hate that this man, who can be so incredibly generous and sexy and kind when he's not bruised and beaten like this, is embarrassed more because of me. I hate that even though everything between us has been a mess of epic proportions, I still look at him and can't help wanting him. And most of all, I hate how much I love the fact he was watching us on his phone.

So I give him the chance to embarrass me in return.

"But I want you," I whisper.

His eyes open and snap to mine, a frown marring his face.

"Yeah? Xander paying you for that too? Part of the upgraded package where you make sure all my needs are met?"

"That's low. Even for you." I shake my head, pulling my hand back but he doesn't let go.

"No? Weak men just do it for you then? Turns you on to see them fucking struggling?"

"You're not weak, Tobias. You're just being a giant asshole

right now. Unfortunately, the rest of my body doesn't listen to my brain when it comes to you."

"Yeah, you do always look at me like you're dying to get fucked. It's why I can't stop watching that video. The way you fucking look at me, like you don't want anything else in the world but me inside you. So desperate to have it. No other woman's looked at me quite like that. Gets me so fucking hard every time I see it, knowing how bad you want it. I bet you still fucking touch yourself thinking about me, don't you?"

"I'm glad your ego is intact." I shake my head, sorry I ever felt bad about his embarrassment.

"Yeah, lucky for you the parts you need are, so you better ride me."

"What?" I stare at him blankly, sure that I must be hearing him wrong.

"You fucking heard me."

And God help me because I'm actually considering it. I want him, and the tension between us is too much at this point. If we're going to make it through this arrangement, we could probably both benefit from getting off. But climbing in his lap seems way too dangerous with his hip.

"If I do that it's gonna put pressure on your hip."

He smirks, and his eyes flick over me.

"I don't mean ride my lap, sweetheart. I mean my face."

Oh.

"Strip down and climb up here." He lets go of my wrist and pats the stack of pillows he's resting against.

"I don't have that kind of balance."

"That's what the headboard's for." He glances back at it and then dark eyes fall on me. "Get up here."

I take a step back from the bed, questioning my sanity and his.

"I think maybe you should just—"

"You should just get naked and get up here. *Now.*" The way he says it turns my entire body into a warm quivering mess, and I unbutton and unzip my jeans while he watches. Sliding them and my panties off.

I take a tentative step forward and he clicks his tongue and shakes his head.

"All of it off. I want to see every inch of you."

I slip my shirt off over my head and let it fall to the chair, reaching behind to undo my bra and slipping it off too. His eyes land hard on my breasts, and he reaches under the blanket to stroke himself.

"Fuck your breasts are so perfect. All of you really." He closes his eyes as he takes another long stroke. "Get up here, Spitfire. I need you to come on my face for me. I want you so fucking wet you're dripping down my chin. You do that for me, I'll make sure you come harder than you have in your life." A promise he's already made good on before. It's also the first time he's called me by my nickname since I've been here, which I'll take as a good sign.

I climb onto the bed, kneeling next to his shoulder and hesitating. This was not a position I ever considered attempting with my general clumsiness but now I don't want to let him down. But I'm also terrified of hurting him. So I carefully move my leg over as his hand slides along my thigh to help guide me, and I hold onto the headboard as tight as I can to keep from losing my balance as the pillows shift underneath us.

"Fuck," I whisper as I nearly slip.

He catches me though, his arms wrapping around my legs. I spread wider to get into a more comfortable position and then I feel a whisper of self-consciousness. He senses it and pulls me toward him, his tongue sliding over me with just enough contact to tease.

I moan and press my forehead against the headboard.

"Now ride me." He grabs my ass, and I buck forward, grazing over his mouth. The stubble on his cheeks scratches the insides of my thighs, and I love the sensation. I roll my hips again.

"Ride. Me. Like you actually fucking want my mouth, Spitfire."

"I just don't want to hurt you."

"Then don't make me beg any more than I already have."

I know what he means, what he needs. To feel wanted again. To feel like he's still worthy. To feel like he's something other than broken and hurting. To know a woman can't stop fantasizing about him even when he is miserable and lashing out because of it. And that much I can give him if he needs it.

I rock forward and his lips and tongue slide over every nerve ending I have, lighting them up in the perfect order. I can feel my stomach twist and the first little sparks of pleasure tease my clit. I'd already been wet for him just from seeing him half naked in the bed with his hand on his cock. But now between my legs like this, begging for me to ride him, it's making me soak his lips and chin just like he asked.

He pulls back for a moment, catching a breath before his lips slide over my clit and he sucks, softly at first and then slowly teasing more and more pressure until I'm moaning for him while I slam my palm against the headboard. He lets go just before I come, and I whimper at the loss.

"Holy fuck." He takes a breath of air and then takes me in his mouth again, his tongue dancing over the tiny bundle of nerves. I dig my hands into his hair, twisting my fingers into the dirty blond, and writhe over his mouth as one of his hands grips my legs. I glance over my shoulder and see him fisting his cock out of the corner of my eye.

"Tobias, please. Let me come, so I can finish you with my mouth." I have to stop to gasp for air just to get the sentence out, and he groans his agreement. That touch of extra vibration takes me so close to the edge that I have to white-knuckle the headboard.

"I'm so close. Please," I whimper, and he digs his fingers into my thigh dragging me down tighter onto his mouth. He sucks hard and his tongue strokes over my clit until I cry out and come hard against his lips.

When I can finally see straight again, I take a breath and carefully slip off his chest and down his side. I glance up at him for permission and his tongue slides over his lower lip still tasting me.

"I'm not gonna last after that, so if you—"

"I want you to come on my tongue just like you did for me," I cut him off.

"Fuck. Okay..." He nods and I position myself to the side, too scared to accidentally hurt his hip to climb between his legs.

His thumb glides over his cock in slow teasing strokes, and I slide my hand in place beneath it, following his rhythm until he lets me take over. Then I add my tongue, running it along the length to the tip just before I take him in my mouth.

"Holy fuck. Spitfire. Fuck." Stuttered curses leave his mouth, and his hand grips my hair pulling me back and tightening until I can feel the burn at the nape of my neck. It spurs me on, and I take him deeper, wanting to make him come as hard as he made me.

I hear him groan as I swirl my tongue over him and then I suck harder, sliding my hand in rhythm with my mouth until he grunts out a warning. The warmth of him pools in my mouth, and I swallow down as much as I can before he pulls me back.

His chest rises and falls, a sheen of sweat making the tattoos there glisten. The last tiny bead of come forms, and I lean down to lick it up while he watches.

"Fuck me." He closes his eyes and leans back against the

pillows. He releases his grip on me, and his hands rub over his face like he's trying to come to. Which means it's only a matter of moments before the fantasy is over and post-accident Tobias returns. I move to stand when his hand grips my forearm. His eyes search mine for a moment like he might say something, but then they shutter again, and he lets me go.

TWENTY-SEVEN

Tobias

WE DON'T TALK about the incident, and she's barely looked me in the eye since it happened. She seemed done with me even before the accident, so I don't know how to explain the other night. The broken parts of me tell me she's just a good girl who feels sorry for me. Who gave me a pity fuck to make me feel a little better and make up for the fact that she walked in on me. The tiny bit of my ego that's still intact argues she got turned on by finding me jacking off to her and still wants me even though she knows better. A mutual moment of weakness.

I'm not up for discussing it with her though, and not entirely sure she'd tell the truth anyway. She treats me like I'm cracked glass that's likely to shatter if she taps on it just the wrong way. Nervous and quiet whenever she's around me, and even quieter when she's in other parts of the house. I'm finally starting to feel well enough that I want to try to get around with the crutches more and not always be summoning her for something as simple as a glass of water. So I'm currently hobbling my way with the pair of them toward the kitchen.

As I get to the living room though, I pause. She's sitting in the window seat on the far side of the room, leaning against the glass with her eyes closed. A small circle of fog where her breath hits the cold glass. She must have fallen asleep watching the rain out the window. I can't imagine it's going to feel good waking up in that position, so I hobble my way over to her.

"Scarlett," I say softly, but she doesn't wake.

Now that I'm closer I notice the little bit of drool on her lip where her head's tilted to the side, and I grin. She looks even more innocent than normal like this. Serene even. I pause to watch her for a bit before I realize how awkward it'll be if she wakes up like this. Me hovering over her just watching her sleep like I'm a serial killer.

"Scarlett," I say her name louder this time, and she jolts and then blinks. She jumps back from the glass like she's confused about where she is. "You must have fallen asleep."

Another little jolt and she turns toward me, looking up at me as she wipes at the drool on her lip with the sleeve of her cardigan. Her gray eyes studying me and the crutches for a moment.

"Did you need something? Did I not hear my phone? I'm sorry." She stands up abruptly.

"You're fine. You just fell asleep, I guess."

"Oh, yeah. I forgot my books at home."

"You could watch TV." I nod to the massive TV over the fireplace.

"I couldn't figure out how to turn it on."

"You could have asked."

"I didn't want to bother you. Especially if you were asleep. I know the painkillers knock you out."

"I was awake, and you can wake me up to ask something

like that. I don't mind. I'll show you how to turn the TV on if you want."

"Nah. It's okay." She looks down at the time on her phone. "I'm going to make dinner in a few and then head out unless you need me."

"All right. Well, I'll show you tomorrow. You can also get a book out of the library if you want."

"You have a library?" She looks at me curiously.

"You really don't snoop, do you?"

"You told me not to. And I kind of learned my lesson about opening doors without knocking and all that." She smirks at me.

I raise a brow at her, surprised she's mentioning it and that she's making jokes.

"Come on. I'll show you the library. You can go in there whenever. If I can't trust a curator in that room, I don't know who I can trust."

She follows behind me at a slow pace, and I can tell she's studying how well I'm managing on the crutches. I wonder if she reports back to Xander every day. I'm starting to think she does, or at least to Harper who reports to Xander. There's been twice now when he's asked about something that only she could have told him. So perhaps less of a snoop and more of an informant.

I unlock the double doors to the library and push them open, turning to watch her reaction. This room and the office where I keep all my football awards are my two favorite rooms in the house. This one in particular is my pride and joy and a huge reason why I purchased the house in the first place. I knew it had the potential to be an amazing party house, but I also wanted somewhere I could keep my collections close. I didn't like the idea of storing them off-site or having to pay someone else to care for them on my behalf. So I made the realtor find me a place that had something like this.

Her eyes go wide, and she steps inside, turning around and then looking back at me. The front part of the room has massive reading tables and walls lined with bookcases that flow back into the rest of the room where I've got more bookshelves and display cases, big comfy couches, and a small bar. I had them knock down walls and combine rooms to make this space. But there's also a spiral staircase that leads up to a mezzanine area and then a second floor. The mezzanine sits in front of a massive picture window that overlooks the rest of the property, the pool, and the pool house, and the second floor has even more books and curiosities I've collected over the years.

"Oh my god. This is yours? All of it?" She walks through, her fingertips running over one of the reading tables as she stares upward.

"Yeah, Spitfire. It's all fucking mine. It's in my house, isn't it?"

"I didn't know you read." She stops abruptly when she realizes what she's said and turns back to look at me. "I mean I know you read, but I didn't think you *read*. You know?"

"Yeah. I read. I decompress in here when I'm..." Normal. Not weak. Not fucked up. When my whole life hasn't gone to shit and left me stuck in bed while she cares for me like I'm a child.

"No, I get it. This would be amazing to relax in. Pour a drink and just read for hours. Wow. I'm so jealous." The look of awe on her face stirs the little bit of pride I have left.

"Well, like I said, you can read in here if you want."

"Really?" She walks up to one of the shelves and her eyes run over the titles there.

"Yes really."

"You've got a lot of history. Good ones." She looks up at me curiously.

"I was a history major."

She blinks at me. "You never mentioned that."

"You never asked." She glances down and then back at the shelves, something flickering over her face I can't read. "Don't worry. I have a collection of vintage Playboys too if you're worried that I'm too nerdy now."

She smiles. "We have some of those at the museum."

"You have a porn collection at the museum?"

"Previous curator, I guess. Thought they were good cultural ephemera. Zeitgeist and what not. Which I mean, they are, but there's probably a better museum for them than ours. They need to be deaccessioned because they don't fit the mission statement, but deaccessioning means it has to go before the board. I have to write up a summary of the contents, take photos, and explain why they should be removed from the collection. I haven't been looking forward to that board meeting." She smirks.

"Don't want to give all the little old ladies on the board heart attacks?"

"Or have the Vice President making lewd jokes."

"Fair enough."

"Anything else scandalous in here?"

"A few things. It's a mix really. Whatever I see on auction or sometimes I go to garage sales and find something cool."

"Huh." She glances at me and walks around a case in the room that has a WWII bomber jacket in it. "Relative?"

"I wish. Auction. I do have my great-grandfather's stuff from the war though. He died overseas but my grandmother kept all his letters and the personal items they sent back with him."

"I'm sorry, especially for your great-grandmother. But what a family heirloom to have. That has to be interesting."

"I haven't had time to go through it yet. That's the only problem. Kind of chaos in here. Nothing really stored properly. I come in when I have time to decompress but otherwise, I keep it locked up."

"Yeah, it's impressive you've kept all this safe when you have the parties you have."

"No one's allowed in here. Well except Xander, Colt, and Ben. People I trust."

"So I'm part of the inner circle now then?" She grins at me, and I can't help but return it.

"I guess you are now."

"Well, if you want to deputize me, I can go through some of the stuff. Organize it. If you give me a small budget, I can order some archival boxes and things. It'd give me something to do during the day while I'm here... Rather than just getting paid to read and clean." She looks up at me bright-eyed.

Like I could say no if I wanted to.

"Yeah. Honestly, I think I need to start getting out of my room anyway. So maybe we can work on it together."

Her grin returns.

"As long as you keep your leg elevated and everything." She glances at me standing on my crutches.

"I will. There's plenty of places to sit and put my leg up. I have to start doing something though, or I'm going to go stir crazy."

"All right. Well, it sounds like it could be a good deal. I'm allowed to explore in your sacred library and in return I'll get things organized for you." She holds out her hand for me.

"Deal." I shake her hand, and she beams at me like I've just given her the keys to a castle.

TWENTY-EIGHT

Tobias

I'M SITTING in the library watching her climb the ladder again. It's the best part of the fucking day when she does it, especially when she's forgotten I'm in the room. She climbs the steps, and I get to watch every single movement and sway of her body, the long line of her legs, and if I'm lucky, she bends over to reach for something, and I get to see the tops of her thigh highs while she does.

I watch her as she leans over to reach for something when she squeals and bounces on the ladder—add that to the list of fucking things I need to see her do again.

"What?"

She holds the side of the ladder and swings around, one foot off as she stares at me with her jaw dropping. "You have an early edition Austen? How did you not tell me this."

"Oh. Yeah... That's not mine. It's my sister's. I just keep it for her because she's been traveling a lot and doesn't like to keep stuff at my parents'."

"How did she get one?"

"Our parents bought it for her for her birthday, I think. She was obsessed in her teens. The books. The movies. The fashion. It's all she fucking talked about. I think she even went to a cosplay event one time."

"I think I'd like your sister."

I tilt my head. "It's possible. She's a lot like Joss. Chaos incarnate most of the time. She might be too much for you."

"I love Joss. And I love chaos. I just also need a nap sometimes after hanging out with her." Scarlett smiles.

"Fair enough."

I watch her as she stares at the book.

"You can take it down if you want and look at it. She won't mind. She just put it up there because she was worried that someone would damage it."

"No. I don't want to move it unnecessarily. It could be fragile. But I got this close to one. That goes on the life achievements checklist." She laughs and whirls back onto the ladder in the proper direction, sliding her heel onto the rung.

"I feel like you're going to fall off of that one of these days."

"Nah. I'm like an archives ladder gymnast. Depending on what museum you work at, how old it is, and when the last time was that they had a supply budget you never know what the hell kind of ladder you're going to have to climb in any given warehouse. It's ladder roulette. Then you have to balance taking objects down while not falling or bumping them. You learn a lot of tricks fast."

"Tricks, eh?" I smirk at her, and she glances over her shoulder and shakes her head.

"Your mind would go to the dirtiest place possible."

"It's a gift." I grin and she turns back to what she was doing.

"So... Darcy? Knightley? Wentworth?"

"Have you actually read them or are you just repeating your sister's knowledge?"

"I've read them. It's been a while, admittedly."

"Then who do you think I pick?"

"Darcy." I don't hesitate.

"Darcy over Knightley and Wentworth?" She tilts her head as she works.

"He's very main character. You seem to like that."

"But the quiet pining is so hot."

"Yes but pricks who do the quiet rescues seem to be a thing for you." I make a more pointed comment and watch for her reaction.

She pauses as she moves to put a book back on the shelf.

"I think I'm more of a Knightley girl. Fighting with her now and again, but always there for her. Quiet pining."

"Quiet pining is your thing. Got it."

"Yes. It is. So which heroine then for you?"

"None. All too proper for my tastes."

"Of course they are." I can see the eye roll from here.

"So have you had time to go through any of my great-grandfather's stuff?" I decide to switch subjects before we're fighting again.

"No. Not yet. I'll make sure I get to it soon though. Do you want me to prioritize that? And do you want me to wait for you to do it when you're not at PT?"

I'm back to PT full time now and around the house less, but I asked her to stay on those hours anyway and work in the library. It means she's still around and she has work, so I figure it's a win for both of us.

"No, you can start it without me. I don't mind. Just if you find anything interesting—keep me posted."

"Of course. There's a box of it on the table over there. All the letters and a diary in it. I'm going to put it in archival boxes and put them in order. Then you can go through it when you have a chance."

"Over here?" I move to the other side of the table where the box is.

She looks down at me and nods. "Yep."

Sitting on top of the box is a printout with a bunch of annotations on it—highlights and notes scribbled all over. I pick it up and skim it, realizing quickly it's nothing to do with my great-grandparents and everything to do with her history channel. I'd been watching episodes of it while I've been laid up, and I'm nearly caught up on them now.

"Next episode is Morse Code, eh?"

"What?" She stops abruptly and looks down at me, noticing what I have in my hand. "Oh. Um... Yeah."

"How are you going to sex that up for your Filthy Friday episode?" I ask absently as I'm still half reading her notes. She does a normal educational episode on Tuesdays, but Fridays she has a subscriber only episode that's more in line with the harlot side of her History Harlot channel.

"How do you know about Friday episodes?" She's coming down the ladder.

Well. Now I've just told on myself accidentally.

"I subscribed when I ran out of regular content. Nothing better to do when you're stuck in bed." I try to play it off.

Her face goes from anxious to offended in record time. "Thanks for describing my content as 'nothing better to do.'" She snatches the notes from my hands.

"I didn't mean it that way."

"Right. Also, don't subscribe. That's my like... personal space."

"A public subscription site is your personal space?"

"It's… crossing this employee/employer line, yes." She's grasping for straws.

"Is working on your private projects during the time I'm paying you to be working in here crossing that line?" I raise a brow.

"Not if you're already watching the channel and subscribing."

"I should get a discount."

"Yes, because the man with the immense personal collection and library needs a discount."

"Fine. Then I should get bonus content."

"Like what?"

"I can give you a list of ideas." I smirk.

Her brow raises and she shakes her head, her eyes raking over me.

"Yeah? Submit them in Morse Code and I'll think about it."

"Challenge accepted."

TWENTY-NINE

Scarlett

HARPER, Joss, Violet, and I are all sitting in a booth having drinks and enjoying the atmosphere of the bar. It's a feminine little place accented by pink and lace made for a girls' night out, and all the drinks have adorable names and come with over-the-top garnishes and fancy glasses. We're still on the fence about the decor but the drinks are delicious, which is the most important part.

"So... how goes the new job?" Joss looks at me with a grin.

"Going okay. Mostly just getting caught up on all my reading for the year most days."

"Reading?" Joss looks at me quizzically.

"She gets him his food and checks up on him, and otherwise keeps to herself in the living room reading books." Harper offers.

"So the two of you don't talk or interact?" Joss raises a brow.

"We do when the situation calls for it, but otherwise I stay out of his way. He's been pretty miserable and in a lot of pain. Even now that he's getting better, he's still not much for company, or at least my company. The guys going over tonight seemed to be something he was looking forward to. I'm sure he misses having his parties."

"He needs to quit with all the parties. Cancel them for the foreseeable future and probably sell that house too." Violet frowns.

"That's going to be a hard sell." Harper raises her brows and takes a sip of her drink.

"If he wants to keep his career, he'll do it though," Violet adds.

"You sound like your husband and Colt. Always a buzzkill." Joss shakes her head.

"Maybe, but I just want to see these guys get the things they've been working so hard for. Screwing it up at the last minute because you party too hard and then make dumb decisions like getting on a motorcycle in the rain with no helmet? I love Tobias. Don't get me wrong, but he's his own worst enemy so often."

"He is. It's strange too, given how smart he is. I just feel like he could do so much more with his life if he wanted to. Be more like Ben and Colt, but he chooses not to. I don't get it." I shrug.

"Yeah. He's got depth." Joss gives me a curious grin.

"What?"

"Just the way you're talking about him. Seems like you might have a crush."

"I do not have a crush." I flash a look at Joss, worried she's going to spill more information than I'm ready for the rest of the table to have.

"It would be normal if you did. All that time you're spending together cooped up in his house. Taking care of him while he's injured and needs you."

"It's not like that at all. In fact, Harper was just talking about setting me up with a friend, and I agreed. Right?" I look to Harper to save me from this conversation. I didn't need anyone to think I was crushing on him, let alone anyone who might report that information back to him.

"Right." Harper side eyes me in the process though. In a way that makes me think she might not totally disagree with Joss's assessment of our situation. "He's a cute professor. I think they'd make a great couple, so I'm trying to get the two of them together," she explains to the rest of the table.

"Ohh. A nerdy guy. I like those." Violet smiles.

"Tobias is nerdy. That entire fucking library he has? He's like king of the nerds," Joss pipes in.

"You know about the library?" I look at her confused.

"Uh... yeah. I've been in the library."

"When?"

"At a party a while back. Colt took me there." Joss grins.

"Colt took you there, or Colt fucked you there?" Harper laughs.

"Both." Joss shrugs.

"Good for you." I grin at her, but I'm busy being jealous, thinking of the fact that she and Colt have fucked in that room and Tobias and I only sort through boxes.

"Also... didn't you try one of Harper's setups before and need to be rescued from that? By Tobias if I remember correctly?" Joss grins deviously.

"Maybe."

"So see... I think maybe the complete nerds aren't it for you. Maybe you need a bad boy. Or an athlete. Maybe an all-in-one. If you're saying you're not feeling it with Tobias, maybe we could find you someone else on the team."

"I don't know about that..." I hesitate. Thinking of how weird that could get given the past between me and Tobias.

"Oh, I do. I've already got a couple of guys I can think of who might be good for you. I'm sure Harper can think of some too. And Violet?"

"Count me out of your matchmaking. I'd rather see Scarlett make her own way. I don't want to be responsible for another failed setup." Violet shakes her head, giving me a sympathetic smile.

Joss rolls her eyes at Violet. "We just want her to be as happy as the rest of us. Sometimes that takes a little work."

"Or a little time." Violet points the end of an umbrella garnish at Joss.

"Or both." Harper smirks.

"Okay all of you. I can really find my own dating prospects."

"Oh yeah? How's that going? Any dates lined up currently?" Joss bats her lashes at me expectantly.

"No, but I could. I just need to download a dating app, and I'm sure I could find some. It can't be that hard. I've just been busy with work and my history channel."

"Ah yes. Busy with work."

"Don't say it like that. He is a lot of work some days."

"Oh, I'm sure he is." Joss grins.

"Which is exactly why you need downtime and someone to take you out and treat you to dinner and a movie."

"Fine. If you find someone... I'll go on a date or a double date."

"Or a quadruple date," Joss suggests. "See, this is why it would be better if it was someone on the team. Someone who already gets our dynamic and fits in with the group. Trying to adopt some nerd she finds in a university or a dating app... I don't think so." Joss shakes her head in disbelief.

"I'll consider someone on the team, but he has to be able to hold a conversation about something other than football. Don't get me wrong. I love the game, but I need something more than that," I concede to the idea.

"All right. Just give us a little time. I'll plot—I mean plan something good." Joss slides the cherry out of her drink and into her mouth, crushing it with her teeth as another devious look crosses her face.

"Why do I feel like I've just accepted some sort of dark fate?" I look to Harper.

"Because you probably have."

THIRTY

Tobias

THAT NIGHT after they finish practice and dinner, Colt, Xander, Waylon, and Ben all come over to my house to play some video games and hang out for a bit. We've ordered some pizza and we're sprawled out across my living room. It almost feels like old times except for the fact they're playing and I'm not, and right now things are dire.

"So how's the mood in the locker room?"

"Not fucking great since I can't stop throwing interceptions," Colt grumbles, keeping his eyes on the TV as he and Ben try to take a fictional compound of aliens in the game.

"It's not all your fault." Ben shakes his head, glancing back at me to give me a look that lets me know Colt is in his head about it. "I can't get open. We're all fucking up."

"Yeah, and our fucking line could use work," Waylon adds quietly. "We need to be more in sync. Give you longer to throw."

"Defense is doing all right. A few things that could be improved but we're confident it's all gonna come together. It's been rough losing Colt and then you. You know? We can't ignore that. And Colt's gonna take a minute to be a hundred percent again. That was a serious concussion."

"Yeah, well... I should be pulling it together faster." He shakes his head.

"Tell me about it," I grouch, adding to the general storm cloud in the room.

"How's that going anyway? The PT?"

"Progress each week. But day to day it feels like nothing gets better. Definitely not as fast as I'd like, that's for fucking sure."

"How are things around here?" Xander gives me a look, and I know what he's really asking.

"She found the library and has a bunch of ideas for how to organize things and care for them better. So I let her have at it."

"Oh yeah? Makes sense she would like it in there. That's a bonus if she gets it in order for you."

"I've helped her a little bit."

"So you're spending time around each other?"

"Like you don't know, and she's not one of your spies." I glance over at him from the TV.

"Spies," he scoffs. "Harper asks how things are going. She sometimes gives a minimal report, and it gets back to me. No one is spying."

"Yeah. She hating it then? Telling Harper what a cruel and demanding boss I am?"

"No. Nothing like that." Xander shrugs, turning his focus back on the TV.

"Then like what?" I ask because I don't like the dismissive tone.

"Like nothing. Just says you guys get along as well as you can. That you're getting better."

"Nothing more than that?"

Xander's neck slowly cranes back toward me, and he looks me over. He glances at the other guys, making sure they're fully focused on the game on the other side of the room before he raises his brow.

"Is there more than that?"

"I guess not if she hasn't said anything."

Xander runs a hand over his face and looks up at the ceiling. "You just... remember she's technically an employee right now, right?"

"Thanks to you. That wasn't my bright idea."

"She would have been my employee if you hadn't been such an ass about it. And this is exactly why."

"Relax. She's not gonna sue me for workplace harassment. If anything I could sue her."

"Do I want to ask?"

"Guarantee you don't. It was once and hasn't been repeated. Yet." I smirk.

"Tread carefully, yeah? She's a good person. She's done a lot for you just by being here."

I grit my teeth. "I don't need a lecture where she's concerned. I have zero intention of doing anything to hurt her."

"The road to hell... and all that."

"Yeah, well not all of us can be all in immediately. Some of us have fucking shit to work through."

"Like I don't have shit to work through?"

"You had years to figure it out first."

"I didn't need years. I figured it out the second I saw her with him. Unfortunately, that was already too fucking late. I don't wish that fate on anyone. Especially if she's got that unicorn thing going that you've been looking for." He gives me a pointed look, and I shake my head.

"Noted."

Scarlett is the closest any woman has ever come to possessing my long list of wants. The one I thought was so long that no woman could ever live up to it and therefore this whole conversation would be moot. But if there was ever a unicorn—Scarlett is mine. A thought that leaves me feeling more than a little adrift.

"All right. I fucking suck at this almost as much as I suck at throwing right now. Tobias you wanna take a turn? See if you can kick some ass?" Colt hands me the game controller.

"Yeah, I'll give it a try. I haven't played this game yet."

"Always a first time." Xander smirks.

And I proceed to glare at him before I start blowing things up on the screen.

THIRTY-ONE

Tobias

AFTER WE FINISH WORKING in the library for the day, she disappears to the bathroom for a bit and reemerges in a wine colored vintage dress, with her hair curled and heels that make her legs look even longer than they already are. I smirk at the sight of it, wondering if she's finally trying to make her move to seduce me. Cause if she is, I'm in for whatever she wants to do.

But when she comes back, she just goes back to putting things away in the library and tapping a few more things into the computer before she closes up. When she stands, I look up from my book because now I'm curious about what she's up to.

"You look nice tonight."

"Oh. Thanks. I have a date...ish? Harper and Joss are setting me up with someone. So we're all going to get drinks."

My blood runs cold. It's pretty much the last thing I

expected her to say. Since when the fuck is she dating and why the fuck is Harper meddling in it? Doesn't Harper know she's busy?

"You have a date but Harper's going? That didn't end well the last time."

"Well, like I said it's not really a date. It's like a setup? I don't know. I'm nervous. Harper and Joss think we should date, but I don't think he's interested in me. So we're meeting him and Xander for drinks."

And my best fucking friend is involved in this plot? Are they serious right now? Harper and Xander are the ones who put her in my house. Shoved us together. Now they're setting her up on dates and going with her?

"Not another guy you used to work with, I hope."

"No. Uh, actually a guy you work with."

"What?" The actual *fuck*.

"Nick Harris? He's on the team, I guess."

Panic wells in my chest. I don't know where it's coming from. Mostly from the fact that she doesn't just look nice. She looks gorgeous. And Nick Harris isn't Oliver or Danvers. One of the guys who would just fuck her for fun. Harris is a good guy. Went to an Ivy, smart as fuck. Exactly the kind of guy who could charm someone like Scarlett if he wanted to. And Harper wouldn't set her up with someone who wasn't interested. Which means my time with her is running out and I'm desperate for a time out.

"Are you sure that's a good idea with the weather?" I suddenly remember my phone flashed an ice warning at me earlier. I didn't think much of it at the time since we didn't plan to leave the house most of the day, but now I'm hoping that it lived up to the hype of the brilliant red banner.

"The weather?" She looks at me skeptically.

"Said there was going to be ice."

"Oh yeah, I saw, but it sounded like that was mostly in the foothills and at elevation. Should be fine in the city."

"Spitfire, we're outside the city here."

"Oh. Right. Shit... I haven't looked outside." She hurries over to the window, and I follow her.

My heart buoys at the sight of a slick sheet of ice across the pool deck.

"Fuck," she mutters, grabbing her phone and pulling it out. "I'll have to text Harper. I should probably leave now. It'll take me a while just to get back closer to the city through this."

"You can't go out in this. You definitely can't drive in it." I look at her like she's lost her mind.

"I'll be careful and take my time. I'll just have to go now." She taps out a message to Harper and then hurries to grab her purse. Then she stops abruptly and looks back at me. "Dinner. Shit. Your trainer gave me some back up meals for you, and I froze them. Do you think you could reheat one of them tonight?"

I want to say no. I want to force the issue to make her stay here with me and tell her she can't leave until she does her job. But then I'm a fucking asshole for no good reason. So I nod my yes.

This is it, I guess. Me sitting at home eating a reheated frozen meal while I watch my unicorn get dressed up to go out to drinks with my fucking teammate. A thing I'm going to fucking ask Xander about the second she's out the door.

It was coming eventually. I knew it. But I always thought I'd have more warning and time to prepare when it happened. Now I've had literally minutes to adjust to the idea and all I feel is the beating of my heart in my chest, rapidly picking up its pace like I'm about to have a panic attack.

"All right. I'll see you tomorrow then. Have a good night."

"Be careful out there. The driveway when it's icy is a nightmare and so is the road to get out of the neighborhood. It's uphill there, and you could slide back," I warn her because I got stuck on it last winter and had to have a tow truck come help. I wouldn't even be able to get to her if that happened now.

"I'll be fine. I've dealt with ice before." She gives me a look like I'm overreacting.

A few moments later after she's gathered the rest of her stuff, I'm watching her walk out the door.

"Scarlett?" I call after her, and she turns around to look at me.

I have no idea what I was planning to say. Stop? Don't go? Stay here with me and sort through shit in my library for a few more hours instead of going on your date?

It all sounds ridiculous. It would only buy me time anyway, and for what?

"Just be careful, okay?"

"I will be." She nods. "Make sure you take your meds and stuff, okay?"

"Yep. Night."

"Night."

She turns out the door and then it's a blur of limbs and skirts and a yelp followed by the slap of skin on icy pavement. She's on her knees and palms before I even realize what's happening.

I start to step out toward her, not even thinking about the risk or the fact that I don't even have a crutch or a cane right now on the ice.

"Tobias! No!" she yells, holding her hand out to stop me. "You'll fall too. Just stay there."

"I can—" I try to figure out how to get to her, feeling helpless that I can't do anything in this situation. Another insult to injury.

"No. I'm okay." She swipes at her palms and then slowly inches her way back to the door on her knees across the ice.

She grabs the door frame and hauls herself up, refusing to take my hand when I offer it.

"If I fall again, I'll take you with me, and I can't live with you re-breaking your hip or worse." She shakes her head.

I take a breath once she steps back into the house, but I'm immediately eyeing her knees.

"Come on. Let's get you to the kitchen, and we can clean them up." I start moving slowly with her after she takes her heels off.

I grab towels, soap, and water and prep it for her, handing it over as I survey the damage. Her cheeks are pink, and I'm not sure if it's embarrassment or just the cold.

"You okay? Nothing broken?" I ask as I hand her the dry towel.

She shakes her head in response again. "I'm fine. Just clumsy."

"I think you need to stay here tonight. If that's any indication of how the roads are, it's too dangerous."

Bonus that it means she'll have to cancel her date and stay the night locked in with me. I'm an asshole for finding joy in this, but now that I know it's just skinned knees it feels like I've been saved by fucking fate.

"I think if it wasn't for my heels, I'd be fine." She sighs, wiping at the blood on her knees and then rinsing the towel and washing the soap off her knees too. "Of course, now I look like a mess."

She checks her dress and at least seems satisfied with that.

"Please stay. I... you know the roads were wet when I did this. It's giving me anxiety that you're still even thinking about it. You can blame it on me, and I'm sure Harper and them will reschedule things for another night."

She looks at her knees and then at the floor for a minute, seemingly contemplating my argument.

"Okay." She nods at last. "I'll text Harper."

THIRTY-TWO

Scarlett

ONCE I'VE TEXTED Harper and finished cleaning myself up in the kitchen, I look at the time and sigh. I guess I'm staying here, and I might as well get changed back into my daytime clothes and start trying to make something for dinner.

"I can help make dinner," Tobias offers when he meets me back in the kitchen.

"I've got it. I just need to change out of my dress."

"Why? You look beautiful." His eyes meander over the dress and down to my knees again.

I'm rendered speechless for a moment because it's the first honest compliment he's given me outside of us having sex lately. I'm not sure what to say in return at first.

"Um, well thank you. It's just I'm a messy cook. I'll get something on it."

"Apron in the pantry. I have the same problem when I grill."

He opens it up and pulls one out to hand to me.

"Wear the dress. I'll change into something that's not sweats, and we can pretend we're going out. Eat at the table. Would be nice for a change and then maybe the night's not a total loss for you." He gives me half a smile, the kind that's so sweet it makes my heart do weird things in my chest.

"Okay."

"I think I can..." He disappears into the pantry again and mumbles a few things before he comes back out with a handful of boxes pressed to his chest and another apron. "I can make dessert."

I look at the cake mix and raise a brow. "Yeah?"

"Listen, cake mix isn't the best but the way I do it is..."

"All right. Deal. Can I make something unhealthy for dinner for once though? I know your trainer wants you on a strict diet to help you heal but—"

"Yes. Please. Jesus. I'm dying for some real food. I didn't want to ask you to go off script and feel like you were gonna get in trouble but, yes. We'll just blame the storm or something if he finds out."

"I think we can keep the secret." I grin at him, and he sets the ingredients down on the counter.

"Deal. All right. I'm gonna get everything prepped, and then I'll change."

"Sounds good."

The two of us quickly start moving around the kitchen together, gathering the things we need and preheating the oven. Before I know what's happening, I've entered some sort of domestic moment with the least likely man on earth to be caught in it. I grin a little to myself as I watch him lean over a bowl measuring things carefully and pulling out the mixer.

I'm pretty sure it's a sight very few people in the world have seen, and I'm feeling pretty lucky. Because a concentrating-onbaking Tobias might be the hottest version yet. And while I'm interested to see what he's going to change into, the sweats and tight tee he has on right now are doing things for me just the way he is.

Which is exactly why I need to remember to keep my mind straight tonight. Or I'm likely to make a mess of this whole situation. One I don't need—one I've successfully avoided since I stumbled in on him. No use breaking that track record now. Especially when there's a good guy on the horizon. One who might actually want to be in a relationship someday.

I smile at my phone when I see a text come in from Harper as we're finishing dinner. She explains she went ahead and met up anyway because she didn't want to cancel so late; they're having drinks and he can't stop talking about rescheduling to meet me. Xander's still running late but she wants another date we can meet up. I quickly text her back with a few good dates for me, and she sends me a "Please hold" and smile emoji as a follow-up.

"Something good?" Tobias looks at me and then his eyes drop to my phone.

"Harper. Xander's late, but she and Nick are getting drinks and talking about rescheduling."

"I'm surprised Xander's not having a heart attack about that."

"About what?"

"Her out with another guy."

"Oh please, she's out with him to set *me* up."

"Still." He raises a brow. "His temper and all."

"I'm sure he knows he has nothing to worry about. Harper's obsessed with him and rightly so. He's hot as hell and adores her. No way some random guy compares to him."

"Huh. Maybe Harper needs to be worried about you."

"Me?"

"Sounds like you're crushing pretty hard there."

"Oh please."

"Just saying." He raises a brow and smirks.

"I do not have a crush on Xander. He's too much for my tastes, plus the temper is just not for me. If I had a crush on any of you it'd be—" I stop abruptly.

"Oh no, go on." He grins, and I hate that he's so smug.

"Colton," I say smartly.

"Colt?" He sounds incredulous.

"Yes. Obviously."

"Why is that obvious?"

"Umm. He's dream-man material. He's gorgeous, talented—I mean the quarterback, come on—he's so incredibly sweet and such a good guy. The way he treats Joss like she's the only one he sees? And he fucked her in a library. That's hot."

"We're gonna circle back to that last part, but do your friends know you're crushing so hard on their men?"

"They know I'm happy for them and just a wee bit jealous which is why they're on a mission to set me up now. Joss has been joking that they're in a competition to see who can get me a date for her wedding."

THIRTY-THREE

Tobias

JOSS and I are going to have a talk about her stabbing me in the back like this after I worked damn hard to help push Colt in her favor. Then I'm going to ask Xander why the fuck his girlfriend put her best friend in my house to torture me day in and day out, only to try and torture me further by setting her up with other guys on my fucking team while I watch. I'm starting to think there's a fucking conspiracy afoot with these women.

"A competition, eh?"

"Yeah. Joss wants to set me up with a football player. Harper thinks I'd be better off with someone academic. I guess Nick is the compromise?"

"This is how you spend girls' nights? Talking about where you're getting fucked and who's going to fuck you next?"

"Yes. How do you spend guys' nights?"

"Well, not bragging about the sex we've had anymore since they're all locked down."

She laughs as she puts the dishes in the dishwater.

"And what do you mean a library?"

Her eyes lift to meet mine, a smirk forming there. "Joss knew about your library and when I asked how…"

"He fucked her in *my* library?"

She shrugs.

"Wow. I trusted him." I'm half amused that Mr. Rules would, and half proud that I must have rubbed off on him a little bit.

"Don't you dare tell him I told you." She gives me a threatening look.

"He fucked someone in my library. That's cold. The whole rest of the house I don't give a fuck about, but my sacred inner sanctum. Really?" I continue with my pretend shock.

"Oh please. Like you haven't fucked a dozen women in there. It was romantic. Leave them alone and get over yourself."

"Uh, I will have you know I've never fucked anyone in there. That's like a no-fucking zone. Or at least it was. And it's romantic for him to fuck her in *my* library?"

"I mean, I don't think it matters that it was *your* library. Just that it was a library, and he couldn't wait to have her anymore."

"He couldn't wait to have her because I pushed him."

"You?"

"Joss leave that part out? Figures. Little minx would. She wanted my help with him. So I agreed."

"And you got what out of this exactly?"

"The chance to torture Colt over a woman? Priceless."

"You would torture that poor innocent soul."

"Not very innocent when he's fucking women in my library is he?"

"Oh you'll live."

"I won't. That's like… worse than fucking her in my bed. The guys know how fucking weird I am about that space."

"Don't you dare say anything, or I won't share gossip with you again. I shouldn't have in the first place." She pokes me in the chest, half a smile on her face because she's amused at how much this is getting under my skin.

Her phone buzzes again, and she looks over and picks it up. Her smile grows brighter at whatever Harper's saying, and I feel the jealousy claw its way up my throat as she hurriedly types out a response.

"Reschedule your date?"

"It's just drinks, but maybe. Later this week or after the holiday." She sets the phone back down and looks at me briefly before she resumes putting dishes in the dishwasher.

Later this week? This guy is on a fucking mission.

"Sure he won't be an asshole and bring his girlfriend like the other guy?"

"She assures me that particular mistake will not be repeated."

"Good. Couldn't rescue you as easily this time."

"Hmm. Good point. I'll have to have someone else on speed dial to whiteknight it for me. Will have to talk to Joss about another guy..."

The fuck would another guy replace me there too.

I help by adding some of the glasses to the dishwasher and wiping down the counter. I briefly try to tell myself not to do the thing I do next, before caving the second I see the small smile reappear on her lips just thinking about him while looking at her phone.

"We could fix the library situation."

She glances up at me, an amused look on her face as her brows knit together. "Fix it?"

She puts the tab in the machine and then shuts it with her hip and turns it on.

"Yeah. Since it's already defiled... least I can get is the chance to have someone in there myself."

She gives me a look and then turns to hang the dish towel up.

"I don't know what that has to do with me. Have one of your women come over one night. Just make sure you Lysol the table I have to work at after though, okay?"

"One of my women?" I ask trying to figure out what she's talking about.

"I assume you have company at night."

I frown at her. "The guys once or twice. Xander sometimes. But that's it."

"Don't be obtuse. I helped Ed put away stuff after the shopping trip the other day. I've seen the condoms. I don't care what you do, Tobias, but I'm not stupid. I know you're not celibate. I appreciate that you're trying to be discreet given the past, and me having to be here all the time. But we don't have to play a game over it."

Ed was lucky he's been such a great assistant for so many years before he started doing everything in his power to cockblock me with this woman. He bought condoms but only because I was nearly fucking out and I had stupid hope where one woman in particular is concerned. How to admit any of that without it being humiliating in this context is going to be fun.

"You know I haven't been able to have sex while my hip is healing."

She gives me a knowing look. "I know you have limitations right now, but you didn't seem to have a problem finding workarounds in the past."

"Oh, are we done pretending that didn't happen?"

"Tobias..." She sighs and turns away from me, starting off into the living room, and I follow her.

"Don't do that."

"Do what?"

"Ignore what I just said. I'm tired of it."

"You've been ignoring it too."

"You're right."

Her face contorts at the easy admission and then she eyes me carefully like she's trying to figure out my angle in this. So I continue on.

"You're right. We've both been ignoring it. It's my fault for putting you in that position in the first place, and for that I'm sorry."

"Are you apologizing for fucking me?"

"No. I'm apologizing for making you act like it didn't happen. I was fucking embarrassed that you found me like that, and my ego's basically been ground to fucking dust. And then even still I couldn't resist the pity fuck." I scrub a hand over my face. "And don't tell me that's not what it was. I saw the way you looked at me. Like I was about to break, and you just wanted to stop it. I took advantage of it wholeheartedly, so you don't have to feel bad about it. I can't even really say I regret it if I'm being honest. But I regret that we're trapped in this fucking limbo where we pretend like we're half-friends and half-strangers and you're assuming I'm here having substitutes come in."

"I didn't say that. I said—"

"I'm saying it. You run around here all day looking like you do, taking care of me, talking me up, and being supportive... And fuck... I know how you taste, the little sounds you make for me, the way you look when I'm inside you. I don't want to fuck someone else."

She glances at me and then away again, her telltale blush starts to creep over her freckles, and she folds her arms across her chest before she begins to shake her head like she can't believe it.

"And I know you don't want me. You want the dream guy. A guy like Colt. The guy who rides in on the white fucking horse and tells you how in love with you he is and asks you to marry him. And we both know I'm not that guy. I don't expect anything from you. I'm just telling you where I am."

"I've been ignoring it because I didn't want to be a distraction to your recovery. And I knew I embarrassed you—on accident—but still, no one wants embarrassing things dragged up out of the mire. I liked the time we spent together before the video and the accident. Even if it was the one-night kind of fun instead of the fairytale kind. But then stuff got so messy, so fast. I just... I like you as a person. A friend. I do think of you as a good friend, you know? And I wanted, *want*, you to get better, Tobias. I want to see you play again. Laugh. Be your old confident self."

"I appreciate that. I know you have good intentions."

"Not always. Before the accident, there was a flicker of hope in me. I thought..." She shakes her head and laughs. "I thought maybe I could change you, you know? I have no idea what the hell kind of audacity got into me to think that. It's embarrassing. But I hurt my own feelings. You were always clear about where you stood. About who you were and about what you were offering, and what you couldn't offer. So I'm not mad at you if that's what you're worried about. Just seeing that video of you with someone else. Hearing everyone talk about how hot it was at that particular time... Shattered a lot of illusions for me—ones *I* created. Anyway... I'm just trying to move on, which is hard to do when I have to be here every day. You know?"

"Which is why Joss and Harper are setting you up."

"Harper doesn't know. Or at least, if she does, she hasn't let on."

"But Joss does?"

"She guessed before the video and the accident. She doesn't know anything else."

I have a sneaking suspicion about what Joss is up to then. She and I are going to have words. But there's no point in telling Scarlett right now.

"Got it."

I don't know if I can ever be what this woman wants—what she deserves. I don't want her stuck with a broken version of me who can't play anymore. One who's bitter and hasn't worked through the aftermath of everything that's happened. I want to earn her. *Deserve her.* But I'm panicking a little at the idea of these other guys. I've been imagining her in the same bubble as I am—in this house. In our own little world.

But she isn't broken like I am, clawing her way back to something even approaching normal. She's fucking sweet and perfect. So thoughtful and smart. Everything I've ever thought I wanted. These guys are fucking idiots if they don't try to lock her down. She has every right to want to move on from me. I've given her no reason to think I can or would do any better than I have in the past.

But fuck, I want a shot at something with her. A fair one. If that means competing for it, I don't fucking mind. I have advantages they don't have with her. I just have to try to get one without scaring her.

"This awkward silence here is the other reason I didn't want to bring it up." She flicks her gaze to the ground, looking like she wishes it would swallow her whole.

THIRTY-FOUR

Scarlett

HE BRIDGES the space between us a moment later and his hand wraps around the back of my neck, pulling me forward and pressing his lips to mine. He kisses me with soft strokes at first, ones that become more insistent and pleading. His other hand wraps around my waist, pulling me flush against him. I kiss him back before I know what I'm doing. So easily swayed by just a few touches as his cologne envelops me, dragging me under by the hold he has on me.

"What are you doing?" I press my palm to his chest to create distance.

"Killing the awkward silence." He grins, leaning forward and brushing his lips over mine in one last gentle sweep.

"Clever."

"If we're stuck in limbo until this is over... maybe we just call a truce."

My heart skips in my chest and my fingertips press softly into his.

"A truce?"

His fingers slide down my throat and his mouth trails behind them. I already feel the kick of my heart rate speeding up.

"Yes. This one's gotta last a little longer though. Might need to think about what a peace treaty looks like. How many bottles of rosé will I need to make that happen?"

I can't help but laugh. But I don't know if I'm understanding him the way my heart is hoping I do.

"A peace treaty sounds nice, but I just rescheduled my date."

He stops kissing my neck and pulls back, grabbing my chin as he looks at me.

"He's not here tonight, Spitfire. Right now, you're mine."

He kisses me roughly, wrapping his hand around the base of my throat and taking anything I'll give him. He grabs my hand a moment later and tugs me along behind him. I follow blindly. It's stupid, I know it is, to go down this path with him and start this all over again. But when it comes to Tobias, I don't make good decisions. I make the ones my heart tells me to.

He takes us through to the library, and I realize now he wasn't kidding about christening it himself. He walks us between the tables and pins me up against one, sliding between my legs as he presses me back against it. His hands slide up my thighs as he kisses me, his mouth on mine and over my jaw.

"Being with you in here has been torture. Watching you work. Bending over these tables to study things. Climbing that fucking ladder to where I can almost see up your fucking skirt. The way you tap your heel on the ladder when you're thinking. Drives me fucking mad that I can't touch you when I want to so badly."

"It's been hard for me too," I confess.

"So hard you're going out on dates with Nick. Wearing this fucking dress."

"I wanted to look nice," I say defensively. "I told you I was trying to move on."

"Meanwhile for me, it's only been you since this all started on your last fucking date with what was his fucking name? Cal... no..."

"Carter."

"Carter. Right. And you were all fucking dressed up for him too, wearing that skintight dress and see-through fucking lingerie." His eyes light and his hands slide up my thighs, hooking into the sides of my underwear. "What kind are you wearing tonight anyway?"

I swallow because it's a similar pair to what I wore the last time. Just a different color and the dress I have on is one of my favorites. He pulls on the panties, and I let him take them off me. He holds them up, glaring at them, and throws them on the table, his eyes meeting mine again in accusation.

"I can wear nice things if I want."

"Yeah, well I'm fucking tired of seeing the ones you wear for other men." His eyes flash with something. "You came out here tonight in that dress and I thought..." He trails off shaking his head as he laughs.

"Thought what?"

"Maybe you were finally going to try to fucking seduce me. Maybe it wasn't in my head that you've been fucking teasing and taunting me. That some part of you still wants me after everything." He looks down at the floor.

"Tobias..." I whisper. "I didn't think this was still a possibility. That you still saw me like that."

"Climb the ladder." He steps back abruptly and points to the antique ladder that leads up to the higher shelves.

"What?" I blink, trying to figure out what he's asking for.

"Climb the ladder." He nods. "Don't say what again." He gives me a sharp look, and I do what he's asking. Taking a few steps up and glancing over my shoulder.

"That's good. Now turn around."

I teeter a little on my heels but manage to brace myself with the handrails. The ladder's more like a very steep set of stairs and I can lean back on it to help balance myself. I raise my brow at him in question, hoping there's a point to whatever this is we're doing.

He walks up to me, his eyes level with my waist at this position. His hands slide up the back of my thigh highs and under my skirt. His lips press against the inside of my knee before he begins a tortuous ascent, pausing every couple of inches to kiss me again. My skirt bunches higher with every inch he moves up and the slow anticipation of it has me getting wetter by the second.

"Lean back and spread for me."

I tighten my grip on the handrail and lean back, hooking one heel into a rung of the ladder. He tucks the edge of my skirt up, so I'm half exposed, and the cold air of the room sends goosebumps over my upper thighs.

"This right here. This is how I see you. Every single fucking night. Telling me you can't stop watching the videos we made. Begging me to put my mouth on you."

"I do."

"That what you planned to think about when you let him touch you tonight?" He steps forward and slides his fingers between my legs, a muted groan escaping when he finds me exactly how he wants me. "Wishing it was my hands and my voice talking you through it." His fingers dip inside me, working me slowly and teasing me with just enough to make me want more.

"I wasn't going to let him touch me."

"No?"

"No."

"Fucking right. Because no one touches you like I do."

I whimper when his thumb brushes over my clit, bringing the teasing up another level to torture.

"You promised you were going to think of me when you watched that video. Do you?"

"Yes."

"How often?"

"Whenever I watch it." I give a non-answer because I'd rather play this game a while longer.

A self-satisfied grin forms. "I bet you work here all day and then go home and watch it. Every night using your nightstand arsenal and wishing it was my mouth on you again. Don't you?"

"Not every night."

He lets out a short laugh. "Yeah, some nights you probably don't make it home. But that's okay. Sometimes I don't wait until you leave."

"Lucky I haven't caught you again."

"I wish you would have. So I could put you on your knees. We both know how much you like being there for me. See it in your eyes every time I watch that video we made."

"Fuck Tobias. Stop torturing me."

"Torturing you?" he answers with a question, feigning confusion like he doesn't know what I'm talking about.

"You're holding back. Not giving me enough of anything, and it's cruel."

"All you have to do is ask for what you want. That's all you've had to do this whole time."

"I want your mouth, please."

"Want it where? You'll need to be more specific. I want to hear you ask for it, Scarlett."

"I want your head between my thighs and your mouth on my clit until you make me come."

"There's my dirty girl."

He slips his thumb out of the way and replaces it with his tongue. He takes long slow tortuous drags while he slides his fingers in and out of me. I rock my hips forward, trying to carefully balance, and his arms wrap around my thighs, steadying me and helping with this delicate little act we're performing.

I want to melt when I look down at the sight of him between my thighs like this. He's so beautiful and the way he works me into a slow-building wave of pleasure, carefully taking his time, measuring every response, and giving me more and less as I need it, has me drowning in it in a few short minutes.

As I come down from it, he trails kisses along the inside of my thigh toward my knee, stopping there to look up at me.

"You're fucking gorgeous, Scarlett, but having you here has been nonstop torture for me." He takes my hand and helps me back down the library ladder, and my legs feel wobbly when I hit the ground. He grins at me and wraps an arm around my middle, pulling me close and kissing the side of my neck.

"Do I make you unsteady?" He teases.

"You do have a habit of it, yeah." I smile.

"It's mutual." He kisses me on the lips and then takes my hand, leading me back to his room.

THIRTY-FIVE

Scarlett

IN THE AFTERNOON we're working in the library together when his phone rings. He answers it, and it's his agent. I don't hear the first part of what he says to the guy on the phone, but I definitely hear the next few bits.

"Are you fucking kidding me? You can't be serious."

A long pause ensues.

"So it was her, this entire time? The whole time she was playing coy and acting the victim?"

Another pause.

"Yeah. Yeah, I'm fucking pissed. Who wouldn't be? All because she wanted some extra cash? Jesus, she could have come to me, and I would have given her some of it. Was it that fucking dire she wanted to release poorly lit homemade porn? Fucking hell."

"I'm not going to say anything. Frankly, in some ways, it's a relief. I was worried about what else a hacker was going to leak.

I can hear a raised voice on the other side of the phone.

"I've already got it handled, Jim. The forensic guy consulted for me, and we got extra security on it. Encrypted passwords. All that mess that he suggested, so I'm not as worried going forward."

My heart skips a beat as I listen. It sounds like maybe we're in the clear. That maybe it was the woman who released the sex tape and not someone else. I nibble my lower lip while I wait for him to get off the phone, and he paces around discussing more details of his current physical therapy and progress. When he finally gets off the phone, he looks at me and grins.

"We're in the fucking clear, Spitfire. No home pornos for us."

"Seriously?"

"Yeah. It was her. She released it. I guess she got some deal to have her own makeup line or whatever. The marketing campaign wasn't going well, and they told her she needed to do something to get more attention, or they were going to pull it from shelves. Poor numbers or whatever."

"So she released the video she made with you?"

"Yeah. Makes me feel fucking sick." He shakes his head. "But on the upside, you're in the clear. Which is a huge fucking relief. I couldn't have lived with fucking up your life like that."

"You wouldn't have fucked up my life. That would have been the hacker's fault. We made the video together and while I definitely did not want to share it with the world, I also kind of feel like we shouldn't have to be embarrassed about it at the same time. You know?"

"Yeah. Doing a thing tons of other fucking people do, but we have to pay the consequences because people recognize my name. Like I said, it makes me feel sick. This whole thing... It's changed a lot for me."

"What do you mean?"

"Just fucking hard to trust people in general. Now knowing it was her. Just so she could make some money? Fuck... I doubt she even once considered what it would mean for me. Probably just figured I wouldn't care 'cause I'm a fuck up anyway."

I walk over, hugging him as I sit down next to him on the couch and curling my feet under me after I take my shoes off.

"You deserve to be treated better than that. Period. No matter who you are or what's happened to you in the past. It doesn't give her or the tabloid or anyone for that matter the right to use you in that way. I hate them for it to be honest."

He turns and grins at me. "Yeah? Feeling protective, Spitfire?"

"Oh, hush." I poke him in the side when his grin widens. He kisses me on the tip of the nose.

"Protective Scarlett is pretty fucking hot."

"Don't start. I have stuff I want to show you. But before that... did your agent say anything else?"

"Just that I need to talk to my lawyers and publicist. Figure out what we want to do with the information."

"Do you know what you want to do?"

"I need to think about it, I guess. I'd rather never have to think about it again, but I don't think that's an option. For right now though... what did you want to show me?"

"Your great-grandparents' letters."

"Find something interesting?"

"I mean... yes? I think you should read them. They're love letters mostly. He talks about how much he loves her and can't wait to be home. She tells him she's counting down the days until he returns."

"I think this might be more of a you thing than a me thing, Spitfire. I'm not into the sappy stuff."

"Well, they're not my grandparents, so it's not quite as meaningful."

"Great-grandparents. I didn't know either of them. He obviously passed away during the war, and she died when I was young."

"Still. They're your great-grandparents."

"Also if you knew my family—like my dad—you'd have a hard time buying any of it. Probably just what they felt they had to say to each other in case anyone opened the letters someday. Like you. Right now." Tobias's lip tugs up at the corner as he looks between me and the letters on the table.

"Just read them, please? If not today, sometime? They're really beautiful. I can understand keeping them private if you want, but some of the things in them... I'd frame them if it was my family."

"I'll read them sometime, Spitfire. I promise. But right now I'm starving. You want to get some dinner to celebrate our sex tape not going viral?"

"Yeah, I suppose that sounds like a plan."

AFTER DINNER, we sit on the couch watching TV for a while. We've gone down a rabbit hole of archaeology and history shows on television as well as a few about mysteries in space, and we've started watching them occasionally during his downtime. He's been lying back against the arm of the couch, looking at things on his phone and typing away. I assume texting someone but after a while, he looks up from it and smirks at me.

"Check your texts."

I raise a brow at him, but he just shrugs and nods toward

my phone that's sitting on the coffee table. I pick it up and open the text from him. It's just one long stream of dots and dashes.

"You sit on your phone?" I give him a confused look.

"No. It's Morse Code."

"Morse Code?"

"My list of desired bonus content in the format you requested. You know, if you plan to keep researching and filming during the day while you're on the clock, and I'm at PT."

My cheeks heat a little when I remember I filmed one of my short episodes and some promo content in the library last week without asking. I made sure there was nothing identifying in the shot but some of my regular subscribers were curious about where I was working. I also keep forgetting that he watches at all, let alone that he watches regularly.

"I should have asked, I'm sorry. If you saw though, you know I was careful about where I filmed. I just got behind and had to finish it. I won't do it again."

"You're good, Spitfire. But you'll need to pick at least two pieces of bonus content as repayment for facility rental." He smirks.

I glance down at the dots and dashes frowning at the fact I created extra work for myself.

"Don't worry. There's a few on there I think you're going to love."

THIRTY-SIX

Tobias

"WE'RE GOING to have to talk about your cunning little future wife, St. George."

"Oh yeah?" He looks up at me as he opens up the takeout boxes he brought over.

"Whatever he says, it isn't true. Don't listen to him." Joss kisses his cheek and then flashes an amused grin in my direction.

"What did she do now?" Colt looks between us.

She lets out a pretend incredulous gasp and slides a plate and fork in front of me.

"I have reason to believe she's meddling in my personal affairs."

"I have no idea what he's talking about."

"What affairs would those be? I didn't think you had many at the current moment."

"Just one, really. But it's enough."

"Relatable." He flashes a look at Joss before he looks back at me again. "So?"

"I'm still trying to figure that particular affair out, and a certain raven-haired matchmaker is trying to marry her off to a white knight before I can even have a chance with her."

"Is this true?"

"From what I can tell he's been sitting around doing nothing while she's played house and taken care of him. I just thought she could use some post-work sex to help her relax after all the grueling Cinderella-era stuff she's got going on around here."

"Is this why you were asking about Danvers?" Colt raises an eyebrow at her.

"Maybe." A mischievous little grin spreads on Joss's face before she takes a bite of her spring roll.

"Danvers? Are you fucking serious?" I grouch at her.

"What's wrong with him? He's hot with all those tattoos." Joss frowns at me.

"The guy's a good football player but he's dense as fuck. He probably couldn't even tell you when WWII happened. That's the guy you want to set up Scarlett with?"

"Listen, Harper's trying to find her the smart one who will set all her nerdy girl bits on fire and white knight her. I'm just trying to get her railed by something tattooed and muscular in the meantime. She deserves it putting up with your grumpy ass these last few weeks."

"If she needs to get railed, she doesn't need Danvers."

"Jesus. You better not be railing anyone and refracturing your fucking hip. Have you seen the games? I need you back on the field if we even have a chance at the playoffs."

"I'm being careful. It's modified and physical therapist approved. And you'll get into the playoffs with or without me."

"So you are fucking her finally? Good. It's working then." Joss grins.

"I submit to the court a near confession," I say as I look up at Colt, and he looks between us.

"Remember when I said that someday I would get payback for this?" He points between the three of us.

"Payback for what? Making sure you got engaged and didn't fuck things up here?"

"The torture that came before that, if you remember."

"Oh, it was just some minor torture. And you're so hot when you're jealous." Joss grins at Colt.

He grunts in response and then turns back to me as he takes a bite of his food.

"If you're fucking her, then why are they setting her up?"

"Because she wants more than that."

"And you don't?"

"I'm a fucking mess she doesn't need."

"Except when you're fucking her, apparently," Joss interjects.

"I never said I wasn't selfish."

"That didn't answer my question," Colt counters, giving me a meaningful look.

"I don't know. I don't know how to be that guy. That was part of the reason I wanted to talk to you two. If you made it work, then..."

"Why not just ask Xander? Given Harper is her best friend and you're Xander's... seems like it would be a better line of correlation."

"Because Xander was always in love with Harper," I answer.

"And *you* turned a hoe into a housewife." Joss grins. "So now he wants to know if he can turn into a househusband."

They both laugh, and he kisses her before he turns his attention back on me.

"I'm glad my suffering is a source of amusement for both of you," I grumble and take a bite of my food.

"So how do we help?" Colt asks leaning back in his chair. "That's assuming I want to help and not just watch you struggle after all the shit you pulled."

THIRTY-SEVEN

Scarlett

HARPER AND I are sitting at a quaint little bistro near her office downtown, the one she shares with Joss and her photography studio, eating our lunches and people-watching out the window. She's been telling me about the plans she and Xander have to walk the Camino in the spring and all the walking she's been doing lately to prepare for it. I love how animated she is when talking about him. How much her eyes light up and how often she smiles when she mentions his name. It's so different from her ex, and it makes me so incredibly happy for her.

It also makes me realize that I really want to be able to talk to her about my own situation. I guess that's what I can call it. Whatever is evolving between Tobias and me, and the fresh hope I have for it after we were both iced in together.

"Harper, I need to tell you something. Come clean about it, I guess. I feel bad it's gone on this long without telling you."

"Okay." Her brow furrows. "Is everything okay?"

"It's nothing bad. It's just... I wish I'd told you sooner, but then I didn't. Then it felt like it went on so long with me not telling you that I felt like I couldn't." I take a sip of water, buying time and trying to stop talking in circles about it.

"Is this about Tobias? Because if it is. I know..."

I nearly choke on my water.

"You know?"

"That you guys slept together. I suspected. And then I told Xander I had my suspicions. He made a face, and I badgered him into telling me. Tobias swore him to secrecy, but you know... I can be persuasive. I just didn't want to put you on the spot if you weren't ready to talk about it. I figured you'd bring it up if and when you were." She gives me a sympathetic look.

"Yeah well... it wasn't just us sleeping together. We kind of... made our own video?"

"What?" She drops her fork, and it's her turn to almost choke on something. She coughs a few times, taking a big gulp of her water to try to stop it.

"Are you okay?" I look at her worried and our server even stops to look.

"I'm fine. I'm fine. Wrong pipe there for a second. But I'm fine." She looks at me and holds a hand up and smiles to assure everyone she's good.

"Okay, if you're sure..."

"I mean I'm not sure I'm fine about what you just told me. You made a sex tape? With Westfield?"

"Keep your voice down!" I say in a hushed tone, glancing around to make sure no one heard her.

"Sorry! That's just a lot to digest... Wait. Oh shit. Does this mean yours could be next?"

"No. He found out that it got leaked by the woman, and he wasn't hacked. So ours should be safe."

"Oh wow. That's fucking cold."

"Right? I feel awful for him. It definitely isn't helping his trust issues that started since that's all happened either."

"Well yeah... of course. Shit. That's terrible." She frowns and then looks up at me. "But I need you to elaborate on your situation... Does that mean you guys were a one-time thing or you're together or...?"

"We're in limbo, I guess. When the video came out it blew everything up between us. Then the accident happened immediately after, and well you know how hard all of that's been on him. Any feelings I had seemed silly in comparison to everything he was going through."

"Your feelings are important too," she admonishes me.

"I mean I know that, but I wasn't going to start asking how he felt about me when he was trying to figure out how he could play again."

"Right."

"And all indications felt like he was over it. Well... sort of. We kind of hooked up a bit that first week I was there, but then it was like awkward silence on the topic after."

"Hooked up the first week? When he was still in bed? Um... not that it's my business, but how exactly?"

"Creative solutions." Because I'm not keen to explain how I rode a man's face in the middle of a bistro in the daytime.

"Okay. Understood. So then there was silence and then?"

"When he found out I was trying to date again, he flipped out a little, I guess? I don't know if he was jealous or what. But the night we were iced in together and I couldn't make the date. We talked and it was good. Felt like we were getting along again and breaking through some of the awkward silence. And then he... kissed me. Which had not been a thing before. I mean in all the times we hooked up. It was insanely hot. But not like... romantic hot? You know?"

"Yeah. Sometimes it's just a different kind of hot. Just as

good but different. I get it. And I can see how Tobias wouldn't exactly be romantic."

"But that night, it was more. We talked about our feelings. Like a real adult conversation."

"Huh. No fighting?"

"No. Well, a little bickering but you know that's our thing."

"Of course."

"There's so much I didn't realize about him. How much we have in common. How alike we are in some ways. I really think I might have real feelings for him. I mean... I thought I did before but then it's hard to tell when you're having that kind of sex you know? Like is it the sex or is it deeper than that?"

"Oh, I know." She grins. "Thankfully it was a lot more than that, but I had the same worries with Xander."

"The two of them are both so freaking hard to read sometimes."

"A lot of the time. Until they let their guard down, anyway. They're so used to being walled off. And they were both raised by men who taught them it was work first and feelings later. Boys don't cry. All that toxic stuff that doesn't exactly lead to healthy emotions. Not exactly shocking that they ended up the way they did."

"Yeah. I know Coach Westfield's reputation, but not much about him and Tobias. He's mentioned they don't get along but not much beyond that."

"I don't know a ton. He and Xander keep each other's confidence pretty tight. They're like brothers that way."

"Except when it comes to whether we had sex." I raise an eyebrow.

"Minus when I badger him into telling me, yes." Harper has the decency to look guilty. "Don't fault Tobias for telling him. It was when Xander was trying to get him to have you come on. He was resisting it. Saying it wasn't a good idea to have you in the house. And when Xander wanted to know why..."

"Ah. Yeah. He was probably afraid I'd be more trouble than I was worth."

"I didn't get that impression. I think it was more... he knew he was being a giant asshole and didn't want to subject you to it. Xander said you'd be perfect for the job and not to make your decisions for you."

"Ha. Well... I guess it's worked out pretty well."

"I like the idea of you two together. For the record, I mean."

She smiles.

"You would say that."

"I mean that. Even if it didn't mean we could double date all the time and take trips together and all the other amazing things. Oh my god. You could be up in the box with me and Joss and Violet. How amazing would that be?"

"Let's not get ahead of ourselves. It's not that serious."

"No?"

"No. He was even fine with me still dating other people. Said he doesn't mind competition. He told me flat out he couldn't be the kind of guy I want... but he still wants what he can have *for now*. Wants to see what will happen if we try."

"Oh. But that's kind of romantic honestly. It's more than what Xander was willing to do the first round and look how that turned out."

"I don't want to marry someone else for years though."

"But you want to marry Tobias?" A devious grin spreads across her face.

"Again. Way, and I do mean way, ahead of ourselves. I just mean... if things are going to happen. I don't want to have to wait for some distant moment in the future after we've gone our separate ways. I want a chance for things to work now."

"So you like-like him?" she teases.

"Yes, I like-like him." I roll my eyes and shake my head at her before I smile. "A lot. I had no idea how much. But the last few weeks being with him... I have all the butterflies and heart twists. All the stuff you could possibly want, you know?"

"Uh huh. Tell me more."

"I just... He does seem like he's grown a lot, and I believe him when he says he wants to know where things will go. I just also keep trying to remind myself it's Tobias."

"Well. I don't want you to get hurt, and the guy has been through it lately. So much to take on and I know he's struggled hard with all of it. Things seem to be on the upswing for him though. I think you should listen to him. Be cautiously optimistic if he tells you to be."

"I'm not crazy for doing that?"

"No. I mean keep your options open. Joss and I have put hard work into it, and if he says he's okay with you dating other people—do it. Don't preemptively commit to something he hasn't committed to. I didn't commit to Xander the first time and as much as I wish it would have turned out differently, if we had tried then I don't think we'd ever have had what we have now. You know? Let Tobias continue to work through his shit while he figures out what he wants to do."

"Right... Thank you."

"For what?"

"For not judging me. Or being mad I didn't tell you right away."

"That's what best friends are for, silly."

"Well, I'm glad I have you."

"I'm glad I have you. And I can't wait until we can go on double dates together." She grins.

THIRTY-EIGHT

Tobias

NOW THAT I'VE learned my infamous sex tape is the result of a leak and not a hack, I want justice. I feel like my co-star and her publicist think that we should all just put this behind us, forgive and forget. Move on. But the tape cost me a lot—the relationship I'd been building with Scarlett before this, a good portion of my dignity, and temporarily, my sanity when I decided to hop on a motorcycle in the middle of the season to escape it all.

I can't lay all of that at her door. I made my own decisions, both to film the video and to hop on the bike. But her using me to increase her visibility and fame while she was releasing her own makeup line is unforgivable. Her selling it to the tabloid to make an extra buck on top of it all? More than I can swallow. So the idea that I'm just going to pretend like none of it ever happened just to make it go away? Hell *fucking* no.

While it was a humiliating experience to have it revealed in this way and have way too many people holding unflattering angles of my ass in the palm of their hand, I also feel like people like me shouldn't have to be ashamed of the fact we're normal people. Sometimes we make a sex tape. Sometimes we take nudes. We like to have the same kind of fun as everyone fucking else, and that doesn't make our personal lives any less personal. Doesn't give people the right to access that just because I play ball a few nights a week.

So I told my publicist to put out the truth. That we investigated and found out it was leaked for fame and profit, and I was an unwilling participant in the whole scheme. That I'm denouncing the tabloid that publicized the tape. I'd held back on the idea of suing either of them or pursuing it further. That is until I talk to my father.

"You can't be fucking serious with this, Tobias. This was almost out of the news cycle. They were focused on your injury and your recovery, and instead you what? Fucking drag it all back out into the light."

"Did you read the statement or just get mad that one exists?"

"Oh, I fucking read it. You sound like a fucking crybaby who can't handle fame. Looks like some woman duped you because you're too stupid to know better. The statement doesn't make you look better. It makes us look worse."

"Us, eh?"

"Us. This family. I wish you'd fucking think of your brother and sister when you do this shit."

"Easton and Madison both know about it and supported my decision to come out against it. So I think there might be one person you're concerned about."

"I'm concerned about this whole fucking family and what your off-field shit means for us. Jesus Christ, Tobias. Even Xander has his shit together these days. His agent fucked him over royally, but do you see him whining about it in the papers?"

"He's suing his agent for a fuck ton of money and trying to destroy his whole business. He can't talk more than that because they're in legal proceedings. If he could, I'm sure he'd be very vocal about his agent profiting off his name and image while he blackmailed him and his ex-wife."

"Fuck. You boys just can't take your licks these days. Just sit it out and let things roll in and out. You don't need to have an opinion or make a statement on everything. You're out there to play a fucking game."

"You're right, Dad. I am out there to play a fucking game. Which is a lot fucking harder to do when everyone wants to talk about what I look like fucking naked because someone I trusted released a personal video. I might be to blame for fucking trusting the wrong people. That's on me, but standing up and saying I don't want to see that happen to other people? That seems fair."

He lets out a disgusted chortle, scoffing at the idea I have any sort of say in these matters.

"Next thing you know you'll be following Xander into the court system."

"You know, I hadn't given it a lot of thought. But after talking to you, I might just sue the tabloid for publicizing the video. Why should they fucking profit off my cock instead of me?"

"Are you out of your goddamn mind, boy? Did I teach you nothing or are you just too fucking stupid to know better?"

"If I'm so fucking stupid, why do you keep talking to me?"

"Because you're my fucking legacy and you're supposed to be better than this. A better player and a better fucking son. I wish I knew where the fuck I went wrong with you."

"Probably the day I learned to think for myself. Goodnight. Dad."

I toss the phone onto the counter of the kitchen. Every time I talk to that fucking man, I want to fucking punch shit by the end of it, and I can get through almost anything without feeling that kind of rage.

When I look up though, I notice a cake sitting inside a domed cake stand perfectly frosted with "Happy First Day Back" with a little 50-yard line and green frosting grass on the edge of it, and I can't help but smile.

"Spitfire?" I yell out, hoping she's within shouting distance.

Less than a second later she appears dressed in some kind of fifties housewife outfit complete with an apron.

"Was already headed out when I heard you raising your voice on the phone. Everything okay?"

"What? Oh uh..." My mind goes blank. That's the power this woman has over me. I forget my asshole father and everything else I'd just been pissed about. "Did we have some sort of bonus content situation I forgot about?"

"Ha! No. I was filming an episode until it got loud in the background. If you don't want them to know I film here, probably shouldn't talk so loudly."

"I don't give a fuck if your subscribers know that you film here."

"Then everyone will know you're a secret nerd." She makes a pretend gasp and covers her mouth.

"They already know exactly what my ass looks like from all angles, so what's one more thing?" I grumble.

"Is that what the raised voices were about?"

"They were about my dad being... my dad actually. There is no word that properly encompasses how much of an asshole he is. So we'll have to settle for that."

"I see. Well, I'm sorry about that."

"But then I saw this cake. Did you have this made?"

"I made it. From a 1950s cookbook, so I don't know how good it'll be, but I thought I could kill two birds with one stone. Make a cute cake and get some short-form content for socials."

"Fair enough. Thank you though. I love it. Again with the little hints that your subscribers might put together. I've seen the comments. They've been sleuthing about where you are and what you're up to these days."

"I like to maintain an air of mystery." She grins.

I slide my hands around her waist and pull her close, kissing her softly before she returns it in more pressing strokes of her tongue.

"I missed you. Was it a good first day otherwise?"

"Yeah. It was really great to be back in the locker room with the guys and on the field. I didn't get to do a ton. A lot of just taking it easy and observing. A few catches here and there. But feels like I'm headed back to normal even if I'm not there yet."

"Good. I'm happy for you." She hugs me. "Now I've got to finish this shot, and then we can get dinner and have some cake?"

"Can I watch?"

"Watch what?"

"You film. You get to see me on the field. Or at least you did. I want to watch the making of the magic."

"Um. I guess we could try it. I feel like I'll be nervous with you in there, but I guess I won't know until we try."

"Up to you. I don't want to make you uncomfortable."

"No, let's do it. It'll be fun, and I have to do a live anyway." She smiles up at me, and I kiss her one last time.

I could get used to this. Having her working here in the library, filming for her job, and the two of us having dinner together after a long day. While I'm excited, fucking thrilled frankly, to be back on the field part-time, I know every day I'm closer to being one hundred percent is a day closer to when I won't have an excuse to keep her here. I might be able to drag out the idea of her working in the library a while longer, but eventually, she won't be stuck with me. She'll have to want to see me, and that makes me nervous if I'll be enough for her when the time comes.

THIRTY-NINE

Scarlett

WHEN I WRAP up the live, Tobias practically jumps out of his seat and grabs me, hauling me onto the library table before he shuts the laptop at our side. His mouth is on mine in fervent strokes and after a few moments, I have to press for air.

"That was hot as fuck to watch in person. Is this what it feels like when you watch me play football?"

"Funny."

"I'm not fucking kidding. You're fucking brilliant like that. This like super sexy nerd girl thing. Especially in this dress. I swear to god, Spitfire, I was trying to listen and not objectify you, I promise. I did so fucking well for most of it, but by the end, I started having ideas."

"Yeah. Well, I need some food for stamina and fortitude."

"Fuck. I totally forgot. Should have ordered something before you were done. How do you feel about cake?"

"Better than nothing. I hope I didn't mess it up. I used the recipe from a historic cookbook. It called for tomato soup."

"I'm sorry, what?"

"I heard it's not bad."

"Uhh, I guess we'll see. Sounds like maybe it should have stayed in the historic cookbook." He laughs as we walk to the kitchen.

"Hey! I worked hard on that cake. And I even used your frosting recipe."

"Oh yeah? A fan now, are you?"

"It's pretty good. I see the appeal. Not sure I understand the whole food kink thing. I don't think it's one of mine, but the frosting is good regardless."

"Have you tried the food kink thing yet?"

"No. Just the way I imagine it... It's not for me."

"Spitfire... you gotta try things before you decide you don't like them." He takes the glass top off the cake and dips his finger in the white frosting ribbon at the bottom and turns, brushing it over my neck. He grabs me by the throat with his free hand, pulling me toward him, and licks the frosting off, holding me still while I writhe under the sensation of his tongue over my skin.

"Fuck," I whisper.

"Yeah?" He grins, his eyes searching mine.

"That's not what I imagine when I think of food play."

"It's what I imagine." He repeats the process on the other side of my neck, and I'm surprised at how well it's working on me. How much I want him already.

"That so bad?"

"No."

"You up for trying something new? We stop anytime you want."

"Okay."

His fingers go to the buttons on my dress. It's a 1950s shirt cocktail-style dress with buttons all the way down the front and a small collar. Buttons he's slowly undoing as we stand here.

"Fuck me... you're so gorgeous." He leans down and kisses the top of my breast, working his way down as he pulls the clasp loose at the front of my bra. His hand slips underneath, his thumb toying with my nipple as he takes another dip in the frosting and spreads it over the tip. His tongue follows a moment later and I'm practically melting against the counter.

"Okay... maybe I do like it."

He takes his time with the next round, spreading the frosting around and taking time to admire his work. His lashes are low, and his eyes are heavy with lust. I reach forward and palm him through the sweats he has on, and he leans into my touch, his eyes closing.

"Scarlett... fuck. Seeing you like this, with this frosting all over you. There's something I've been fantasizing about but I don't know..."

I slide my hand down the front of his sweats, wrapping my fingers around him and sliding over his cock in slow, languid strokes. Wanting to torture him the same way he always does whenever he touches me.

"Does it involve you inside me? Because I'm thinking I need that even before dinner."

"On you."

"Hmm... explain." It's my turn with frosting and I use my free hand to put a small smear across his neck before my tongue runs over it. I grip him tighter as I stroke him, and he groans.

"Fuck you're going to be the death of me."

"That's not an explanation."

He takes a breath, opening his eyes to stare up at the ceiling before closing them again.

"Your breasts are fucking gorgeous and I—" He stops mid-sentence because I've dropped to my knees, taking his sweats with me, and run my tongue along the underside of his cock. I'm fairly certain I know what he wants and given how often he gives me the things I like, I'm willing to try it for him.

"Want to come on me?"

His eyes open and he looks down at me, his fingers running through my hair.

"We don't have to. If it's something that turns you off... That's the last thing I want."

"I've never tried it before, so I guess I don't know until I do." I take him in my mouth again, swirling my tongue over the head and his fingers tighten in my hair.

"Fuck. You're such a good fucking girl when you do that, Scarlett. Your tongue is fucking magic."

I use it on him again and he bucks forward, sliding deeper into my mouth, teasing the back of my throat before he pulls back, groaning my name as I take him again. He watches me, leaning back against the counter to brace himself as I continue, a series of curses and praises leaving his lips in rapid succession until he finally tells me he's close, and I pull away.

"You sure about this?" His brow furrows with concern for a moment before I nod. "Fuck..."

I use my hand to take him over the edge, warm streams of him falling over my chest and neck as he grips the counter and curses. He's still recovering when I dip my finger in a swirl of the frosting and come that's running down over my nipple and lick it off my finger.

"Holy fuck, Scarlett." He grabs me up off my knees and pushes me back against the counter behind me. "You can't do that to me."

I'm not sure what I'm doing, but I don't get a chance to ask because a moment later his lips are on mine, kissing me roughly and forcing me to climb up on the counter as he steps between my legs.

"Fuck. Tasting me on your lips like that... I need more of it." He leans down, his tongue flattening as he slides it through the frosting and come before he swipes it over mine. My stomach flips at how fucking hot it is, and I wrap my legs around his waist.

"You like that?" he questions, his eyes searching my face.

"So much."

He picks me up off the counter a second later, and I gasp. "Your hip."

"I'm lifting weights heavier than you at PT. It's fine."

"Still." I release the grip I have on him with my legs and drop to the ground.

"Still," he echoes, glaring at me and giving me a small slap on the ass. "Go to my bathroom and take the dress off before I rip it off."

I do as he asks, and he follows behind, flipping on the water in the huge shower that spans one of the walls in the room. One I've jealously cleaned before, hoping I could have the same someday. He watches me as I undress, and I can practically hear his jaw tighten when he sees I don't have panties on.

"You've been bare this whole time?"

"Yeah. I had this whole little plan about bending over a desk in the library and asking if you could help me. But you had other ideas." A wry smile crosses my lips, and his eyes darken.

"You do that again when you're on a live, and I'm going to slide under the table and fuck you with my tongue. See if you can keep a straight face through it."

"I know you meant that as a threat, but I hope it's a promise," I taunt him.

"Oh, it's a fucking promise." He strips his clothes off as he crosses the room, and I watch each piece fall to the floor.

He's already semi-hard again, and I raise a brow, one that's returned in kind. "Turn around." He presses on my hip, and I turn my back to his front as he moves us in front of the mirror.

He kisses the side of my throat as he looks up at us in the mirror, bringing his lips to my ear.

"Touch yourself while we wait for the water to heat. I want you wet and ready for me."

I slip my fingers between my legs, sliding the pads of them over my clit and close my eyes at the sensation. Listening to the water and the sound of his breathing next to me.

"Nah, dirty girl. Open those eyes. Look at you covered in the frosting you made for me and my come. Your cheeks still fucking pink from sucking my cock. Touching yourself for me like this. You're fucking gorgeous, and you need to see it."

I open them again and the sight of myself like this, with his arm wrapped around my middle as his other hand slides over my hip makes me desperate to have him inside me. I can feel his cock grow thicker against my ass, and I spread my legs slightly as I bend forward, so he slips between.

"I want you to fuck me like I'm your whore." His eyes come up to meet mine in the mirror, surprise, and lust in them. "I want to feel you come inside me."

He nips at my neck and kisses me again as he closes his eyes like he's contemplating it. His brow furrowing like he's worried.

"Please, Tobias. I want to try it," I whisper, softly kissing him to reassure him that I mean what I'm saying.

"Let me get a condom," he whispers back.

"If you're good with it... I'm on birth control." I kiss him again.

"I got tested with everything else that was going on... but are you sure that's what you want?"

"Yes. Absolutely sure. I've been fantasizing about it, honestly." His hand slips over my mouth and he closes his eyes leaning his forehead against my temple.

"Fucking Christ, Scarlett." He breathes against my skin and then kisses his way down, his hand sliding over mine while I continue to tease my clit. "I want to see my come dripping out of you so badly. Since that first night. I just thought you were too sweet to want someone like me."

"You're the only one I'd want it with."

"Fuck me." He grins, grabbing a fistful of my hair. He pulls and my head tilts back as he kisses my throat. "You are my whore, aren't you? Made so fucking dirty just for me."

"Yes."

"Good." He nips at my neck. "Bend over then and show me how well you take me."

I do as he asks, holding the towel bar for support as he slides inside me.

"I can't fuck you as hard as I want, Spitfire. Not yet. But soon. In the meantime though, I still want to hear you."

"Yes," I moan when he slides out and back in again. Nothing and no one—no vibrator or former boyfriend—compares to how good he feels. How perfectly he fills and stretches me when he fucks me. I'd pay for it if I had to. I smirk, and he catches it in the mirror beside us.

"Something funny?"

"How good you feel. That I'd pay for it the same way you'd pay to watch me as a cam girl."

"Yeah. You like it when I watch don't you? Like when you were parading around in soaking wet see-through underwear because you were desperate to have me fuck you."

"Yes."

"Love it so much you had to ride my face when you found me. Even when you got off you still needed to suck my cock. And fuck... do you suck me well. Like my own fucking whore."

He hits me in just the right spot, his cock sliding in and out and over just as he calls me a whore, and I moan out his name because I'm close. His fingers dig into my hips, and I circle my clit faster as he takes me closer. Every little nerve ending I have is on fire between his touch and his voice.

"Gonna take more of me when I fill this tight little cunt." He pulls on my hair as he takes me deeper, and I start to come apart. All the touches and sensations are way too much for me to hold out any longer.

"Don't stop touching yourself. Keep going. I want your fingers on your clit when I fill you up. You fucking hear me?"

"Yes," I whimper, the sensation of my last orgasm dulling as I try to bring another one up.

"Fucking fuck. Your cunt is so tight..." he curses as he starts to come inside me, filling me as I try for one more wave of pleasure. Desperately chasing the edge of it.

When he opens his eyes and sees me, he turns me around and pins me up against the wall. His hand around my throat as he dips his fingers inside me, a sly smile as he feels his come slipping over his fingers and down my legs. His fingers pump in and out of me while his thumb slides over my clit as he follows the same rhythm I had a moment before. I start to shiver under his touch, feeling another orgasm bloom under the weight of it, and he smirks.

"Yeah. You just needed me. My come. My hands. I know, Scarlett. Come for me like a good fucking girl."

I collapse against him a moment later, a whimpering, gasping mess from how much stronger it is the second time around. Every nerve ending I have is raw and exhausted by the time he's finished with me.

He kisses my temple and pulls me into the shower, kissing my lips and throat as he slides us both under the water.

"I don't deserve you. You're too fucking good for me. But I

love watching you fall apart like that. Love how much you like to try things with me."

I wrap my arms around his neck, and he holds me, running his fingers gently over my hair as the water soaks the strands and they start to cling to my skin. It feels like we start to cling to each other, melding into one perfectly satisfied mess.

We don't say much as we get cleaned up, he helps wash me and I wash his back as my lips chase the rivulets of water down his spine. This man is going to be my undoing. There's very little chance at this point, I don't fall for him if I haven't lost myself already to it. But I don't care. Even if it crashes or burns. I just want more of him as long as I can have it.

FORTY

Tobias

WHEN WE FINISH OUR SHOWER, I bundle her up in a towel, keeping her close so she doesn't get too cold. At least until I can get her into my bed, naked and gorgeous where she belongs—her big gray eyes looking at me like I'm the only thing in her world. Something I've wanted from her for longer than I'm willing to admit.

Because I'm fairly fucking certain I'm in love with her. A thing I'm still trying to process. I have no idea when exactly it happened. I'm not even clear when I figured out that's what this gaping, gnawing fucking hole in my chest, which feels like it's only full when she's around, is. But I can't live without her now. Not now that she occupies that space. Now that I've seen all the ways we fit together flawlessly.

I kiss her as I lay down next to her in the bed, cradling her jaw in my hand and seeking the feel of her mouth against mine over and over. Until we finally break for oxygen.

"Are we good?" I ask, wanting to be sure. "I didn't take things too far for you?"

"No. It was everything I wanted." She smiles, her eyes drifting over my face before she kisses me again. "You're perfect. Frighteningly so." Her fingertips run along my jaw, over the now fading scar the accident left on my face.

"Even scarred?"

"Scarred. Broken. Whatever you are. I don't care. I'm here and I want it." Her words wrap around my heart and anchor it. I hadn't realized how much I needed to hear them after everything that's gone on lately. The conversations I had today. The way my own father turns on me if it suits his mood.

"You okay though? You seem like you're a million miles away," she whispers after a bit.

"Just thinking about a lot and things that happened earlier today. Nothing about you. You're the one person who gives me peace." I sweep her towel-dried hair off her forehead and kiss the freckles on her nose.

"Anything to do with the raised voices conversation on your way in?"

"Something like that, yeah."

"Do you want to talk about it?" Her brow furrows with genuine concern as her eyes study me, and I'm opening my mouth to talk about it before I even know what I'm doing. She just has that effect on me.

"It's my dad. He's been an ass about everything that's happened. Now he's telling me I'm not handling the news about her leaking the tape the right way. Always has comments about my career. It's a lot."

"I'm sorry. That must be awful."

"Part of inheriting the Westfield name. My brother and sister have had to deal with it too over the years. Just that I'm frequently one of his favorite targets."

"Yeah, I can see that from someone like him. Just what I know of his public persona anyway. You're the oldest. And Easton, he's good but you're better. Probably better than your father was even at his prime."

"Don't let him hear you say that. In his view, I'm a subpar WR2 who gets worse every year."

"What?" She sits up abruptly. "Fuck him. Are you serious?"

I shrug. "Yeah. It's his usual bit. He thinks he runs everything. That he's better than everyone, and I've just turned into a poor imitation."

"What an asshole."

"Yeah... but sometimes I think it's true. Some of what he says. He's not a good man, and neither am I."

"How are you not a good man?"

I give her a look.

"I'm serious."

"Well I'm sure as fuck not Colt involved in all the nonprofit stuff and looking out for everyone."

"You looked out for me when I needed it. For Xander when he needed you. You helped Colt and Joss work through everything and end up together. You donate money just the same as everyone else. You've been dragging out the work I have to do around here so I can feel like I still have a shred of dignity while I wait for the museum to open back up. It might look different for you, but you're good Tobias. Good comes in a lot of different forms."

"I'm glad you see me that way, Spitfire."

"It's not just me. When you got in the accident, everyone was at the hospital. Everyone wanted to be there for you. You're loved Tobias. Everyone loves you on that team."

"Until I didn't die and then they were furious."

"Because Xander and the rest don't like seeing you do this

to yourself. They don't want to see you hurt and suffer. Miss games and being on the field. You know?"

"I heard you were at the hospital that first night."

"I was."

"Thank you. For staying with me. Not leaving me alone there. I'm sure it was awkward, especially at the time. I wish I'd woken up to be able to know. To thank you."

"Of course. I wanted to be with you. When Xander got the call, I was terrified, being able to see that you were still there, keep you company, made me feel like I was at least doing something useful."

"I don't deserve you." I kiss her again, and she curls up against my chest.

FORTY-ONE

Scarlett

TOBIAS IS BACK to practicing full-time, and I had a couple of appointments today, so I don't make it to his house until the afternoon. Normally I wouldn't bother to come, but he told me he wanted to at least get dinner and see me for a few before I have to go home and do my History Harlot live show. So when I get to Tobias's place and let myself in I stop dead in my tracks, blinking when I see the gorgeous blonde woman standing at the other end of the hall staring back at me in her PJs. My gut turns and my brain starts to go to terrible places.

She stares at me, her eyebrow going sky high. She turns putting the spoon she's holding back in the jar.

"Since when does he let his random hookups have a key to the house?"

"Excuse me? Who are you?"

"Oh, sweetheart. Don't try that attitude with me. I've been

in his life a hell of a lot longer than you and will continue to be long after he forgets whatever it is he liked about fucking you."

"Wow. Aren't you lovely."

"Oh. You don't know the half of it. You should probably run along now. Tobias has enough on his hands without you around. And leave the key. Wherever you stole it from, it's going back."

I toss the key to the floor at her feet and grab my purse back off the entryway table. I have no idea who this woman is, but I'm not doing this today.

"Who the fuck are you talking to?" I hear Tobias's voice, and he rounds the corner. I stop because I want to see his face when he realizes it's me. How the hell he could have forgotten I was coming over to dinner tonight when he invited me is a fucking mystery only time will solve.

"Oh no. No. No, no. We are not doing this again." He hurries down the hall and grabs my forearm. "You are not leaving. I am not running you down again. And you!" He turns to the gorgeous blonde. "Is this how you fucking treat company? Did Mom not teach you any manners?"

"I didn't know we were treating your late-night company with such dignity these days. Especially given what some of them have been up to lately."

"This is not my fucking late-night company, Madison. This is Scarlett."

"Oh. Ohhhhhh." Madison grits her teeth, and her lips turn down in a grimace. "Oopsie?"

"Fuck. I am so sorry, Scarlett. My sister here is a bit aggressive. She works in PR fixing people's issues, and she treats everyone she doesn't know well like a problem. It's a failing of hers, honestly." He glares at her.

"Your sister?" I ask confused.

"Yes. I wanted it to be a surprise. I thought it would be a good one. We could all have dinner. You could meet some of my family not in a hospital setting. You know... Then my sister has to be herself and ruin it."

Madison gives me an apologetic look.

"I'm really sorry. I forgot that he had a... you, now. And I thought you were some random hookup. I'm having a shit day, and I didn't want to deal with some random he's fucking right now. I assumed the key was stolen. My fault," Madison apologizes immediately.

"You're fine. I should have introduced myself. It's just the way you were talking to me and then you being here, like this." I motion to her being in loungewear eating straight out of a jar like she owns the place.

"I get it. Looks a bit like I'm the random he's fucking. My brother's only recently reformed. A year ago you would have been absolutely right."

"Well, I'm sorry you're having a shitty day. That sucks," I say flashing a look to Tobias because I don't know how much I should say.

"It's fine. I just found out the love of my life is in love with someone else. I came out here to surprise him. Had a speech all ready in my head and then found out I don't have a chance in hell."

"If you had given me any sort of warning, I would have told you." Tobias shakes his head.

"Then it wouldn't have been a surprise. You would have told him, and I didn't want him to prepare some speech about how you're his best friend and I'm your sister and blah blah blah. I've heard it all before," Madison grumbles and sticks a graham cracker teddy bear into the Nutella and into her mouth.

"Your best friend?" I look to Tobias.

He grimaces.

"Yes. Xander. Have you met him?" Madison asks.

"Uh, yes. A few times."

"Well I've been in love with him as long as I can remember, but thanks to asshole over here I've been nothing but 'like a little sister to him'. And when I finally get the guts to prove it... When I think we're finally both single, and life's too short... Then I find out he's been in love with someone else for years. And I can't even be mad about it because they're adorable. Have you met her? Harper? That bitch. Not really though. She's very sweet. I bet we'd be friends if she didn't steal my man."

"Madison..."

"What? I'm just saying. Hoes before bros, but she could have at least thrown me a bone. I couldn't sleep with him once? It's unfair. He's literally the most beautiful man in the world. No one else even comes close. Well... him and Undergrove. But I hate him. He doesn't deserve it. Xander was—"

"Madison!"

"What?"

"You didn't let me finish introductions. This is Scarlett. Scarlett, Madison. Scarlett and I met through *Harper,* they're best friends."

"Oh fuck!" She slams her spoon back into the jar and looks guiltily at me.

"It's fine. Didn't say anything that wasn't true. She's very lucky, and Xander is hot as fuck."

"Hey!" Tobias complains.

"I don't really hate her, you know. I'm just being a jealous bitch right now. I'll get over it."

"You're fine. I'd be crushed too."

"Okay. Well, I'm not fine that you're over here calling my best friend 'hot as fuck.'" Tobias frowns at me.

"I mean not as hot as you."

"She's lying, brother. He's definitely hotter than you. She just doesn't want to damage your brittle ego."

"Trust me, she cares very little for my ego."

"Good. See, I think I like you. We'll be friends as soon as I stop being jealous of your bestie." Madison grins at me. "Now to find a romcom to remind me that there are other fish in the sea."

Tobias waits for me to take off my shoes and coat and then laces his fingers with mine, dragging me back into the library and promptly depositing me on the table where he kisses me like his life depends on it.

"Fucking sorry about that. She's... a lot sometimes. A force of nature really."

"It's okay. Misunderstandings happen."

"Don't mention her declaration of love to Harper? She's dramatic, and I don't want them to get off on the wrong foot. Madison and Xander's sister are close. I have no idea how the fuck she did not get the memo, but here we are."

"I won't mention it." I smirk at him amused.

He kisses me again and smiles.

"Thoughts on what you want for dinner?"

"I feel like that's up to your sister. Although, she seemed pretty attached to the Nutella she was eating."

"She claims she's in mourning. Over what, I don't know."

"I mean maybe she is a little heartbroken over Xander. Did she really like him?"

"She might have mentioned something over the years. But no way was that happening. He wasn't interested and even if he was... Harper."

"All those years?"

"He didn't talk about it much. But I figured. Once he met her... And before that, he was... well a lot like me."

"He changed his tune pretty quickly."

"Had to if he was going to get his shot."

"I see." I smile, his lips brushing over mine again.

"She's really going to put a damper on our whole routine. But I think you'll like her. She's staying through Christmas. Says she doesn't want me to be alone with everything going on, but I think she's hoping for some family time too. Then she's off again. Something about starting a resort with Xander's sister. Some sort of retreat, I guess? Madison always has a lot of ideas. We usually have to wait to see how well they actually manifest or if they just stay half-formed."

"She seems nice when she's not telling me to get out of your house."

"She's protective of the people she cares about. She wanted to run point on this whole scandal-injury thing I've got going on, but I told her I couldn't deal with someone from the family that close to it. She'd have to watch the video and having my sister watch me have sex... yeah. No fucking thank you."

"Yeah. I don't blame you. I would not want to see my brother in that state, even if I did want to help him."

"I get to meet this brother some day?"

"Maybe. He's a fan of yours, so I'm half afraid he'll embarrass me."

"Because my sister very definitely did not just embarrass me."

"Well... fair." I laugh. "Maybe sometime in the future if you want to."

"I'm interested. Have to learn more about the elusive redhead who lives in my library." He kisses me. "And my head." Another kiss from him, and I'm leaning into it, running my fingers over his shoulders.

"Ahem." Madison's standing in the doorway clearing her throat. "I thought we were doing dinner."

"Like I said about ruining our routine," he whispers to me before he turns back to her. "I thought you were watching a movie?"

"Nothing good. And I decided I want to talk to your..." she trails off while she debates what to call me, "friend some more."

FORTY-TWO

Tobias

"SO THAT WAS THE INFAMOUS SCARLETT?" Madison grins at me from her spot on the other side of the living room once Scarlett has gone home early for the evening, claiming she wants to give us some time together but just as likely fleeing the bombardment of questions Madison's been throwing at her.

"I'm not sure she's infamous, but yes."

"Oh, I think any woman who's threatening to take you into commitment territory is infamous by default." She grins. "But I like her. I get it. Not quite what I imagined, but I honestly think she's better. Her being such a nerd, just like you. I was worried you'd settle down with someone vapid."

"Let's not get too ahead of ourselves about settling down. We're still feeling each other out. I need to figure out if I can even be the right kind of guy for her."

"And what is the right kind?"

"Someone who can be there for her when she needs them. Make a difference in her life. Show up. Be less selfish. Someone who can commit."

"I think you've checked all of those boxes already." Madison frowns at me, and I raise a brow in return.

"I don't think so. She wants the good guy. The one who drops everything for her and worships the ground she walks on. I've never been that guy."

"Well first, I don't think that's what she wants. Women don't want magic, brother. They just want someone who can hold on tight through all the ups and downs. Have their back. See them through it all. I think she wants someone as driven and smart as she is. Someone who can hold their own against her. I think you need the same thing. Probably why the two of you are always fighting, but also why you've fallen in love with her."

"Again with the dramatic words. I like her. A lot. Love is a pretty strong sentiment though. Fallen makes it sound like I can't get back up."

"Can you? If she disappears tomorrow, how would you feel? You keep letting her date other people, and she finds someone else. Runs off with them and tells you that you took too long... What then?"

My chest aches at the thought of her being gone. Her dating someone else I can stomach. I don't even hate it—the thought of proving to her that she wants me more than anyone else. I like the competition because I like the challenge. I like what it says if she says yes. If she picks me. But if she wants someone else, if there's someone better for her out there. I'd want that for her too.

"I'd hate it. But I'd understand it."

"Why are you tempting fate like this if you'd hate it?"

"I want her to pick me. Have her chance to be with

whoever. See what that's like and decide she wants this. Not just fall in with me because I'm here and she's been stuck with sick me for weeks."

"My God you are dense. She picked you already. She picked you when she agreed to come and be here with you at your worst moment. To help you get back on your feet, when she had literally no good reason to do it. You just had a sex tape released that didn't star her. You were in serious danger of losing your career and all the money and fame with it. You were from all accounts a complete and utter asshole to everyone around you. And she signed up for that wholeheartedly."

"I hate when you make good points."

"I hate when you can't see things that are right in front of you. You're still struggling. I know you are. Wondering if you're worthy. If you deserve something good. And we know why that is, and it has nothing to do with you or her."

"This what you do to your clients? Psychoanalyze them?"

"If I think they need it. Usually I try to just send them to therapy while I try to fix the rest. You are in therapy, right?"

"Yeah. East and Colt helped me find someone."

"Good. So talk to them about it. You're going to come to the same conclusion though, and then you're going to have to work through your daddy issues."

"I don't have daddy issues."

"Oh, you do. You and East both. Don't worry, I have my own set thanks to him. But he didn't try to mold me in his image the way he did the two of you."

"I'm just tired of being lectured about my mistakes by a man who cheated on his wife and treats his sons like they're disposable extensions of himself. I'm not sure that's daddy issues so much as just wanting a little bit of fucking sanity in my life."

"And not to turn into him."

"What?"

"That's what you're worried about. At least in part. It could be a lot more than that too, but don't pretend like that isn't a worry for you. Trying to define yourself separately from his legacy. Make sure people know that you might have the name but not the same die-hard black heart that he does."

"Of course I don't want to fucking turn into him."

"Which is a good thing, until it makes you not take chances where your heart is concerned."

I frown at my sister, shaking my head.

"You're fucking annoying sometimes you know?"

"When I'm right? I'm okay with that." She grins, and I toss a pillow at her face that she returns in kind.

"When are you settling down anyway? Going to give Mom her grandchildren?"

"Don't fucking start." She turns a withering glare on me.

FORTY-THREE

Scarlett

MY FAMILY DOES all their Christmas celebrations on Christmas Eve, so Christmas Day is wide open, and when the Westfield siblings invite me over to spend it with them while they eat cookies, drink spiked eggnog, and watch football—I can't say no. But I did have to spend part of my holiday yesterday last-minute panic shopping amongst the crowds of people with similar gift problems. I don't know Madison well enough to know what to get her, and Tobias has everything he could ever want, so it's the worst of both worlds trying to get a present for each of them.

But I manage to show up on time, a bottle of rosé and some homemade cookies in hand in addition to the presents I purchased as they let me in the house. Madison's dressed in a festive sweater, and Tobias looks handsome as hell in a button-up shirt he has rolled up at the sleeves.

"Perfect timing. We just got off a FaceTime call with East

and his wife. Long distance Christmas morning ritual in case these guys have games." Madison smiles at me as she takes the champagne and cookies, so I can set the presents down and work my way out of my coat.

"Not your parents?"

"My mom was on the call briefly. Dad has a game, so there's not a chance we'll hear from him today. Holidays are forwarded to more convenient dates in his mind. Too much strategy and work in the morning to be on the phone you know?" Madison explains as we walk down the hall to the kitchen.

"Missed you, Spitfire." Tobias kisses me on the temple and wraps his arms around me.

"How was your Christmas Eve?"

"Good. Watched a couple of Christmas movies. Made some cookies. Ate takeout."

"Missed a certain redhead because he has an obsession," Madison adds, smiling at her brother.

Tobias rolls his eyes and looks at me. "Don't listen to her. It's not an obsession. It's an addiction. How was your family Christmas?"

"Really good. Got to see my brother and his family. Mom made all the usual stuff. Dad and I watched some football with my brother while my nieces played with the new toys that Santa brought them. Then Mom and I watched White Christmas until we fell asleep on the couch. So all in all a good one." I grin at him.

We settle into an easy holiday routine while we work on getting things ready for our small dinner party. Madison and I get to talk about what her life in public relations has been like, some of the celebrity clients she has, and what her plans are for the future now that she's seen what Tobias has been going through. We manage to whip together a pretty decent

Christmas dinner and spend most of it talking about things that aren't football.

After dinner, we go to open presents, and I hand mine nervously to Madison and Tobias. Madison opens hers first.

"You really didn't have to do this. You didn't even know I'd be here, and I didn't get you anything."

"It's not much. Don't worry. Just a little something to help you through the current situation." I smile at her.

She pulls the paper back and looks down at the little kit I put together for her. There's hot chocolate, marshmallows, extra Nutella, cookies, three different rom-com movies, and a couple of books that I think will fit her life at the moment.

"Oh my god. I love it." She grins at me and then elbows her brother. "This one is a keeper. You better not fuck this up because I like her a lot."

"I'm doing my best." He glances up at me and smirks.

"All right, Spitfire. What'd you get me? Motivational sports movies?"

"Something like that."

He opens the box slowly, peeling back the wrapping and the tape until he pulls out the first couple of things I bought him from a kiosk. Two silicone wristbands in Seattle Phantom colors. One says "WR1" and the other says "You got this."

He looks up and grins as he slides them on his wrist.

"They're just meant to be silly. But you know, in case you ever doubt yourself."

"Oh no. I love them, Spitfire. Can't wait to show Ben this one." His finger slides over the WR1 band, and he grins. We laugh and then he reaches into the box for the next one. A Polaroid camera with a note attached. He pulls it off and reads it out loud.

"For future photo opportunities that you don't want the

public to see." He smirks as he reads it, and his eyes darken as he lifts them to look at me.

I blush a little, mostly because Madison is nearly having a giggling fit.

"Okay, but that's kind of genius. Like I said. She's a good one." Madison shakes her head at us.

"Oh, I intend to keep her around." Tobias kisses my temple. "Got to put this to good use."

"Okay. Let's not overshare though," Madison jokes.

"All right. Your turn," Tobias says, pulling something out from behind him on the couch.

Tobias slips me a black box, one that looks distinctly like a jewelry box and a devious grin flashes over his face. My hands shake a little as I go to open it, feeling like whatever's inside is going to be more than I deserve. I lift the lid and pull it back to reveal a beautiful silver beaded necklace.

I bite my lower lip and then grin at him before I get up to give him a hug.

"It's gorgeous, thank you."

"Here, let's put it on." He takes the box from me and unclasps the necklace while I turn around for him to help me. "This isn't one of those fancy ones you only wear on special occasions. I specifically told them I needed something you could wear every day."

"Every day, huh?" I smirk as I run my fingers over the beads.

"Every day," He reiterates.

Under the necklace is a small business card size piece of paper with the name of the restaurant that we went to on my birthday.

"What's this?"

"That's a promise. I want to take you there when I'm fully back to playing and better. Just the two of us. We'll get a quiet table, and you can actually enjoy the food. Make up for him fucking it up the first time."

"Oh, you didn't have to do that. You were so sweet that night."

"Still. I want a redo. Just the two of us."

"I love it, Tobias. Thank you so much." I kiss him, and he pulls me into his lap.

When I look up, Madison's staring at us a little wide-eyed before she breaks out into a grin.

"Um... I love this. Every bit of this." She waves her hand over us. "I'm not entirely sure how to process it, but I love it."

FORTY-FOUR

Tobias

"TOO BAD YOU don't have a date tonight. You could join the rest of us." Colt stands next to me at practice later in the week, smirking like an asshole.

"Yeah, well I'm trying to stay focused on us winning it all. Shouldn't you be?"

"Oh, we will. But Joss has me focused on that work-life balance thing. Nick and I were just talking about it the other day. Making sure there's plenty of downtime when we're not on the field, you know?"

I turn on Colt. "If Nick gets his downtime anywhere near my girl, I will break every finger he puts on her, and you'll be out a wide receiver and a long snapper in the playoffs. That what you want?"

Colt just laughs. "We both know you're smarter than that. And don't say playoffs until we know for sure."

I give him an annoyed look as I toy with my mouthguard, rocking it between my teeth. He's right that the physical violence is a baseless threat on my part. But he won't lay a fucking finger on her if he knows what's good for him. I've already warned him twice this week that he better treat her like a fucking lady and keep a fucking bubble between them at all times.

"She won't touch him anyway. No reason to when she's got me every day."

"You're seeing her today?" Colt raises a brow.

"No, but she knows where she can come after."

"I don't know. Joss said she was pretty excited for the date. She was into the idea of a younger guy. Joss talked it up, I think. You know we last a little longer than you senior citizens."

"You're fucking cold-hearted these days," I grouch at him. "That her wearing off on you or just the way you kids act now?"

"Probably both." He laughs. "Speaking of Joss. Did you ever get the remote-controlled vibrator she told you about?"

"No. Why?"

"Works long distance with an app on your phone. Comes in handy when we're not at the same place at the same time." He shrugs. "Could be useful if that situation ever happened for you and a girlfriend. Assuming you ever have one."

I glance over at him and raise a brow.

"Just a thought... All right. Let's get out there and see if you can still run a fucking route old-timer." He nods to the field and starts jogging on.

"I'm not fucking old!" I call after him.

"Whatever you say ol' guy!"

AFTER PRACTICE IS OVER, I glance at my phone. Scarlett hasn't responded to my text yet, and I barely have enough time to get to a store and then go see her before she has to leave to meet them. So I hurry through my shower and change to make good time, praying that the traffic on I-5 isn't a complete fucking nightmare.

When I get to her apartment I knock, and it takes a minute before I hear her at the door, unlocking it and opening it to give me a surprised look.

"What are you doing here? I have to leave soon."

"Good to see you too," I answer her, closing the door behind me as I step in.

"I'm sorry. I'm just running behind. Still trying to fix my makeup and get my dress on. If you want to talk, it'll have to be in the bathroom while I finish up."

She's in a robe with thigh highs and underwear underneath it, curls tumbling over the back of the silk fabric. I follow behind her, and I already want to be buried in her. I lean against the doorframe as I watch her apply mascara.

"What did you need?" She glances back at me through the mirror.

"Do you need to get this dolled up to go to Gabe's with some friends?"

"Do I need to get this dolled up to go on a first date with a pro football player who's five years younger than me?"

"Well, he can enjoy the view but he's not touching you."

"Excuse me?" She turns to look at me. "I hope that's a request and not an order."

"Yes, I'm requesting *you* not do it. He already got the order."

"Tobias..." She sighs and caps the mascara. "What happened to 'I don't care if you date them. I like competition'?

How am I supposed to have a normal date if you're threatening them?"

"First... not a threat, a promise. Second, it's a competition. I just have unfair advantages. Like seniority on this team and knowing how to make you come multiple times in a row. He still wants to stay in the game knowing that that's on him."

"So now I have to make the first move. Thanks for that." She swipes on lipstick and glares at me through the mirror.

"The fuck you do." I throw the bag on the counter and wrap my hands around her waist pulling her back against me where I'm already going hard just from watching her bend over the counter in these clothes. "You need fucked tonight? I'm right fucking here."

I reach into her robe and slide my hand under her panties, brushing my fingers over her clit. She closes her eyes and rocks back against me, dropping her hands to the counter. She's already getting wet, and I smirk, leaning forward to kiss the side of her neck. She's wearing the necklace I bought her and seeing it around her neck while her ass brushes over my cock gets me impossibly hard.

"Already wet for me? Or does us fighting over you turn you on?" I spread my fingers to the sides of her clit, just barely brushing against her and wrap my hand around her neck, kissing and sucking my way down the side.

"I like that it irritates you." She smirks, her long dark lashes shadowing her eyes.

"I bought you a present. Open it." I nod to the bag on counter.

"A present?" Her lashes flutter, and she pulls the box out of the bag raising an eyebrow when she sees what it is.

"Joss and Colt said we should try it. Put it on."

"I think I have to tell her to warn me when she gives you ideas. You want to do this *now*?"

"Now."

She pulls it out and washes it off, drying it on a towel while I slide a finger inside her and nibble her earlobe. She grins and scrunches her nose.

"Tobias, you are going to make me late."

"For a good reason. Put it on and hand me the remote."

I slide my hand out from her panties and take the remote while she takes the disc and slides it on, using the magnet to secure it. I turn it on to a low setting and her eyes close, a stuttered breath leaving her. She puts her hands back on the counter, bending over with the sensation.

I kiss the shell of her ear. "It works remote on an app. And you're gonna wear it for me tonight. But first I'm gonna fuck you."

I set the remote on the counter and pull my sweats down, setting my cock free as I slide her panties to the side and pull her hips back against me. She makes a gasping noise when I'm all the way in, one that wakes up every fucking nerve in my body as I start to fuck her. She counters me with a roll of her hips, and I grin when her fingers slide between her legs to press the disc flush with her clit.

"Oh fuck. It's so fucking good. Having it and you. Fuck," she curses.

"Yeah? Open your eyes and look at me." I slide my hand around her throat and tilt her chin up as she opens them.

They immediately cloud with lust as soon as she sees me in the mirror, her lashes dropping, and a little smirk threatens before she bites her lower lip.

"Jesus Christ. The faces you make, Spitfire. You would have made a killing as a cam girl."

"Might still," she taunts me, and I tighten my grip on her and take her a little harder.

"Yeah? You think so? I think you're too busy taking my cock

to have time for that. Need me so badly you're gonna be late for your date just so you can feel me come inside you first."

Her eyes narrow but she doesn't deny it, so I up my pace, digging my fingers into her hip as I fuck her harder and faster. Loving how she watches me in the mirror. It doesn't take much more of that before she's crying my name.

She comes, breathing hard and shallow, little gasps as she presses the disc against her clit, and I fill her as her body shivers around my cock, taking me like she was made for me. I suck a little hickey on her shoulder, just far enough away from her neck that she might have bruised herself but close enough he'll have to wonder.

"Tobias," she scolds me when she realizes what I'm doing.

"All's fair, Spitfire. Besides, I want him to know where you've been. How you had to have your sweet little cunt full of me before you make it to dinner."

"You're an ass," she mumbles as I pull out of her, but her face betrays her because a satisfied grin spreads over it. She goes to reach for the disc, and I grab her wrist.

"You're wearing it at dinner. And after. I meant what I said. He doesn't touch you."

"I'm not going to go home with him."

"Good. Then there's no reason you can't wear it."

She sighs but relents on any further protest. I grin, turning her jaw toward me, so I can look at her. Taking her mouth with mine and kissing her roughly. I slide my hand between her legs and under the lace edge of her panties, dipping my fingers inside her as I kiss my way down her throat, loving the way both of us coat my fingers.

"I have to get cleaned up and change. I'm already late," she whispers but she doesn't move to stop me, letting me take my time with her.

"I know you do, but first..." I take my thumb and brush the

mixture of us over her lush lower lip, letting her suck the rest of us off it.

I smile against the side of her cheek as I whisper, "Just in case he gets any ideas about kissing you goodnight. He can taste the man you already belong to."

FORTY-FIVE

Scarlett

I'M EXCEPTIONALLY late to my date and hurrying to the back corner of Gabe's where everyone else is already sitting down having drinks and appetizers. They've taken up two booths across from each other and Nick has made space for me. I make apologies and Joss makes introductions between me and Nick before I slip in to sit beside him. Ben, Violet, Xander, Harper, Joss and Colt fall into an easy rhythm talking about the team's late season comeback and how everyone spent their abbreviated Christmas holiday.

Nick asks me questions about myself and the museum, and even asks about how working with Tobias has been. He's incredibly sweet and gives thoughtful answers as I ask him more about how he likes Seattle and how his first season here has been. We're just finishing up dinner and looking at dessert menus when Tobias and Madison appear at the end of the table.

"Oh hey! I was just bringing Mads here because she loved it so much the last time. No idea you all were going to be here."

Colt laughs and shakes his head. "What a coincidence."

"Coincidence my ass," I grumble, flashing a smile at him and his sister anyway.

Tobias's eyes rake over me and Nick, his eyebrow raising at how close we're sitting.

"Think we could join you?"

"Sure, we can make room," Nick says and then looks to me. "You mind sitting in my lap?"

I start to say no, but then I see the playful look on his face, and I nod. "Yeah. That's perfect."

"He's too fun to fuck with," he whispers as I slide into his lap.

"Agreed," I answer.

Madison slides in next to me.

"I actually need to go to the restroom anyway. Want to go with me?" Harper asks Violet, and she nods. Xander gets up to let Harper out, and Tobias uses the opportunity to slide all the way to the end of the booth, opposite Nick and me.

I feel the wave of tension as his eyes flick over all the places Nick's body and mine meet before they come up to meet mine. Tobias manages to look calm, but I know the man well enough to know what he's thinking. Xander and Madison start talking, and Tobias pretends to be interested while Nick joins in.

A moment later I feel my phone buzz, and I open it up under the table in my lap.

TOBIAS:
We need to talk.

We can talk later tonight.

It can't wait.

He glances up from his phone and looks at me, his eyes stormy and his brow creased. A quick nod of his head before I shake mine subtly. Returning my attention to Xander and Madison as she tells him about some of the work she's being doing lately and her plans to go out to Colorado.

My phone buzzes again, and I look down at it.

TOBIAS:
Fine.

I give him a false smile and then Nick asks me if I've ever been to Colorado and tells me about a guy's trip he went on there. I'm looking over my shoulder at him, leaning back against his chest when I suddenly feel the vibration between my legs. At first, I think it's my phone, sitting awkwardly against my lap, and I wrap my hand around it to press the button to stop it. But the vibration intensifies making every nerve ending I have wake up as I realize what's happening.

He wouldn't fucking dare.

My eyes snap to Tobias's as I continue to listen to Nick talking. A growing smirk on his face as his eyes taunt me, his hand under the table, and I watch his forearm flex the tiniest bit as he presses the button to intensify the vibration. I close my eyes, biting my tongue, thankful that with the way I'm sitting it isn't perfectly lined up with my clit. Otherwise I'd probably be under the table right now moaning and wanting to die of embarrassment.

I grab my cell, barely able to hold it still while I type. Not even trying to correct the many typos that follow.

S topjt it now

TOBIAS:
Come talk to me at the bar.

> It ca nn waiit.

Nah. Gotta give my girl what she wants.

> TOBIAS I am in his lap

I close my eyes and try to focus my way out of this. Think unsexy thoughts. Pretend like it's not happening. I can do it. Except then my phone buzzes again dragging me out of my concentration.

TOBIAS:
Eyes on me.

I look up at him, and the look on his face is positively devious, and hot as fuck. I can feel how wet I'm getting, and the fact that it's happening while I sit in his teammate's lap in the middle of a bar hits me hard. Another thing for the list of things I had no idea I wanted.

His lips pull into a dark smirk like he knows exactly what I'm thinking and who I'm thinking about and hits the button again. The shift is intense, and I bite down hard on my lower lip to stifle a moan. So tempted to rock forward for more of the friction. Anything to put me out of my misery.

Nick shifts underneath me, and I'm mortified when I realize the vibration is probably enough that he can either hear it or feel it while I'm sitting in his lap. He might have even heard me moan over the music and chatter in here.

"Are you... Are you vibrating?" Nick asks quietly, laughing nervously. I shift again, hoping I can shield him from it. When I suddenly realize why his laugh is nervous because I can definitely feel Nick's dick going hard against my ass.

"Yes. Sorry. It's my phone. I should..." I stop mid-sentence because as I move the vibrator presses closer to my clit and I nearly see stars. "Madison, can I get—"

I stop again, and she frowns at me, but seeing the pained look on my face, she shifts out of position and lets me up. I start walking as quickly as I possibly can back toward the bar to where the restrooms are, so I can take this thing off. Right before I strangle Tobias.

But I don't get far before an arm wraps around my waist, and I'm pulled back through a door that's behind the bar. It's dark in here, but there's just enough light that I realize it's Tobias who dragged us in here.

"Turn it off. Now." I press my palm to his chest and the firm tone of my voice makes him react quickly, the vibration coming to an abrupt halt. I take a deep breath, leaning over and resting my hands on what appears to be a desk in the middle of the room.

"Where are we?"

"Gabe's office."

I look around and it's like a sunken office behind the bar, surrounded by glass on all sides. Glasses of alcohol stacked on shelves on the other side and brightly lit behind the bar.

"Is it see-through?" I puzzle at it, trying to figure out where the hell we are.

"Two-way glass. We can see out, they can't see in. Gabe thinks he's clever."

"It is pretty clever, in like a 70's detective series kind of way."

"Or a 70's porn kind of way." Tobias smirks.

My cheeks pink as I look around and notice the couch and desk don't have a lot on them. I lift my hands off the table quickly.

"It gets cleaned every night."

"You would know?"

"He's told me because he's offered to let me use it."

"Have you?"

"Not yet." He smirks.

"Were you planning to ask Nick to join us?"

His brows knit together in irritation.

"Fuck no."

"Because I definitely know what his dick feels like now thanks to you making me vibrate and moan in his lap." I glare at him.

"Oh fuck." He laughs, his eyes bright with amusement.

"Yeah. *Oh fuck.* I'll never be able to look at him in the eyes again. Thank you for that."

"Like you didn't enjoy it."

"Well, I hope Nick enjoyed it."

"I told him what he was in for, and he chose to do it anyway. If he gets a little cock tease in the process, seems like fair punishment." He shrugs.

"You seriously warned him? I thought you were kidding."

"Just a few words on the field."

"Your sister is still out in the bar. You want to warn off her suitors you can try that old-fashioned stuff and see if she doesn't kick you in the balls for it. But you don't do that to me. What did you say to him?"

"Not much. But enough. One being that he not touch you, and he broke that rule. So..."

"Tobias! I'm going to fucking throttle you!" I reach up to grab his neck and he grabs my wrists and pins them behind my back, pushing me back on the desk in the process.

He looks over me in amusement and leans down to kiss me. I nip his lower lip. He lets go of one of my wrists and runs his thumb over the damage.

"Fuck, I think you drew blood, Spitfire."

"Good!"

He pulls out the remote, a glimmer in his eyes. "You want it again?"

"Sure. I'll go back out and sit in Nick's lap, and we can both come that way."

"He doesn't touch you again."

"Maybe I want him to touch me."

"He doesn't deserve to touch you. And there's no way he gets you off, let alone as many times as I do. You'll have to slide your hand between those pretty fucking thighs and finish yourself off anyway. We both know who you'll be thinking of then—whose name will be on your lips when you come. So I'm just doing us all a favor."

He's not entirely wrong. Nick is nice—a lot of fun and it seems like we do have some things in common. But I'm not exactly thinking about taking him home with me—now or ever. It's why I'm so mortified that we had that awkward little scene out there.

Except he'd probably be better for me than Tobias. Grounded. Self-effacing. Lacking the massive ego that Tobias has. Not nearly as rich or as famous. The kind of guy who would probably retire to a semi-normal life in the suburbs after football with all the things that come along with it.

"He's a good guy," I argue as much with myself as with anyone.

"Good for someone else." Tobias sets the remote down, and his hand slides up my inner thigh as he watches me. "You're only good for me."

"Bad for you. Bad for me. A downward spiral that makes me think you'll change for me—"

His hand slides along my jaw, his fingers anchoring in my hair, and he cuts me off with a kiss. One that feels like the end of all the others we've had before it. It's long and slow, like he's taking his time and proving a point.

"I have changed for you. I haven't even looked at another woman since you. Because you're the only one I want. I just wanted to be sure I wasn't going to be some broken has-been with no career and no future first."

"I didn't care about any of that."

"The jersey in your closet says otherwise."

"I like watching you play, but I fell in l—" I stop talking immediately when I realize what I'm about to admit. I feel my cheeks heat with embarrassment, and I sit up, pulling away from his touch. "See this is what I mean."

He smiles at me though, his eyes warm and thoughtful as he looks at me.

"I know you're in love with me. If you think I would have let you go on a date with someone else if I wasn't fucking positive about that... Nah, Spitfire. Not a fucking chance."

"That was a slip of the tongue. I don't mean I'm in love with you. I mean I love you... you're my friend. I care a lot about you and—"

He cuts me off by slipping his thumb over my lips, and the look in his eyes nearly melts me in place. Some combination of heat and adoration that I've never seen on him before.

"I love you, Scarlett. A maddening fucking amount if we're being honest. Have for a while which is why I had this made." His hand drops down to my neck and his finger slips under the necklace I'm wearing, the one he gave me for Christmas. I glance down at it and back up at him.

"I mean, I love it, but I don't understand what it has to do with anything?"

"You never noticed it's a combination of short and long beads?"

"Yes, but..." I frown and then I suddenly realize. "Morse Code?"

He smirks.

"What does it say?" I ask, feeling stupid I never noticed

before. Knowing that I've been running around with it on my neck saying god knows what.

"Westfield's."

"That is... simultaneously the sweetest and most infuriating thing."

"Pretty sure that's how this whole thing is between us in general."

We both laugh then until the air turns thick with tense silence in the wake of our confessions.

"Now what?"

"In general? I guess we gotta figure out how we make this work. That's a problem for another day though. Right now? I'm going to fuck you on this desk, while we watch everyone around us, and they have no idea what we're doing."

"They're going to wonder where I went."

"Nah, Spitfire. They're not going to wonder. I guarantee they know exactly where you are." He slides his hand under my skirt and pulls my panties off, kissing me softly in the process.

"I thought you weren't fucking me in things I wear for other men anymore."

"I'm not. You put this pair on when you soaked the ones you were going to wear for him—with me. So they're mine, just like you are." He pulls his belt off and throws it on the desk next to me.

FORTY-SIX

Tobias

I LOVE the way she looks up at me, her lashes low as she spreads her legs, and her hands go to the button and zipper on my pants. She takes me out a moment later, stroking me gently and leaning over to tease the tip of my cock with her tongue. I wish everyone could see the way she is for me. How much she fucking makes me feel like I'm the only one she's ever looked at like this.

I slide my fingers between her legs, gently teasing her as she gets wetter for me again. Still ready from the torment of the vibrator. I kiss her again, leaning her back on the desk as she lines me up with her. Her eyes shutter and she bites her lower lip as she takes me.

I fuck her slow at first, just watching the way her lashes flutter and listening to the small sounds she makes while I kiss my way up her neck. Feeling the way her fingers travel down my back until her legs wrap around me and she urges me on.

She begs for more of me, and her moans get loud enough that it's possible if the bar wasn't so raucous some of the bartenders would be glancing over their shoulders knowing someone was getting thoroughly fucked in here. I fuck her harder then, running my thumb over her clit to take her closer to the edge. I want her to fall apart with me. Feel her come around my cock like she belongs to me.

"I need you to come for me like a good fucking girl, Scarlett. I want to hear you—everyone in here to hear you belong to me. You think you can do that for me, gorgeous?"

"Yes."

"That's my girl. So perfect for me," I say as I take her deeper and she wraps her hand around the side of the desk bracing herself as she curses and moans my name. She takes me with her a few moments later, and I come harder than I have in my life, too fucking gone on her to care when I tell her how much I love her.

We stay that way for a moment, me kissing her throat and running my hands over her thighs and her with her hands in my hair and dancing down the back of my spine before I pull away from her. It takes even longer for her to stand again, and she kisses me when she does, smiling sheepishly as she pulls her underwear off the desk and brushes her dress down.

"All right. I'm going to the restroom now, I guess. Finally." She grins up at me with amusement. "I'll meet you back in there in a few."

I wrap my hand around hers and take the panties back.

"I think I earned these, and when you come back, I want you in *my* lap anyway."

A small frown mars her face. "That's kind of rude to Nick, isn't it?"

"Spitfire, you're going back to the table with my fucking DNA in you. I wouldn't worry about manners right now. But

I'll explain the situation before you come back to the table if it'll make you stress less about it." I shake my head as I put my pants and belt back together again.

"Just be nice, please. I feel rude."

"Don't worry. I'm fairly certain he was well informed of our situation before he volunteered to take you out. So he took the risk and lost. I'm sure he'll find someone else. Not nearly as fucking good as you, but too fucking bad." I grin at her, kissing her temple before she leaves me.

"All right. I'll see you back there." She opens the door and hurries out back across the hall to the restrooms and I grin as I watch her go.

A minute later Nick appears, peering into the room and smirking when he sees her panties in my hand.

"Just making sure it was that and not that she got lost or something. Didn't want to be derelict on my date duties." He smirks.

"Yeah. Sorry about that. I did warn you."

"It's all right. I don't mind playing the wingman in this particular case. I knew going in that's probably where things were headed based on what the girls told me. I was going to ask if your sister is single."

I laugh then because any man who thinks he can handle my sister definitely hasn't spent enough time around her. She would tear Nick to shreds before they could even make it to a date.

"Yeah. She's single, but I like you, so I'd recommend steering clear of her."

"Ah. Not fond of guys you know dating your sister?"

"If my sister thought I was giving out permission slips to date her, she'd kick my ass. She makes her own decisions. I'm just saying I think you're a good guy, and she's hell on fucking wheels."

"Noted. You and Scarlett together now then?" He gives me a curious look.

"Yeah. We are."

"Good. I'm happy for you. Seems like everything's coming back together again for you."

"I hope so, but let's not fucking jinx it. Okay?"

"Fair enough."

We walk back out to the table together after I finish smoothing my shirt and tucking her panties away in my pocket. We get knowing glances from several of our friends.

"No blood or broken bones, I'm impressed." Colt gives me an amused once over.

"Yeah. I'm not Xander. I can settle things without any of my teammates needing an ER." I smirk at my friend.

"Yeah well, Jones isn't half the guy Harris is."

"I also know how to gracefully take a loss," Harris pipes in.

Scarlett appears then, returning from the restroom and all eyes turn to her as her cheeks heat. She straightens her spine under the weight of their gazes though and grins at Joss.

"What? A girl can't get railed in a bar without everyone staring?" she huffs and then sits down in my lap as Joss reaches over to high-five her.

FORTY-SEVEN

Tobias

THE ROAR of the crowd is deafening tonight, and it feels good to be back on the sidelines even if I can't play. Having my black and teal back on, being with the guys while we play this last season game feels right. I pace the sidelines for the thirtieth time though as the game seesaws back and forth on the board. First we're ahead, then the other team. Back and forth a nauseating amount as we approach the last quarter.

Ben comes off the field with Colt after an unsuccessful drive, both of them looking demotivated.

"Hey. You guys are doing good. Don't let me see those faces." I pat Ben on the shoulder, and he gives me a look while he tries to catch his breath.

"Fucking need Jones to stay on his feet, so I've got fucking time to throw." Colt glances down at his linemen as they rehydrate, and the defense prepares to take the field.

"That would be a fucking plus, but you got this either way.

Just keep moving and watch your right side. That's where they keep coming for you. They've realized you've got a bit of a blind spot there, so you've gotta keep them guessing."

"Yeah." Colt tosses his helmet on the pin behind the bench, staring out at the field as we punt the ball. "We need fucking points though."

"You'll get them. Just wait for Xander and the guys to clear their offense off the field, and then go for it. You've got this."

BY THE END of the fourth quarter though, the game is still tied, and it stays that way well into overtime. The exhaustion and frustration is showing on everyone's face—including mine. Moments like these are the hardest to watch. I want to be suited up and subbed in. Give them a fresh set of legs and perspective on the field when they need it, but I haven't been cleared to play yet. Another week at most, I hope. But that doesn't do anything to solve today's problem.

We sit and watch the offense start to get penetration on our defense, moving downfield more efficiently than they have the last several drives, and I feel the familiar sense of nerves in my stomach. Even Colt's attention is rapt as he worries at how close they're getting to field goal territory.

There's another throw and the wide receiver gets a few yards, but it's still not quite enough to justify the kicking team coming on yet. I watch their quarterback huddle his guys again, shouting the plan at them. I turn around to the crowd, throwing my arms up and signaling for them to get loud.

Luckily, they see me and react, stomping, jeering, and loud screams echoing off the walls and causing the stadium to be deafening. I grin as I watch the quarterback put his hands over his helmet, desperately trying to hear the calls and failing on the next play. He points wildly and then throws his hands up in frustration.

I throw my hands up again, watching as the scoreboard lights up with "GET LOUD SEATTLE." This is our biggest advantage in moments like these, the volume of our fans and the acoustics of the stadium making it damn near impossible for visiting teams to hear on the field. It pays off beautifully when there's a false start on the next play, and the team has to back up yards as a result.

I turn around to the seats again, clapping and throwing my fist in the air to cheer them on. They get loud again as he sets up for the next play. The quarterback trying to scream at his guys over the din in the stadium. They line up this time without a false start though and I frown, watching him drop back in the pocket.

But this time Xander is on it, charging through their offensive line and getting his hand on the ball just as their quarterback throws. It tips the ball, and it tumbles end over end through the air. It feels like we're all collectively holding our breath until it lands in the hands of a Phantom player—Jones to be exact. He grabs it and falls on it, doing his best just to maintain possession, and I can't blame him for that.

The crowd erupts now that we've managed to take our ball back, and I slap Colt on the back.

"You're turn my guy. You fucking got this."

"I got this," he repeats as he grabs his helmet.

"Any thoughts on how you want to do this?" Ben sidles up beside him.

"You should do a flea flicker. Right off the bat. Just hit them out of nowhere with a special play. Their guys will never see it coming. They'll assume you want to try the steady march. It's up to coach, but if he lets you call it—think about it, yeah?" I look at him, and he nods his support for the idea.

. . .

THE TIME it takes them to get back on the field is interminable. The referees checking and rechecking the footage to confirm that overturned ball. I start pacing again while I watch the clock ticking down, and Colton and the rest of our guys get out on the field. This moment right here is one of the most frustrating of my career because all I want to do is be on the field to help make the play happen.

With very little time on the clock, Colton calls the flea flicker play and the ball gets snapped. He launches the ball, and Ben for his part is wide fucking open in the end zone. The touchdown gets called, and the stadium goes fucking wild.

I run onto the field with the rest of the guys to celebrate, slapping Colt on the ass.

"That's my fucking quarterback!"

"Good call. You got a coaching job in your future." He laughs, and Ben and I run up and slap each other on the back.

"Fucking amazing play, Lawton."

"We're going to the fucking playoffs!"

Fireworks go off on one side of the stadium just as he says it like it was perfectly timed, and the lights flash teal and white. I just wish Scarlett was here to see it in person, but I know she's just as happy as I am watching it on TV with her dad at the bar. Which is the next place I'm going to celebrate, and hopefully the guys will come too. All of us too fucking excited to have the chance to make our championship run.

FORTY-EIGHT

Scarlett

I'M LEANING against the bar, watching the screens above it flash with stats about their win tonight. I haven't gotten a text from him yet, but I know he's busy with after-game celebrations and interviews. I'm sure that even though he didn't get to play that he's insanely happy he was on the sidelines for their win.

Harper and Joss have both texted me copious amounts of photos from the family box to make me feel like I'm there with them while I celebrate my dad's birthday with family and his friends. I'm still trying to figure out how to explain to him that I'm dating Westfield. I imagine it's going to give him a heart attack for about five different reasons, and I'm not sure what emotion he's going to land on when that's over.

"Fuck, Spitfire. I love seeing my name on your back." His hand wraps around my waist and he kisses the side of my cheek as he pulls me against him, and it takes me a second to realize I'm not daydreaming.

"Tobias!" I turn around and wrap my arms around him, kissing him for real as he tugs me in closer for a hug. "Congrats on your win. So excited you guys are going to the playoffs!"

"Well, thank you, but I didn't do much. It's these guys you want to congratulate." Tobias nods over his shoulder, and I see Xander and Colt there, standing with Joss and Harper.

"Oh my god," I mumble. "You guys are gonna cause a scene here. This is a diehard Phantom bar."

"I know. But I wanted to see you, and if you won't come to the stadium, I gotta come to you. They came so we can surprise your dad. I hope that's okay. I thought he might like it."

"Like it? He's gonna die, Tobias. You're going to kill him on his 60th birthday." I laugh and then I hurry over to congratulate the rest of the guys on their win.

"Ben and Violet are coming shortly. They went to get dinner with Mac and Waylon first. They gotta get home with the kiddo, so they didn't want to come all the way out here."

"Oh, of course. They don't have to come all the way out here either." I shake my head. "Really. It's thoughtful of them but tell them they don't have to."

"It's kind of on their way. But I'll let them know you don't want them." He smirks and I poke him gently in the side.

The bartender returns with my pitchers of beer, and I go to grab the cash I tucked in my pocket, but Tobias waves me off.

"Can you start a tab for me? Put those on it and whatever all these guys want?"

The bartender's eyes go wide. "Holy fuck, man. Good fucking game. Oh my god. All of you?"

"Yeah. Try to keep it low key though? We're here for a family party."

"Sure. Sure. Of course. And no tab. It's on the house."

"You sure? I'm happy to pay."

"Yeah, this bar exists because of you guys, so I think we're good. I'm the owner's son, Danny. Nice to meet you." He holds out his hand, and Tobias shakes it.

"Well thanks, man."

"Can't wait to see you on the field again. Hopefully next week?"

"We'll see." Tobias smiles, and I hug him again as he wraps an arm around me.

"All right. Give me your orders, and we'll get them going. Let us know if you need food too."

The guys all put their orders in, and Joss and Harper go off to find a table near where my dad's party is happening. Which reminds me, I have to tell Tobias I haven't told him yet.

"One thing," I say as we start to gather our drinks and the pitchers I ordered.

"What's that?"

"I haven't told my dad yet. Honestly, I thought he would have a heart attack, so I just was waiting until after his birthday and stuff. Plus I wasn't sure if he'd believe me."

"Oh. Do you not want him to know?" There's a distinct change in Tobias's tone.

"No. No. It's not that. I just have no idea how he'll react, and I guess if we're giving him a heart attack already then might as well see it through." I grin at him.

"If you don't want to tell him for a while, we don't have to. I get that my recent history isn't the best."

"Um, I absolutely want to brag to my dad and all of his friends that I'm dating his favorite player. I also want to see my cousin Becky have a meltdown that you're dating someone and it's me. Priceless family memories right there."

"All right. As long as you're sure. I don't want to create tension on his birthday."

"Nope. But just... prepare yourself. Because once they realize you're here, this place is going to erupt."

When we get close, I have Tobias hang back with the rest of our friends and go to talk to my dad.

"Dad!" I yell over the TVs and the chatter, but he doesn't hear me at first. I have to cup my hands around my mouth and bellow to get his attention. His friends hear me too and part down the middle, so I can walk up to him.

"What's up, Scar?" He looks at me.

"Well first, here's your beer refills. Try to share and not down one all yourself."

"Thanks, dear. Appreciate it. What's second?" He looks at me skeptically.

"I have a surprise for you. My boyfriend came tonight, and I want to introduce you."

His friends howl and holler at my announcement.

"On his birthday? You're a cold one." One of his friends laughs.

"He'll like this one. Trust me."

"All right. Let's see him. Honestly, I feel sorry for the boy, Scar. All us guys here. Trial by fire."

"He can handle it." I smile, and then motion for Tobias to come over.

I can tell on my dad's face the second he sees Tobias. His eyes go wild, and his face goes pale and then bright red. I hear his friends cursing under their breath, and I just watch amused as it all unfolds.

"This... How the hell, Scar... this is. Wow."

"Nice to meet you, sir." Tobias holds out his hand, and my dad takes it, shaking it absently as he tries to make sense of it.

"Jamie Edgar. My daughter here's a comedian. Telling me you're her boyfriend, although I can't figure how she got you here otherwise."

"Oh, that's true. We've been friends for a while."

"I mean, I knew she had some friends who knew guys on the team, but... Scar. Don't joke on an old man's birthday now."

"Yes, Dad. We've been friends. I helped him with some stuff while he was recovering and then we ended up dating," I explain because I'm gonna skip right over the part where we almost had a sex tape go viral. That *would* give him a heart attack.

"I adore your daughter. She's honestly a good part of the reason I'm even back on the field at all. If I play next week, it's because of her."

"And she's throwing me parties like this. Gotta be proud of you, Scar." My dad grins at me, and I give him a hug.

"There's more though." I grin at him.

Tobias waves Xander and Colt over, and now my dad is ready to keel over.

"Scarlett's told us all what a huge fan you are. So when she said she couldn't make the game because it was your birthday, we thought we'd stop by." Colt grins and holds his hand out for my dad.

I smile at all of them and kiss Tobias on the cheek. "I'm going to go and talk to the girls while you guys talk football for a bit. Just let me know when you need a rescue."

"Sounds like a plan. And Scar, huh? That what your friends and family call you?"

"Yeah. We tried Lettie for a while, and I didn't like that. Scar sounded more badass when I was a teen, you know? Then it kind of stuck."

"I like it. Might have to try it out sometime. All right. Go have fun with the girls while I dazzle your dad with my football knowledge." He kisses my forehead and lets me go.

As I walk away my stomach somersaults. I'm falling incredibly hard for him. The kind that's for good and instead of being scared, I think I *like* it.

FORTY-NINE

Tobias

BY A STROKE OF LATE-SEASON LUCK, the Wild Card game is still at home despite our record, and we have the chance to keep our playoff dreams alive with a home crowd. Plus I get to fucking play again this season and that's all that fucking matters right now to me. That and the fact that Scarlett is here in the stands along with the rest of the wives and girlfriends to support me.

"You ready for this?" Ben grins at me.

"Fuck yeah, I am."

"It's gonna be a good one. Especially having you back on the field."

"Yes. So happy to have you back." Colt slaps me on the shoulder and smiles.

Xander grins at me from across the room, and I roll my shoulders.

"Fucking can't wait to put points up on the board. We're

going all the way, guys. We have to. Who knows how many more fucking seasons we get with all of us on the same team at once."

I feel the churn in my gut because I know Xander is up for a contract extension, and I will be soon after. Colt and Ben make good money, but Colt's rookie contract will be up, and then he'll have to decide where he wants to be. These guys, this team, we deserve to win it—as a fucking family. Everyone here has worked so damn hard to be where we are, and a few fuck-ups, including the ones I'm responsible for, can't stop us.

"Well, we've gotta take down a certain someone in that last game." Xander smirks, as Ben and Colt look at him confused.

"Certain someone?" Colt looks between us.

"Coach Westfield," I grit out.

"Use the anger though." Xander gives me a pointed look.

"Oh yeah. They get a fucking bye this week, don't they?" Ben looks at me.

"Of course. He'd accept nothing less." I shake my head.

"I'm glad he's not our coach. Sure, he fucking wins but at what cost? Did you see what he did to his quarterback before?" Ben shakes his head.

"Imagine being raised by him," Xander mutters, and I shoot him a look. I don't want any fucking pity or bonuses from my last name.

"Yeah." Colt looks at me, more understanding than pity in his eyes. "No one's winning dad of the year around here, but yours is extra fucked."

"I appreciate that Joss is wearing off on your vocabulary." I grin at Colt, too happy to change the subject.

"Speaking of... They're planning their big final opening gala to coincide with the museum reopening in a little over a month. Everyone better mark their calendars, get their tuxes, etc. because I'm not letting her down when it comes to having a celebrity turnout," Colt says loud enough for most of the locker room to hear and several of the guys grunt their ascension.

"The museum reopens in a month?" I ask, and Xander and the rest of the guys all look at me surprised.

"I figured you of all people would know that."

"Oh, yeah. I guess I didn't realize it was that soon though. Living in my bubble at home, losing track of days and all."

"Yeah well. Just don't lose track of the ball, all right? It's the brown thing flying in the air toward you." Waylon grins at me and slaps me on the back as he heads toward the tunnel.

"Yeah. Yeah. I got this." I grin back at him.

WE'RE STILL CELEBRATING our win and running around the field to take photos with fans when one of the reporters comes up to me. I steel myself for the inevitable onslaught of negative questions. My publicist has prepared me for them. How to answer about the sex tape and potential legal avenues I am pursuing. How to talk about the accident as a learning moment for me. How I planned to move forward.

"All right, Tobias, you were obviously a huge part of the game tonight and your team's win. How did it feel to be back on the field?"

"Fantastic. Never felt better in my life."

"Now we saw that you had something interesting going on with your eye black tonight. A smart guy up in the box said he thinks it's Morse Code and translated it for us as saying 'scar'. Is that a reference to your recent off-field injuries?"

"Well given the league's opinions, I assure you I'd never be stupid enough to try putting a message on my face. So that's probably just a coincidence. But you saying Scar, reminds me of Scarlett—my girlfriend. She was critical to my recovery off the field. It was a long road to get back here physically and mentally and there's no way I could have done it without her. So it was important to me to have her here tonight."

"Well, that will have all the women swooning and then crying into their beers tonight to hear you're taken. But I'm sure all Phantom fans would also want to give her a huge thank you given that pivotal play in the last minutes of the game, just before Lawton scored the winning touchdown. Can you tell us more about how you and Colt prepared in the short time you had before the playoffs?"

I give her some of the soundbites she wants for the game and thank her for the interview before I hurry off back to the tunnel. I'm thrilled to be back on the field tonight, but I'm just as excited to celebrate our win with the team and with my girl.

FIFTY

Scarlett

AFTER THE GAME, we all gather around to wait for the guys, and I can't help but feel a little excited at the fact I'm included with the rest of the wives and girlfriends. Not to mention he loudly told the whole world about us in his end-of-game interview which had practically melted me on the spot.

When he starts walking toward me, I can't help the stupid grin that erupts, and he runs toward me, picking me up and spinning me around.

"Fuck, you look cute in that jersey. I'm glad you kept it all these years."

"I know, but now I'm worried about the signature disappearing in the wash." I grit my teeth in concern.

"Uhh, Spitfire. I can sign you a new one. As many as you want." He kisses me, and I'm lost in it for a moment before I respond.

"But it's not the same. I need the core memories associated with this one."

"Yeah, I think we could do without those." He laughs.

"You were amazing tonight. It was so good to see you playing again." I wrap my arms around his neck and pull him tight.

"Yeah? Not too disappointing?"

"Not at all. Just lots and lots of pride over how amazing you are and how far you've come in these past weeks."

"Yeah well, a lot of that is thanks to you, you know? I tell anyone who'll fucking listen."

"I know. I heard your interview on the live after the game." I offer up a shy grin because I feel special, but I also don't want to take it for granted.

"Good. Cause you're my fucking muse out on that field right now. I just want to make you proud and see how all your hard work and support paid off."

His words twist my heart. "Okay but let's not take away from everything you did."

"Jesus Christ. Is this what we sound like?" Joss turns to Colt.

"Afraid so." Colt grins and pulls her close to kiss her on the tip of her nose.

"Hey. Don't mess with their thing." Harper eyes Joss. "I've been low-key shipping these two for months now, and I need this season to play out in all its mushy glory."

"I don't think there's much chance of that not happening." Joss smirks as she looks us over.

"Yeah, this one is mine for good now. She's stuck." Tobias pulls me close.

"So you all coming over to my house then? We can order in and celebrate?" Colt yells out to the crowd of players who are huddled around the parking garage entrance.

There's a whole chorus of positive responses, and we start heading to Tobias's car. He loads up his stuff in the back, and I hop in the passenger seat, grinning as he waves at fans gathered to cheer him on when we leave the stadium.

A LITTLE BIT LATER, we're at Colt's place, and I'm perched on his lap having a drink while he scrolls social media on his phone with his arm around my waist. I watch the feed as he scrolls. He's been tagged in a million videos and comments, and he responds to some of them—liking and thanking people for their support.

At least until there's a clip of his father. He pauses on it, his finger hesitating over the scroll bar as he stares at it. The sound is off, but the captions tell the story.

"I think he did as well as he can at his age with that injury. Always happy to see my boys on the field. I just hope he can stay there."

He flicks the feed forward before the reporter can ask any follow-up questions, and I feel the shift of his body underneath me. I lean back against his chest, kissing the side of his neck before I whisper.

"He's scared of having to face you guys. Scared of finding out his son is better than he ever was. Ignore it because everyone else is proud of you." I kiss the side of his jaw as he scrolls again. "Look!" I point to a comment that talks about how they normally hate him, but they can't deny he was good today and they're happy to see him playing again. "Even your haters. That's how you know your dad just wants to make it personal."

Tobias glances over at me, his eyes going soft with a small smile that comes and goes quickly before he kisses me back.

"Thanks, Spitfire. I appreciate you saying that."

"I'm not just saying it. It's true. I'd punch him in the nuts myself if I could."

Tobias laughs at that and shakes his head. "Remind me to never piss you off."

"Too late. You lived to tell the tale though because you're too pretty for your own good."

"Yeah?" He grins, tucking his phone away before his hands slip down my thighs.

"Yeah."

"What I need right now is to find out if Colt has a library."

"I don't think so." I frown at him, and Tobias raises an eyebrow at me. "Oh! Oh..." I realize what he's implying.

"I think I deserve a little payback."

I laugh and shake my head. "I don't think he has a sacred library like you do though. So that might be tough."

"Mmm. We'll just have to pick a spot." Tobias jumps up and puts me on my feet in the process.

"Bathroom?" I whisper the question as I follow him, glancing around to make sure no one is following our retreat from the main room.

"It's an option." His fingers thread through mine as we walk down a hall and up a set of steps to the second floor. "But I think I like this one better."

It's a loft. There's no door and only a partial wall that obscures the room from the lower level.

"This feels very... exposed."

"That's the point." He grins at me, his eyes searching my face for a moment. "If you're up for it."

I glance around and then back at him. "How?"

He grins, leaning down to kiss me, first on the lips and then up the side of my jaw until he reaches my ear.

"I sit on the couch. You take those panties off and ride me. Skirt you've got on should give us some cover."

"As long as we're not too loud."

"Hmm." He kisses his way down my throat as he walks backward. "I like hearing you though. You'll have to keep your lips to my ear then. Can't live without all those sounds you make for me."

"Okay." I nod just as we reach the couch. I reach down and slip out of my underwear, handing them to him, and he tucks them into his back pocket for safekeeping. I climb into his lap, straddling it while he pulls himself out.

The party downstairs is loud, but I can still hear strains of conversations drifting up. The music and the sound of glasses clinking with ice follow up behind it. I peer down and take a breath when I realize how close they all are.

His hand slides under my skirt and his fingers brush over me, making me close my eyes when he starts to tease my clit with the slightest pressure. I look down at him, and he grins.

"Fuck, you're so pretty like this. Barely need me to touch you before you're wet for me."

"Watching you today helped."

"Did it?"

"Yes. I was thinking about how much I wanted you the whole time."

"Not about how you want to strangle me?" He grins.

"No. But I did think about your hands a lot." I smirk at him, my hand slipping between us so I can stroke him. His eyes shutter.

"Yeah? I bet you did. I know how much you love them." His free hand wraps around the side of my neck and presses down. "Put me inside. Let me fill that cunt for you."

I guide him inside me, taking a moment to adjust to how full he feels, and then I start to roll my hips. I kiss my way up his throat, and his fingers slide up my neck, threading into the back of my hair, getting twisted in the strands. He continues to softly massage my clit while I ride him.

"Fuck..." he groans. "Come closer. I want to hear your little gasps when you're full of me." His fingers tighten in my hair as I kiss my way up his neck, gently running my tongue just beneath his ear. He starts to move under me, countering my downstrokes until we hit a perfect rhythm. My knees ache a little, and I can feel a sheen of sweat breaking out on my chest. The sound of laughter wrapping around us as it drifts upstairs.

"This feels dirty. With them right there."

"Because it is. But you're a good girl for doing it. For giving me what I need after a long day. Fuck, Scarlett. You take me so fucking well like this. You've already got me close."

I spread my legs a little wider, taking him a little deeper, and he uses rougher strokes on my clit. I feel the edge of the orgasm bloom my nerves, and I press my lips to his ear as I feel it start to take me over the edge.

"Fuck. I love your cock. And your hands. You're so fucking good at that." I wrap my arms around his shoulders, and I can feel the warmth of him as he groans his own release.

We stay like this for a minute, me collapsed against his chest and him holding me tight until we hear footsteps.

"Fuck." I give him a panicked look.

"Just kiss me." He tugs on my hair and pulls my lips to his, kissing me roughly.

"Okay, lovebirds. Colt just bought that couch, and he'll murder you." Joss grins from the hall.

"Yeah, I fucking will," he grunts, glancing at us and then looking away like he's been scandalized.

"Like I'll murder him if he ever did anything in my library?" Tobias grunts as I dig my fingernails into his neck.

Colt and Tobias exchange looks then before Colt grabs the belt loop in Joss's pants and drags her along.

"All right. Let's let them have their little make-out session," he grumbles and then disappears down the hall.

"Great," I mutter.

"Whatever. They're sneaking off to fuck themselves. They're probably just pissed we took their spot."

"He just bought this couch," I repeat, smirking.

"Yeah, so get up carefully." He laughs.

I lean forward and kiss him one last time before getting up slowly, cleaning up, and heading back to the party. He squeezes my ass as we walk down the stairs, leaning forward to kiss me when I pause to give him a pretend-annoyed look.

"Can't help it. You look gorgeous when you're well fucked. Hard to keep my hands to myself."

I shake my head and kiss him, threading my fingers through his before we join the crowd.

FIFTY-ONE

Tobias

AFTER THE WILD Card game we go on to win our divisional round and our conference round, playing the same kind of consistent ball we've been playing all year when an injury isn't sidelining us. But the downside is I've barely been able to see Scarlett. We've been on the road, doing interviews, setting up press sessions with our social media team, doing commercials, and all the other shit that hits a fever pitch when your team is doing this well.

That's doubled now that we're in the championship game and we had to travel out to Vegas a week early to set up for all of the events, press, and training going on this week ahead of the big game on Sunday. But Easton and I were able to get a block of tickets between the two of us and he, Wren, Madison, Scarlett, and Scarlett's dad are all coming to the game and arriving today. We've got a dinner planned for this evening for everyone and, as much as I'm excited for the game this weekend, I'm almost as excited for dinner tonight. Getting to see Scarlett, having our families together at dinner, and spending time with all of them is what I need right now to help settle my nerves and remind me there's ground under my feet.

Because the thing I hoped for and dreaded in equal measure is coming this weekend. We're playing my dad's team for the trophy and the right to call ourselves the best team in the league. The press has been near fever pitch at the implication of our family being pitted against each other. They've seen brothers play, but a father-and-son faceoff is a new one. The questions and theories about how the game will go, what our family will wear to the game, and how it'll all go down, depending on which one of us ends up on top have been endless.

Meanwhile, my dad and I have barely spoken. In part because it seems dirty to cross lines right now, but more seriously because I know he'll have nothing but vitriol for me. Where most families would probably encourage and support each other, happy to see either win... he only cares about having the win for himself. His shithead kid besting him in a year when I've been a royal fuckup? It's likely to destroy his ego. One that's even more massive than mine. So we've kept to ourselves, and I've kept his name out of my mouth even when I talk with my siblings. I'm not about to give him any power over me at the most important part of my career.

THAT NIGHT at a private dinner tucked away in one of the restaurants perched high up in a hotel away from the prying eyes of the press and with a stunning view of the Strip I'd rather not have marred by depressing conversation, the subject of our family rivalry still comes up.

"Well, you don't have to worry about what colors I'll be

wearing. You already know." Easton gives me a look, one only another football-playing son of the asshole could give.

"Me too." Wren smiles at me.

"And of course me. That bastard thinks he can say shit like he did to the reporters and not suffer consequences. It's just poor form on his part. He needs his own PR person if he's going to act like that." Madison shakes her head.

"Like he would listen to them. He always thinks he knows better—no matter who the other person in the room is or their expertise."

"I could get him to listen. I just don't think he's worth the fight." Madison sits back in her seat.

"I'd like to see that death match." Easton laughs.

"You know I could, and I could get Mom on our side too," Madison argues.

"Don't involve Mom. She has to live with him every day already." I shake my head.

"Well, I for one don't think your old man knows what he's talking about when it comes to you. I might not be a pro ball coach, but I've watched a hell of a lot of football, and you're the best wide receiver I've ever seen. Your routes, your speed... Hell, just your intuition. Don't let him tell you otherwise," Scarlett's dad pipes in and everyone gets quiet and exchanges looks.

"Dad, I think it's probably a family discussion here. We're just supposed to eat our food and politely pretend we're not hearing it." Scarlett looks at him and then back at me, giving me a sheepish shrug.

"You guys are family as far as I'm concerned." I kiss the top of her head before I look at her dad. "And thank you. Truly. It means a lot to hear you say that. Scarlett's told me about your coaching career in high school, and it's impressive. Those are formative years for players. Takes someone with a lot more guts, stamina, and patience than someone like my dad could ever have. He gets guys fully formed from men like you and then claims he's responsible for all their talent. Like their high school and college coaches didn't exist. It's bullshit. So hearing it from you... Thank you."

Her dad's cheeks get a little pink as he grins at me and nods, and Scarlett runs her fingers over my knee, her eyes saying everything for her. When I look up, Madison is grinning ear to ear and looking at Wren with a little smirk on her face. Wren grins at me and takes a sip of her drink.

"Oh fuck. They're conspiring again." East grunts and then takes a sip of his beer.

"It's what sisters do." Madison grins and clinks her glass against Wren's before settling back again.

"Just keep anything conspiratorial until after Sunday, okay? My nerves are already on edge." I raise a brow at them.

"Of course, *brother*." Madison gives me an innocent look for all of two seconds before it morphs into devious territory.

FIFTY-TWO

Scarlett

IT FEELS ABSOLUTELY wild to have seats at this game. I'd almost told Tobias no when he offered them just because I knew how expensive they'd be and how many people would want them, but watching my dad cozy up and chat sports with Easton while we wait for Tobias to take to the field is well worth it. And to be in the box with the rest of the girls feels like a dream come true. I watch as Wren, Mackenzie, and their friend Olivia have Joss take a picture of them together with the field in the background. Apparently, Olivia's husband, Liam, is also on the coaching staff for the Chicago Blaze, the team playing the Phantom tonight, and the same team that Tobias and Easton's father coaches.

Harper walks up and leans her head on my shoulder.

"So if I'd bet you a year ago that the two of us would be *here* in a suite... would you have taken it?"

"Hell no. Well, maybe you. I could have seen you here with

your asshole ex. But I have no idea how I would have ended up here."

"And the two of us dating best friends?"

"I mean, I couldn't be the only one with the hot football player boyfriend at our museum reopening."

"Clearly the only reason you're in love with Tobias."

"Obviously. It's all a ruse for the arm candy." I grin.

"So I'm not the only one? Thank God." Joss laughs.

"I seriously need them to win tonight though." Violet joins us as we stare down at the pre-game festivities on the field.

"Agreed." Harper nods.

"Of course they're going to win—" Joss starts, and Madison slaps a hand over her mouth.

"No!" Madison shakes her head. "Absolutely do not say anything like that. It's bad."

"Very superstitious." Joss raises a brow at her when she removes her hand.

"You would be too if you grew up with those three around all the time. Rewearing stinky clothes, everything having to be in a certain order, repeating cheers backward, sitting in the same spot on the couch before the game every time—you name it, one of them did it."

"Oh look we're on the TV." Wren points out.

"Be casual!" Joss jokes, acting like she's about to flip it off.

"Joss, we all know your feelings about the sports reporters but let's maybe not get thrown out of this gorgeous suite. Okay? Okay." Violet wraps her arms around her and hugs her.

Wren turns up the volume on the TV so we can hear what they're saying about us all.

"As you can see, the Westfield family clearly has a favorite in tonight's game, and it's not Coach Westfield. They're all wearing Phantom jerseys or colors in that box save for one person," reporter one says as the screen zooms in on Easton and then Madison in the frame.

"Although their mother is in her own seats with the team owner, and she is very definitely in Chicago Blaze colors" the second reporter adds.

"Apparently, it's that kind of night. We might see some family bloodshed depending on who wins."

"Well, we all know Tobias Westfield is a fan favorite. Especially after his recovery from that awful motorcycle accident that happened mid-season." The screen flashes an image that was taken that night, and I cringe a little seeing it again.

Sometimes it's hard to believe Tobias made it out alive at all given that he wasn't wearing a helmet. The fact that he came out with road rash and a hip fracture to what could have been his death isn't lost on me, or him most days. And I'm glad that after his reckoning with everything he's doing so much better.

But I also can't help but feel like the rest of the girls. Tonight is a must-win game. Not just for the guys as a team and a family, but for guys like Tobias and Xander who have fathers to prove wrong and legacies that deserve championships written next to them rather than asterisks.

WHICH IS why when we're deep in the fourth quarter, three points down with time dwindling fast I'm up on my feet with the rest of the girls, holding Harper's hand as we watch another play blown dead with no gain.

"Oh my god. My heart can't take this!" Joss grouches.

"Get used to it." Violet shakes her head.

"They've got this. It's gonna be fine." Wren looks over at us from where she, Mackenzie, and Olivia stand. "Sorry, Liv. You knew you were in the viper's den when you came up here."

"It's fine. I want Liam to be happy but hard not to root for the guys too." Olivia's brow creases with her concern and divided loyalties.

They set up for another play and one half of the crowd quiets while the other half ratchets up their screaming. Colt steps back in the pocket, looking deep while Ben and Tobias take off from the line. He launches the ball, a perfect throw, before he dodges a lineman who was inches away from sacking him. I squeeze Harper's hand while we watch the ball sail down the field, holding our breath and praying one of the guys is open.

I dig my teeth into my lower lip as I see Tobias's number flash across the field and the ball come down in his direction just as he's about to be hit. He jumps extending his hand and grabbing the ball, holding it up as he and the other player tumble to the ground in a mass of limbs, helmets, and pads. But they're well inside the end zone and the crowd goes wild as the refs hold up their hands to signal a touchdown.

We all lose our minds, screaming and hugging each other. I hear my dad holler and watch as he and Easton high-five before Wren jumps into Easton's arms. Mackenzie jumps up and down and Olivia is a good sport about it all, high-fiving her as she grins at the rest of us.

"Oh my god!" Harper yells and hugs me tight, Violet and Joss piling on a second later.

"I'm so fucking proud of him!" Tears start to come to my eyes, and my heart swells. I watch on the screen as the guys do their post-touchdown celebration, grinning at how happy he looks as he makes his way to the sideline. His coach slaps him on the ass looking like he just won the lottery.

It takes a minute for us all to calm down and catch our breaths. The kick is good, thanks to Nick and Gabe, and we do another cheer for them.

That's when we see the time on the clock. Thirty seconds

still left. The Blaze's QB is famous for two things: his plays under pressure and his ability to throw deep. Olivia's husband, Coach Montgomery, trained him well. What's worse is Coach Westfield is infamous for his clock management, and he has two timeouts still on his side. Which means thirty seconds is an eternity for the Blaze to put points up. One touchdown would mean it's over for us, and we've all just exchanged knowing looks.

FIFTY-THREE

Tobias

COLT, Ben, Waylon, and I all watch nervously on the sidelines while some of the other guys ready the Gatorade. We've burned the time down to twelve seconds, making them fight hard for every inch they've gotten and they're still only at midfield.

Our defense just has to hold them here on this next play. Everyone's up on the line and the ball snaps. I'm counting to ten to keep calm while I watch Xander come off the line with perfect timing. He dodges one lineman and then another and takes five more steps that feel like they take five more minutes.

His hand collides with the quarterback's and the ball goes sailing in the wrong direction. He and two of the other defense guys chase after it, another guy tipping it, and Xander catches it just as they all land in a pile as the game clock hits zeroes.

It takes a moment, more than that really, for me to recognize we've done the thing our team hasn't done in decades—

we've won the whole fucking thing. Waylon slaps me on the back.

"We fucking did it!" His blue eyes light up, and he high-fives Ben before he slaps me on the ass, and we all start running for the center of the field where Xander's holding up the ball while half the defense lifts him up into the air.

I see Gatorade go flying out of the corner of my eye, dousing our head coach and several other members of the coaching staff who didn't flee in time. Confetti falls from the sky, the lights go wild, and the crowd is in a full-on roar while the music hits a crescendo. By the time I get to Xander his feet are back on the ground and there are tears in his eyes.

It makes me fucking cry in response, and we hug each other.

"We fucking did it, brother." He yells into my ear, trying to shout over the noise.

"You fucking did it!"

"We both fucking did it. How much is that going to piss them off?" Xander smirks at me.

"How fucking happy is that gonna make everyone else?" I laugh.

"Damn fucking straight." He holds up the ball and our guys go wild again.

Both teams pour out onto the field, losing their minds and congratulating and handing out condolences in order. It seems impossible that this is real life, and I glance up at the stands where I know our girls and our family are looking down at us. I wave and press my hand to my heart, hoping they see and I'm anxious to get through all the post-game bureaucracy, so we can spend time celebrating with friends, family, and fans after the game. Get back to the locker room, so we have a moment together as a team, as a family, to reflect on what we've done.

But bile surges in my throat when I see my father finishing

his conversation with my coach, and his eyes turn on me. I was hoping he'd just ignore me, but apparently, the man can't let an opportunity to grandstand in front of the cameras go.

He grabs my hand and pulls me close, throwing one arm around me like a half-hug before he leans in covering his mouth to speak.

"Well for once in your life, you did something right."

I have a million things I want to say in return. Things I would have said—would have shouted—in the past. But none of it's worth wasting on him. Not on this night or any other. Not when I have my siblings and my own family, the one that started on this team and keeps growing.

The best revenge on him is the silence anyway—not giving him the reaction he wants and just basking in the glow of his defeat.

So instead, I just smile at him, grinning wide, and then I walk away. Feeling like I can breathe again the second he's out of my immediate presence. Colt tackles me a second later as he spins off to his side after answering some reporter questions.

"You fucking won it for us, every bit as much as Xander did. You know that right?"

"We did. How does it feel to be 26 years old with a championship ring?"

"Like I see a lot more in our future." He grins.

AFTER WE FINISH MAKING the rounds in the stadium, we all meet back in the locker room. Our coach gives a speech about how far we've all come this year and how much more we can do as a team if we keep up this spirit. He thanks us all for everything we've done, giving mini speeches for all the different players who contributed on the field tonight, and then turns to me.

"And Tobias. You had a rough fucking year, my guy, but you fucking pulled it out and showed up for us when we needed you most. We couldn't have done this without you, and you deserve every single moment of recognition you're going to get in the coming days. Don't let anyone let you fucking forget that or diminish that for you."

Several of the guys holler out their support, and it takes me a moment, my chest tight and my eyes heavy with the weight of would-be tears as I nod my thanks for his words.

"Now, go out there and fucking party tonight in this city. Just make sure it's the good kind of trouble. You hear me?" Our coach smiles at us and then we break to go our own ways.

EAST, Wren, Madison, and Scarlett are all waiting for me and pile into a massive hug around me the second they see me. It's hard not to feel like crying again, seeing them all in their Phantom gear, looking at me like I'm a rockstar.

"So fucking proud of you, bro." East nods at me.

"Yes. Hard to believe you were coming off an injury." Wren gives me a soft smile.

"You kicked ass." Madison jumps and wraps her arms around my neck. "So proud of how badass you are. I get to brag about how my brother won the whole fucking thing!"

When they finally give her breathing room, Scarlett takes her turn. She kisses me while East and Madison whistle and cheer, and I pick her up, holding her tight.

"You're my hero. I hope you know that. Seeing how far you've come. My heart feels like it's gonna burst." She kisses me again, and I feel like everything has been worth it. Having them—having her tell me these things is better than anything any reporter or fan could possibly say.

WE'VE GOT two huge suites to ourselves at the top of one of the casino hotels—one that was given to Colt and one that was given to me when they found out we were going to be in tonight's game. The bars have been fully stocked, the rooms have been catered, and there are gift bags lining the table in the front entrance. But more importantly, they've proven to be a great place to retreat from the bigger parties happening in other parts of the hotel. Because as much as having the whole world celebrate with us tonight was amazing, for the first time in my life I'd rather have the people close to me more.

The party explodes as soon as we get back to Colt's place. East and his friends from Highland—Waylon, Liam, and Ben all chat loudly with Colt. Reminiscing about their days in college, their favorite bars, and what their old coaches and program are up to now. Their wives are having an equally good time with our girls, taking photos, and making mixed drinks out of the bar with the bartender's help. My sister has apparently been inaugurated into the group on Joss and Scarlett's orders, and between her and Joss they're contemplating what other appetizers need to be ordered up from room service and whether or not they should go to try a round in the casinos. A raucous debate breaks out before they pass around a bottle of tequila, each taking a shot and then settling on a game of pool in the other room.

As I sit there watching all of them talk, I can't help but stare at Scarlett and think how fucking lucky I am. That I found someone like her, that she stood by my side through everything and patiently waited for me to get my fucking head in order.

"All right there?" Xander holds out a glass of Scotch for me as he leans up against the wall alongside me.

"Yeah. Just feeling fucking lucky."

He grins at me, holding up his glass. "That makes two of us."

"We don't deserve them."

"Yeah. That's why we spend as long as they'll put up with us earning it."

"Fair enough." I nod "Speaking of, I'm surprised there's not a ring on her finger already." I glance at my best friend.

"Taking her on that hike she's always wanted to do. Going to surprise her with the trip and then propose. Hopefully, she says yes, or it's going to be an awkward flight home." He laughs.

"She'll say yes." I shake my head at the idea that he has any concern about that at all and take a sip of my drink.

"Gonna make you the last one standing." He gives me an inquisitive look.

"Yeah. Does that surprise anyone?" I laugh, but I feel my stomach flip.

"You going to make things with her more permanent at least?"

"I want her to move into my place, but it's pretty far from where the new museum will be."

"Condo's not. And I wouldn't mind having you closer. Scarlett might say yes just to be able to be a few floors away from Harper if we're being honest."

"Didn't think about that." I tilt my head.

"Maybe you should." He clinks his glass to mine and then throws back what's left in it. "Gonna get us another round."

When I look up again, I don't see Scarlett with the rest of the girls, and I look around for her, only to see her and Joss coming down the stairs, Scarlett wearing a number nine jersey across her chest while Joss giggles uncontrollably. Scarlett looks up, clearly surveying the room to find me and when her eyes finally meet mine, she grins. Not the sweet kind or the sheepish "my friends put me up to this kind." But the kind that's absolutely meant as a taunt.

She stops on the steps and raises her brow at me. Joss stopping a moment later, a little tipsy on the stairs as she grabs the rail and looks between us. Joss's eyes go wide when she sees the look on my face, and she hurries out of the way. Right before Scarlett takes off running back up the steps, and I'm chasing her up them like I'm still on the field.

FIFTY-FOUR

Scarlett

I TAKE off running up the stairs and down the hall, but I'm not nearly as fast as he is and when I slip into one of the bedroom doors and try to shut it behind me, his hand stops it.

"Scarlett." His voice is a low growl, and I feel my heart jump in my chest.

I step backward in the dark, enough light pouring through the wall of windows that look down on the dining room to see without completely losing my balance. He shuts the door behind him and locks it, setting his drink down on the sideboard.

"It was just a joke. Joss said you did it to Colt, so it was payback." I stammer out an excuse, taking one step back for each one he takes forward.

"I did it to help Joss. And I saw the look on your face."

"Okay well. I was just kidding." I laugh nervously as he reaches for me, and I jump onto the bed. "I'm sorry!"

"You will be." A devious smirk tugs at one side of his mouth.

"Tobias. Seriously. It's a joke. It's funny!" I crawl to the other side of the bed as he rounds it and nearly grabs me.

"Hilarious. I'm laughing on the inside. I promise." He mirrors my movements as I try to decide which way to run next and then freeze.

"I thought you would be amused. I didn't know it would piss you off."

"Oh, I'm amused." The look on his face says he is very much not, and my heart starts to pound in my chest as I realize I'm probably not going to make it to the door.

"You should yell at Joss and Colt then. I was just trying to do them a favor you know? I'm innocent in all this!" I fake like I'm going to run for the bathroom but hurry to the door instead. But he's faster than me, a million times faster it feels like, and before I can even touch the door handle his arms wrap around my middle and haul me up off my feet.

I kick and scream, half laughing and half truly scared that he's about to tickle me to death or some other form of torture I haven't imagined yet. And despite the fact that I can see through the glass in the room down to people below us, apparently, no one can hear me because not a single person looks up. In fact, I can see Joss and Colt from here, she's sitting next to him, her lips to his ear, telling him something and they both laugh.

"Oof. She just abandons you to your fate. How does that feel?" Tobias sees the same thing I do as he pins me between him and the bed, wrapping my arms with his when I try to struggle.

"Like we're going to have words later."

"Doesn't help you now though, does it?" he whispers

against the shell of my ear, and the sound of it makes everything pool warm and low in my body.

"No," I whisper back. "It was just a joke."

"Mmm. Well... You fucked up, Spitfire. Taunting me like that when I've already been desperate to fuck you all night."

"I didn't mean to taunt—" He nips at the exposed part of my shoulder.

"Don't lie. I saw the look on your face."

"Okay. Maybe a little. I just wanted to see your reaction."

"I know you did. But now you're gonna pay for it." His lips brush over my throat, and I arch back into him. "Yeah, that's what I thought. My girl wants fucked. Don't you?"

I nod, a little whimper following when his hand slides up my shirt and grabs my breast roughly, pinching my nipple before his hands rake down over my sides in their retreat.

"Putting his jersey on and then making me chase you? You know what happens when I have to chase you. You want to play dirty? You're getting fucked the same way." His hand slides up the back of my dress, grabbing a handful of my ass and squeezing before he slaps me.

"I said I'm—"

His hand covers my mouth, and he pulls me close, whispering in my ear.

"No. You're gonna shut up like a good fucking slut and take everything you have on under that jersey off for me while I watch."

His words light me up, making my whole body tingle and goosebumps break out across my neck. My hands tremble as I go to undo the dress I'd put on for the after party and then my bra, slowly pulling them off underneath and letting them drop to the floor until I'm in nothing but the jersey and my panties.

"The panties too." He points with the glass of Scotch he's gone to retrieve off the sideboard. He leans against it, sipping it slowly while he watches me slide out of them and sit them on the bed.

"Good girl." He grins before taking the last sip of Scotch and walking over to me.

I go to grab the hem of the jersey to pull it off, feeling self-conscious about it, and he grabs my wrist, holding me still.

"No. You're going to leave that on." He pats the bench at the end of the bed. "Now get up here. On your hands and knees. Facing the glass."

I glance up at the glass again, seeing the shadow of our reflection in it like ghosts over the people below. My nerves light and it causes an echo of desire in the rest of my body as I move into the position he's asked for.

"Spread as wide as you can for me on that bench." His words are rough as I hear him undoing his pants. The anticipation makes my heart tick up another notch, and I can feel the cool air against my inner thighs as I lean forward.

"Fuck you should see yourself right now, Scarlett. So fucking gorgeous and so very fucking wet for me. I can tell you're desperate." His fingers slip between my legs, testing me before his cock replaces them.

I rock back, teasing the tip of his cock and his hands grip my hips, a stuttered laugh coming out of him.

"Such a greedy fucking girl. You want me inside your pretty little cunt?"

"Yes," I whisper.

"Good. You're gonna take me like the sweet little slut you are, and I want to hear every fucking sound you make." He slides inside me a moment later, rough like he's making a point. I gasp at the sensation, catching myself when my hands start to slip forward over the velvet fabric of the bench.

He groans as he starts to fuck me and digs his fingers into my hips.

"Never gonna fucking get over how fucking perfect you feel. Fuck."

He fucks me hard until I whimper at how close he's taking me, and he grabs a fistful of my hair, pulling me up and back as his other hand slides over my stomach and my breast, and then wraps around my throat, tightening as he presses a kiss to my pulse point.

"You can wear any man's name on your back you want, Scarlett. I don't give a fuck because you're still going to be mine. My name around your neck, my hand around your throat, and my cock buried deep inside you when you come saying my name."

"Fuck. Tobias. Please..." I beg for him to finish me off.

"Touch yourself for me. I want to feel you come hard." His teeth graze over my neck before he sucks on my shoulder where the jersey's started to slip off, his tongue teasing over my flesh like he's imagining it's between my thighs. I circle my clit, so wet and sensitive that it doesn't take much before I'm gasping and he's groaning as he digs his teeth into my skin while he fucks me through his own release.

"Scarlett... Fuck. So good for me. I love you so much. So fucking much."

"I love you too." I wrap my fingers around his forearm as he rides out the last of it.

We're a sweaty mess when he finally slides out of me, still trying to catch our breath when he grabs the jersey and slips it off me. The cool air in the room a relief. I glance back at him, and he grins as he uses it to clean up before tossing it on the floor.

He takes my hand then, pulling me to my feet before he scoops me up and takes me to the bathroom. Planting me back on the cold marble floor while he pulls a washcloth for me. I watch him through the reflection in the mirror. His hair a mess, the light catching the slight ridges of the scar on his face, his tattooed shoulders and arms glistening in the low light with sweat, and his gorgeous ass and thighs on full display. When he looks up, he grins at me, a small sound of surprise and amusement.

"Thinking hard about something there, Spitfire?"

"How sexy you are. How lucky I am."

"Yeah?" He slips the washcloth between my legs, gently brushing it over my skin. "Well, that makes two of us." He kisses my forehead. "I'm so fucking gone for you."

I tilt my head up, kissing him softly for several moments before I take a breath. We finish getting cleaned up and head back to the room to get dressed. Before I can reach for my clothes though he pulls me back until we're standing in front of the mirror of glass staring at Vegas spread out in front of us.

"Have I mentioned lately that you have the hottest fucking body I've ever seen?"

"Not yet today."

"My mistake," he whispers, kissing the side of my throat.

"I'm proud of you. You know? You were amazing today. You deserved that win, but fuck you were so good out there. I don't want to say Colt didn't deserve the MVP, but I wish they could split it between both of you. You deserved it just as much."

"Yeah. You gonna write them a letter about it?" He grins against my shoulder.

"I might," I grumble at his teasing.

"My team has their championship, and I have my girl. I don't need anything else."

"Oh, well in that case." I look over my shoulder to smile back at him, and he takes the opportunity to kiss me.

"Didn't hurt to prove people wrong today either." He rests

his chin against my shoulder as he looks out over the city with me. His eyes drifting down in thought.

"Yeah well, I'm glad you have the ability to say you beat his team. So glad. But I don't think if you'd lost it would have mattered for most people. You're already better than him in so many ways, you know? That's why Easton and Madison were there rooting for you. You're so many things he'll never be—kind, caring, compassionate. I was awful to you, and you rescued me on that date, and then in the rain. You loaned me your car when you didn't have to."

"Spitfire, I desperately wanted to fuck you and then you had me wrapped around your finger pretty fucking quick there. So... I don't know that it's fair to use that as an example."

"You kept Xander safe with all of that stuff with Drew. You helped Colt and Joss get together. You're a good man, Tobias. You focus too much on the things you think you did wrong, and not enough on everything you do right."

He smiles at me as his eyes drift over my face. "I don't deserve someone like you."

"Well, I'm pretty sure I don't deserve you. Hottest guy in pro sports? Would-be MVP of the game? Perfect fucking body and fucks like a god? Sweet enough to buy me candy and this necklace? Yeah, I think if I was a betting girl, I'd be down in the casinos right now."

He laughs and kisses me again a few times before he pulls away, and his lashes lower as he studies my face.

"I was thinking about things. The season being over and the museum opening back up. You not needing to be at my place anymore... how we'd see each other."

"Yeah. It'll be harder when I'm back full-time at the museum."

"What if you move in with me?"

"Move in with you?" I blink at him because I think those

were some of the last words I expected Tobias to say. Even in the heat of the moment.

"To the condo downtown. It can be when your lease is up or sooner if you want. Would be closer to the new museum building."

"But you're usually out at the house."

"We can still go there on the weekends, so I still have a chance to watch you on those ladders in the library. But the condo would be closer during the week. Harper and Xander would just be a few floors away from us. We'd be downtown, so we could go grab food or do things just outside our doorstep. Give me chances to take you out and show off how fucking lucky I am."

"Okay."

"Okay?"

"I don't know how to say no to that, or you. So... okay." I shrug, surprising even myself when I don't even feel a whisper of apprehension.

"Fuck yes!" He grins, grabbing me up into his arms as I wrap my legs around him, and he kisses me again. "As soon as we get back?"

"Works for me." I kiss him softly.

"I love you. I know... I know I keep saying it like some fucking sap, but I never thought I'd feel like this... and I can hardly fucking believe it. I say it half the time just to remind myself it's real." His finger slides under my necklace and runs along the underside of the beads there.

"I never thought it could feel like this either." I kiss his knuckles, and I see the breath he takes, the half grin that plays at his lips.

His arms tighten around me, and I melt into him.

"Now I just have to work on getting that 's' off the necklace." He kisses my forehead.

EPILOGUE

Scarlett

1 month later...

It's the night of the big museum reopening, and we're doing it in collaboration with Joss and Harper's nonprofit. They managed to raise enough money thanks to big donors, Joss's player photograph books, and a donation drive that's gotten us thousands of new members who pay a monthly fee to get unlimited visits, lectures, and a yearly behind-the-scenes tour.

Best—and possibly scariest—of all, I've been promoted to head curator. This means the director and I are joint masters of ceremonies tonight and the place is packed wall to wall. We actually had to turn some people away which is unheard of for our previously very modest museum. The fact that four of the championship-winning Seattle Phantom players are in attendance tonight doesn't hurt, and all the press attention we are getting thanks to them and Joss and Harper's nonprofit means our future looks brighter than ever.

My heart hasn't felt this full in years, and I don't even realize how tired I am until we're well into the late hours of the event. I'm walking across the floor looking around for any sign of one of the caterers who might have some food left when a hand reaches out and grabs mine from behind, tugging me gently. I look up, and it's Tobias.

"Come with me." He nods.

"I have to go to find that donor Joss wanted me to talk to in a minute. I'm just trying to find some food."

His fingers lace with mine, tightening his grip.

"Yeah, Spitfire. You're coming with me first."

I start to protest but relent when I see his eyebrow raise. I know it means I'll be in for trouble when we get home if I don't listen.

"Where are you taking me?" I ask as I follow.

"Your office."

"What's in my office?"

"Sustenance and a few minutes of rest. I already told Joss I was stealing you for a bit, and she said she'd cover in your absence, and Harper can do the curator emeritus thing until you get food. So don't worry, okay?"

"Okay." I can't help the little grin that forms.

We slip into my office mostly unnoticed, and he locks the door behind us. There's a plate of food—with a little of everything that has long since disappeared from the catering trays—and water and wine waiting for me.

"How did you get this? I thought I'd be lucky to get some crackers."

"I had them set aside a plate for you earlier in the night. Only cost me half my soul."

I roll my eyes and shake my head.

"Or an autograph for her son. Might have just been that."

He smirks at me as I sit down in my office chair, and he sits across from me on the couch.

"Thank you. That was thoughtful and smart. I should have asked, but I was so nervous about that speech."

"That's what I'm here for, Spitfire. Now eat."

I eat like a starved raccoon because I haven't had a single bite since breakfast, too nervous and busy to do anything but run on caffeine and water. He tells me about the discussions he's had with some of the donors and all the compliments we've already gotten on the new building. Then he muses about how many of the photography books he's had to sign alongside Joss and the rest of the guys tonight, much to the scandal of some of the board members.

"See. I told you," I say when I finally finish, taking a long drink of water to rehydrate before I go back out onto the floor. "This is why I can't deaccession the magazines."

He laughs, and I stand to toss my trash out. I head for the door before he blocks my way, grabbing my wrists. I give him a puzzled look.

"I haven't eaten yet."

"What? You should have said something. I would have saved some. I'm sorry." I feel guilty now for having devoured it all, but he doesn't say anything. He just walks us backward around my desk.

"Not what I meant." A smirk tugs at the corner of his mouth and when my ass bumps the desk, I realize his meaning.

"Tobias." I feel the desire pooling low even though I know I need to get back out there. "I have to—"

"Have to take the panties off, sit back on this desk, and spread your legs for me like a good girl."

I glance back at the door, checking to make sure it's locked before I look back at him. I give him a doubtful look.

He pulls me close then, brushing a kiss over my lips before he goes for my throat, kissing and biting his way down and back up again before he whispers in my ear, "Unless you'd rather get bent over the desk and told what a dirty slut you are. But you don't leave until you've gotten off at least once."

I melt into him then, letting him pull my panties off while he kisses his way over my skin and pushes me back on the desk.

"What if I want both?" It's my turn to smirk as he sits in my desk chair, kissing the tops of my thighs as his hands massage my legs.

"Then it's whatever you want. Because fucking Christ, Scarlett, watching you tonight, listening to you talk... Fuck," he curses when he finds me wet, and he grabs my thighs and pulls me to the edge of the desk. "It's so sexy. I'm so proud of you. That I get to stand next to you at events like these and tell people I'm your boyfriend."

I laugh, amused that this man—who is still fielding a million new deals from his agent alongside the rest of the guys after their big win—refers to himself as my boyfriend. But I love him for it.

"Between this and your channel taking off like it has... I don't know. Gonna have to make sure I keep you happy. Meet all your needs, so you don't run off with some other guy." He kisses the inside of my thigh before he grins up at me.

I run my fingers through his hair, brushing it to the side when it starts to fall in his face.

"You make me the happiest I've ever been, so I think you're good."

"Am I good?" He leans forward, parting me and running his tongue over my clit in one long perfect stroke, and I close my eyes, biting the inside of my cheek to keep from moaning loudly.

"So fucking good," I say as my fingers twist in his hair. "Oh my god. Fuck. Tobias."

He works me over until I'm a pleading mess under his tongue and hands, begging for him to finish me off.

"Like this or you want my cock?" He brushes a soft kiss over my clit, his fingers still working me gently as he looks up at me.

"Your cock. I need it. *Now*." I'm already having trouble catching my breath, so I might as well have what I really want.

He grins and pulls me up off the desk.

"Turn around and bend over then."

I follow his instructions as he stands up behind me, undoing his pants and lining himself up with me as I bend over.

"Grab the desk."

I grin as I reach for the edge of the desk, just as I hear the rap of knuckles at my office door.

Fuck.

"Just a minute. I'm... changing." I reach for an excuse for why my door would be locked and start to stand up.

"Okay. Come find me when you're out okay?" It's my director's voice on the other side and my heart slams against my chest.

Tobias slides inside me before I can respond, his hand clamping over my mouth when I start to moan at how good it feels—so sensitive and on edge from how close he took me with his mouth that I'm on the verge of coming.

"Scarlett?" my director asks.

Tobias moves his hand so I can answer.

"Yep! Will do," I say, doing my best not to sound like I'm getting fucked over my desk and failing.

"That's my dirty girl," Tobias whispers against the shell of my ear before he starts to fuck me. I don't hear what she says in response, but I hear the faint retreating sound of her footsteps in the hall. "The way you fucking take me when we almost get caught. Fuck me..."

"So close," I mutter, and he digs his fingers into the flesh of my hip, reaching his other hand around to give me the friction I need, and I'm coming a few seconds later—it's so good I don't care who hears us.

"That's my girl. You deserve this. All of it for how fucking good you are."

He tightens his grip on me as he starts to come, and I bend over the desk again, loving the way he feels when he comes inside me. He shudders his release, his hand massaging my ass for a moment, murmuring about how perfect I am before he pulls out of me.

I give myself a moment to catch my breath before I stand, cleaning up and straightening my clothes as he does the same. When I turn around, he slides his hand under my chin and kisses me.

"I love you, Scarlett," he whispers against my lips. "I'm serious about how amazed I am by you. Keeping this place going with the bare minimum and creating what you have here. The vision you have. How tireless you are in the pursuit. I hope you know how much I'm in awe of you every fucking day. And I know I'm where I am because you used that magic on me too. None of us deserve you. But I'm going to work hard at it anyway."

My heart swells with his words. Tobias is a kind and incredibly loving person underneath it all, but I know he's also an honest person at his core, without reserve. So hearing it from him means all the more.

"I love you too."

He kisses me one last time.

"All right. Now that I'm sure you're completely sated, you

can return to your adoring fans." He kisses me on the forehead, and I kiss him back.

"What would I do without you?" I tilt my head, smiling at him.

"Good thing we have each other."

ALSO BY MAGGIE RAWDON

Plays & Penalties Series

Pregame - Prequel Short Story
Play Fake - Waylon & Mackenzie
Delay of Game - Liam & Olivia
Personal Foul - Easton & Wren
Reverse Pass - Ben & Violet

Seattle Phantom Football Series

Defensive End - Prequel Short Story
Pick Six - Alexander & Harper
Overtime - Joss & Colt

Other

Lords of Misrule

ACKNOWLEDGMENTS

To you, the reader, thank you so much for taking a chance on this book and on me! Your support means the world.

To Kat, thank you for your constant help, support, and patience. There's no way I'd ever get a book out without you and your team and I'm so incredibly grateful for you!

To Autumn, for all of your support and help along the way!

To Emma and Shannon, thank you for your humor, encouragement and constant support. I'm so lucky to call you friends.

To Thorunn, thank you for holding my hand through this one and sending cookie and coffee reinforcements on the days I felt like I didn't have any words left. I'm so grateful for your friendship and support.

To Jenn and Candice, thank you for taking time out of your day and beta reading Tobias and Scarlett. So grateful for your feedback and thoughts.

To my Promo Team, thank you so much for all the support you give my characters, books, and me. I wouldn't be able to do this without you and I'm so incredibly grateful!

ABOUT THE AUTHOR

Maggie Rawdon is a sports romance author living in the Midwest. She's writes athletes with the kind of filthy mouths that will make you blush and swoon and the smart independent women that make them fall first. She has a weakness for writing frenemies whose fighting feels more like flirting and found families.

She loves real sports as much as the fictional kind and spends football season writing in front of the TV with her pups at her side. When she's not on editorial deadline you can find her binging epic historical dramas or fantasy series in between weekend hikes.

Join the newsletter here for sneak peeks and bonus content:
https://geni.us/MRBNews
Join the reader's group on FB here:
https://www.facebook.com/groups/rawdonsromanticrebels

- instagram.com/maggierawdonbooks
- tiktok.com/@maggierawdon
- facebook.com/maggierawdon

Made in the USA
Las Vegas, NV
27 December 2023